The
Family
Took
Shape

The
Family
Took
Shape

a novel

Shashi Bhat

Cormorant Books

Chapters in this book were previously published: "Drawing Lessons" in *Bayou Magazine*; "Sublimation" in *The Missouri Review*; "Another Dinner Party" in *Nimrod International Journal*.

The publisher gratefully acknowledges the support of the Canada Council for the Arts and the Ontario Arts Council for its publishing program. We acknowledge the financial support of the Government of Canada through the Canada Book Fund (CBF) for our publishing activities, and the Government of Ontario through the Ontario Media Development Corporation, an agency of the Ontario Ministry of Culture, and the Ontario Book Publishing Tax Credit Program.

LIBRARY AND ARCHIVES CANADA CATALOGUING IN PUBLICATION

Bhat, Shashi, 1983–
The family took shape / Shashi Bhat.

Issued also in electronic formats.
ISBN 978-1-77086-091-9

1. Title.

PS8603.H38F35 2012   C813'.6   C2013-900263-1

Cover illustration and design: Angel Guerra/Archetype
Interior text design: Tannice Goddard, Soul Oasis Networking
Printer: Friesens

Printed and bound in Canada.

The interior of this book is printed on 100% post-consumer waste recycled paper.

CORMORANT BOOKS INC.
390 Steelcase Road East, Markham, Ontario, L3R 1G2
www.cormorantbooks.com

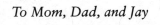
To Mom, Dad, and Jay

Drawing Lessons

FOR MIRA'S SIXTH birthday, her brother Ravi drew a picture of her, pressing so hard the paper warped with the side of his hand. He coloured so darkly the page looked wet, and the markers he used dried out, so a quarter of the drawing faded into pastels. When he gave her the drawing, she said thank you, though she was upset he'd ruined the set of markers they shared. She herself would never have coloured that way; she coloured gently, using only a light pressure. "I don't think this picture really looks like me," she said to her mother, though Ravi was standing right there and could hear her. He looked away, smiling with his teeth, the way Mira smiled in the drawing, her teeth the only white on the page except for the blanks in her eyes. Her nose squiggled and she didn't have lips. She stood on spiking grass but behind her was only a pattern that advanced and receded irregularly, made of shapes she'd only just learned about in school — rhombuses, pentagons, scalene triangles. From her scalp to her shoes, he had coloured her cerise.

Ravi, age eight, had given her the same gift for the two previous Christmases, and for last year's birthday. Always a drawing of her, with identical oval eyes, blackened pupils looking wide and sideways, lacking lashes or brows; in real life such eyes would catch with dust, would water constantly. The figures kept their arms slightly lifted from their torsos, in the shape of an upside-down V, and Mira thought Ravi was the only person she'd ever seen stand like that in real life. She pasted the drawings on the door of her bedroom closet, and the bodies formed arrows aimed at the ceiling.

Mira was a child who valued homemade gifts. For Mother's Day, she wrote a poem on a pink paper heart, glittering in fine lines of silver ink, and along with it a bottle of homemade bubble bath, which they'd showed her how to make at school. She'd emptied a jar of grainy Dijon mustard to put it in, and it looked much more beautiful than mustard — instead of black-speckled yellow, the bubble bath was a layer of pink and a layer of coarse white salt, separated by a carefully cut circle of acetate. Mira thought the salt looked like rocks on the moon. The bottle sat for years on the bathroom shelf; her mother only took showers, as the tub wasn't long enough to sit in. Mira wasn't offended; she thought the potion looked better in the jar than it would in the bathtub. She liked it as a display piece. She had developed a firm aesthetic, which she expressed through her incisively chosen rock collection and her various arts and crafts, and which she spent much of her time pondering quietly, slipping around the house in sock feet, settling into quiet corners from where she startled her mother.

The house had been louder when her father was alive. He had boomed around, his movements characterized by their volume. Her mother had been louder then, too, her voice bouncing and echoing from her body like air through a conch. Both Mira and her brother were mostly silent. Ravi had his drawings, his sweet-smelling dried markers and pointed pencil tips that Mira helped him sharpen when they wore dull or snapped. Mira wondered sometimes if her mother wished she were louder, or that she was more mischievous, that she would cause trouble. She wondered this because of the stories her mother told her, about the things she'd done when she was a girl. While they ate their cereal in the morning, she told Mira and Ravi about how she'd refused to eat any food but chakuli for breakfast, watching her mother and aunts fry the dough into marvellous crunchy spirals. When she brought Ravi a set of coloured pencils, she told them she'd once drawn all over the whitewashed outer walls of her family's home, not just on any day, but on the day of her eldest brother's wedding. Hundreds of guests were to arrive in the valley, and the servants had needed to repaint everything fresh. Mira's mother gathered with Mira and Ravi in the family room, and as they flung whole bananas into the fireplace to roast them, then pulled them out with tongs and peeled off their black skins, she told them about how, once, she'd jumped into a pile of burning dry banana leaves that her father had left to disintegrate overnight in the mud field behind the stables. The leaves, she said, had flown up around her, flaring like fireworks, and Mira had found that image so lovely that she thought perhaps she would try it too, if she ever had the chance.

SEVERAL MONTHS AGO, Mira had waited in the anteroom while the psychiatrist interviewed Ravi and their mother. Those

were the words he'd used — "interviewed," "anteroom" —
and Mira tumbled them over in her head while she waited,
trying to think of situations in which she might say them.
They had come to the psychiatrist because Ravi's teacher said
he was exhibiting repetitive movements: flapping his limbs,
tapping his desk with his curled fingers, squealing during
class, laughing for no reason. Her mother had told her all of
this — people always told Mira things she wasn't old enough
for — as she went around the house collecting Ravi's drawings
to take in to the doctor with her. Mira overheard the rest later,
in the doctor's office building lobby after the appointment, as
she sat in a too-big leather chair and watched her mother on
the payphone crying, using more words — "mild autism,"
"developmentally delayed" — clutching the rolled-up drawings
in one hand like a newspaper, her other hand holding Ravi's.

RAVI'S CLASSROOM AT school was room 314, the special
education room. Once a week, the special education class was
paired up with another class in the school, for game or a craft
activity. When it was Mira's class, the first time she saw her
brother's classroom, she recoiled at its massiveness, the way
the desks were spaced far apart to leave room for wheelchairs,
the way the pencil jars held only the fattest red pencils, instead
of slim yellow ones. Mira could tell her brother was uneasy.
Ravi beat his fingers against his leg and pursed his lips as
he watched other students blur past the tiny window on
the classroom door. At one point, a boy in the hallway came
right up to the window in the door and mashed his face up
against the glass. He smirked at Ravi, and hit his palm flat
on the glass with a startling thud. One of the teachers noticed

and took a purposeful step towards him. When the boy noticed, he pulled his face away. The lunch bell rang and Mira's class was allowed to go outside, but Ravi's wasn't. The special education class never left room 314, except once a week, when their straggling group would adjourn to the gymnasium, forming a circle to heave a rubber ball around.

"What kind of future can a boy get out of a class like that?" Mira overheard her mother say on the phone, probably talking to Lala Aunty. Mira flipped through a photo album in the adjacent room. She stopped at a picture of their family, from a few years earlier, standing in front of the buildings at Queen's Park. She peered in at her amorphous baby face; she only knew it was herself by the context. Ravi was in his stroller, and her mother and father casually propped their weight against the purple brick steps. Mira wished she could step into the picture, like into a Mary Poppins chalk drawing. She could almost. In her imagination, she remembered the atmosphere exactly — the clash of traffic, the parabolic glass of a nearby office building, the people emerging from the subway, cutting across the circle of streets, moving southward like birds. Her family stood away from everything, cushioned by the urban park's ellipse of grass. She would take the camera back from the stranger who'd taken their photo, and she'd take that family, like that, forever, and that father, reincarnated now into God-knows-what. She was Hindu; she knew about being reborn. Now when she saw deer in the backyard, she stared at their deer faces, challenging them to recognize her, but they froze and then ran, the way all deer will, forgetting they were once ladybugs or tigers or husbands or fathers.

IT WAS LALA Aunty who suggested the art lessons. She tended to be the instigator of such things. "He has potential, definitely, there is no doubt about it. You know, postcards, greeting cards, et cetera et cetera, what a star he will be. Probably Hallmark will hire him," her eyebrows fluttered with enthusiasm.

"I have never seen this sort of thing at Hallmark," said Mira's mother, gesturing at the drawings she had spread out on the kitchen table, where the three of them, Mira, her mother, and Lala Aunty, sat eating apple slices. On the bottom of one of the papers, it said CAT, in tilting, boxy letters. Above that there was a cat, though not any cat that Mira had ever seen. Its body was made out of falling stacks of blue squares — several different blues: azures and navy and powder blue. Mira recalled the names of all the marker colours, and the cat had oval, human eyes. She thought it might clatter as it moved. The background, like his other drawings, was completely filled with an indecipherable pattern. Another pattern said HOUSE across the bottom. She recognized it as their own house, but with geometric details that hurt her eyes — a thinly penned grid across the garage door, trees in the yard with exact individual leaves, and bricks drawn on the house walls from the violet grass to the ochre sky.

"He is a true original," said Lala Aunty. "Anyhow, I know someone, friend-of-friend, who teaches art lessons, so we will send him there. And Mira, too, if she feels like," she said, putting her arm artificially around Mira's small shoulders.

THE ART TEACHER'S house was only two blocks away, so Mira and Ravi walked there together after school. The front of the house looked more like the side of a house should look, Mira thought. But it had a door on it, so they knocked. The woman who opened it had hair like the top of an old dandelion. Mira wished it were windy outside, and pictured individual hairs alighting on the grass, reborn as new weeds.

Mira wore her house key around her neck on a string. The woman reached out and tucked the key into the neck of Mira's shirt. "You should wear it on the inside," the woman said, and then introduced herself as Mrs. Heinz. The statement made a lot of sense to Mira, who lived in fear of abduction, of strangers. She thought, shuddering, of a tall thin man wearing a black hat, coming up to her, grabbing the key and pulling her with it, leash-like, demanding she reveal her address. She wondered why her mother hadn't given her this advice.

They went all together down to the basement, which was arranged like a gallery with student art hung on the unfinished walls, pink fibreglass peeking around the corners of frames. Mrs. Heinz sat them down and offered them orange juice, and Ravi said yes but Mira declined, because she had the idea that it was polite to always refuse things that were offered to her in other people's houses, even if she wanted them. On the worktable in front of her was an art set, open like a brief-case. It held pliable tubes of acrylics, pale linen-textured papers, and flat paintbrushes with bristles as flexible as human hair. Mrs. Heinz returned with juice for both Ravi and Mira. Mira worried she would knock hers over and it would paint the paper like a watercolour sunset, and then Mrs. Heinz wouldn't let her paint anything else, and she would never get to use those exquisite brushes.

But that didn't happen, and they spent the hour drawing a pair of sneakers — whose, it was unclear. They were dusty, shoelaces knotted, logo nearly invisible, and Mira painstakingly recreated everything she noticed. She could be an artist, maybe. She had often thought, while being read aloud to at school, the teacher holding up the pages to show the pictures, that *she* could have drawn those pictures, those smiling dogs and hiding, whiskered mice. *She* could be the one to design greeting cards and sell her work to Hallmark. People she knew would go into the store and select a greeting card, and Mira's signature in the corner, a loop dissolving into a line, would be so artistic, so cryptic, they wouldn't even recognize it as hers.

Ravi ignored the details of the sneakers, and instead he drew what seemed to Mira a different pair of shoes entirely, though there were laces and soles; they were in the wrong colour, their necks stood higher in his drawings, footwear from another decade.

The next class, they drew a baseball glove. "Is it a hand?" their mother asked when she saw her son's version. The drawing was colourless then, but Mira saw him in his room at night with the desk lamp on, tinting the sketch brown with a pencil crayon that Mrs. Heinz had given him. And suddenly to Mira it did look like a hand, a horrible webbed hand, or like Ravi's own hand, bloated and soft.

IN THE WEEKS that followed, Ravi's drawings accumulated all over the house. Flipping through the phonebook for the pizza delivery number, Mira found entire pages covered in round, tiny-beaked birds. The back of the TV guide was painted with concentric circles. Inside the cover of one of her chapter books, she found the image of a slender, running boy. Ravi hid the morning newspaper indiscriminately with multicoloured fish in crowded schools, their bodies striped and spotted and finned. "Where did he see these things, to draw them?" her mother asked her, and Mira shrugged. She kept her own drawings neatly in her desk. They were on pads of paper, as drawings should be. And they looked like what they were — a tree with a bird's nest balanced in the nook of its branches, an old woman with a web of wrinkles on her face, which Mira had copied from a book.

The backgrounds of Ravi's drawings were still filled with their patterns of shapes, and the animals still had human eyes. They scared Mira; she believed she saw emotions in those eyes, in the subtle ways they widened or narrowed at one side, or a white dot of glint in their pupils that might signify anger or elation or sorrow of the kind she had never seen in her brother. Ravi didn't have emotions; he was always only himself. He smiled widely, always, or laughed in his frightening Ravi way, a sort of uncontrollable chortling that grabbed him from the inside and shook his whole body. He would cup his brown fist with his mouth to try and stop it. Once, when he'd laughed that way at the breakfast table, their mother had grabbed his glass of milk and spilled it over his head in a single splash, as though to douse him like a flame. He still hadn't stopped laughing. The milk slid down his face as Mira watched, chewing her cereal slowly.

MIRA HAD SEEN the boy who was bullying Ravi at school, but she didn't say anything. Her mother arranged Ravi's drawings into a portfolio, a red folder with large pockets. "Will you make sure Ravi gives these to his teacher?" she asked Mira, on a Monday morning.

"He's supposed to be the older one," Mira said, and walked out of the room.

Her mother's idea, she knew because she'd heard her say so, was that Ravi's school teacher would be impressed with the drawings, and perhaps would go easier on Ravi when grading his tests. It was a far-fetched idea. He could barely read. Mira, two years younger, helped him with his reading homework, and though she knew he wasn't like her, that there was something the matter with him, she couldn't understand why he had so much trouble. She had seen other kids like him, and adults, too. Once, at the mall, she had seen a grown man standing by himself, not doing anything unusual, not making a scene, but she knew from his eyes, and from the low humming noise she heard him make as she passed, that he had more in common with her brother than she did.

Another time, outside the hospital where her mother worked, she had seen a man sitting on the street outside the shoe store, with one dead leg. He wore a bright white shoe on his good foot, but the dead leg was covered in a thick salmon-coloured bandage. She was waiting outside the hospital for her mother to pick up something she'd forgotten inside, thinking of legs, trying not to look at the man, looking instead at the blue baggy legs of doctors, the tan and white legs of nurses, the steel legs of gurneys moving past, *fat-leg-white-leg-steel-leg-naked-leg*, she focused, when the man had laughed and then clutched at *her* leg, as though he meant to prop himself up with it, to use as a cane. She had kicked and screamed, and a lady nearby had ushered her into the hospital lobby, asked her where her mother was, and suggested she wait in one of the chairs at reception. There was something wrong with that man's mind, was how she reassured herself. He didn't know what he was doing. He wasn't going to do anything; he wasn't going to steal her leg, replace his leg with hers. It wouldn't even fit.

She wasn't sure where people like that, the man in the mall, the man outside the shoe store, came from. It was possible that their fathers and mothers and sisters had died. A *career*, her mother and Lala Aunty kept saying, as they looked at Ravi's drawings. They even talked about art school, about galleries and studios and shows. Mira had stopped showing anybody her own drawings after she'd shown her mother a painting she had done of a frog, using the perspective and shading techniques Mrs. Heinz had taught her, and her mother had said, "Pretty, Mira," and put it up on the fridge, then opened the fridge to get out the chutney, as though frogs were pretty, as though it didn't matter if you smudged chutney all over them. *Career* — the word made no sense in relation to her brother. She tried to picture him wearing a suit, or answering a telephone in a professional voice like the secretaries at school: "Hello, this is Ravi Acharya, how can I help you?" or "Acharya here, how may I direct your call." She would probably have to choose his clothes for him and buy him an answering machine. She knew that it would be her responsibility to make sure Ravi didn't turn into a strange man in the mall, or a strange man outside the hospital. She would have to take care of him forever.

Taking care of him was what she should have been doing all those times when she saw the bully chase him. It had started weeks ago. On this Monday morning, when their mother gave Ravi the red drawing portfolio to carry with him, Mira knew it was a bad idea. He didn't even put it in his bag, just held it out in the open. She was about to tell him to put it in his bag, when the boy ambled up the street to their school bus stop after Ravi and Mira's mother had dropped them off. He wasn't large, but he was certainly bigger than Mira; she didn't think she could be blamed. Ravi dwarfed him, actually, but the boy looked mean, he had a mean face, he smirked, his freckled skin twisting as he spat out taunts, leaned his face in to Ravi's and drew back suddenly, then imitated his nervous gestures, pulled at Ravi's shirt and slapped at his sides. Ravi began to run. "Ravi, the bus is coming!" Mira said, falteringly, dropping her purple book bag and picking it up again.

When the bus arrived, her brother was so far away she couldn't see him. "My brother is over there," she said to the driver.

"He's late," the driver said. She didn't bother waiting. Mira took a seat, purposely on the side away from where she could look for her brother. He would go home, she figured. It wasn't like he learned anything at school. She felt the cold brass house key against her skin, its string around her neck. At recess, she saw that the bully had gotten a ride to school. He was there playing tetherball, beating the ball with his fist, whipping it in a violent circle.

Mira spent the day picturing what Ravi might be doing: wandering the neighbourhood, stopping on sidewalks in front of other people's houses to put his hand to his mouth and stare, as he did sometimes, at something nobody else could identify; eating the raspberries from the raggedy bush in the neighbour's unfenced yard; napping on their own back porch, under the monstrous face of their garden's single sunflower.

The bus dropped her off at the end of the day, and she expected to find her brother there outside the house — at least it wasn't winter yet — but he wasn't there on the front porch, or in the backyard either. Even then, she didn't call her mother.

Bullies, Bees, and Spiders

"WE'LL LEAVE NO stone unturned," Lala Aunty's husband said reassuringly to no one in particular, as their small search party — Mira, her mother, and Lala Aunty's husband — left to walk around the dark neighbourhood. Lala Aunty stayed home in case anyone called. Mira thought it was an odd expression to use, hollow, compared with the seriousness of the situation, and because they *were* leaving stones unturned, many, in fact. She eyed every stone she passed with suspicion, thinking that, though Ravi would never have been able to fit under one, turning them all over might reveal some new truths. If they walked around the whole neighbourhood, or the whole city of Richmond Hill, and turned every single stone, would the city look any different when morning came? Would those other Richmond Hill residents, inside their houses now, families intact, open their front doors in the morning and gasp at how different the city looked, now that every stone had been turned? Everything would look darker, bluer, damper, flatter, once the undersides of stones had been revealed.

"Did he leave here after you two came home?" her mother had asked her.

"No, he didn't go to school today," Mira responded.

"He didn't go? What do you mean he didn't go?" Her mother took her arm and shook it and brought her face close. "Where did he go?"

"There's a boy," Mira said. "Who chases him. He chased him down the street and Ravi missed the bus."

"Why didn't you call me? Why didn't you tell anybody? What's the matter with you?" Her mother had kept shaking her arm and then tossed it away from her.

"I told the bus driver," Mira whispered.

Though Ravi wouldn't fit behind a stone, he might fit behind a tree. There was one fat tree in front of each house, and sometimes there were skinny fruit trees. She checked both. Her shadow stretched out and overlapped the shadows of the trees. Every time she saw leaves and branches moving, she thought she might find Ravi standing behind them, his hands clasped together with one finger tap-tap-tapping.

Lala Aunty's husband held Mira's hand. "I can take Mira home," he suggested, after they'd been around the block. "She can wait with Lala?" But Mira's mother said no, and they kept walking. They knocked on the doors of the several neighbours they knew, but nobody had seen him. In one of the houses, Mira could see *Jeopardy* playing on the TV, and the two teenage sons watching. "Jakarta," said one teenager. "Wrong," said the other. In another house, she heard chair legs creaking over a floor and fork-and-knife noises coming from an unseen kitchen. She imagined they were eating sausages with mushroom sauce and frozen vegetables, which was what she'd

Why does no one suggest the police?

had the one time she'd been invited to dinner at a non-Indian friend's house. It was not unlike Halloween, though of course she had no costume, and instead of asking for candy they were asking for her brother. "Did Ravi happen to come by here?" her mother would ask. After the third neighbour had said a very apologetic no, her mother had persisted. "But he knows your house," she said. "He likes the brick driveway. He likes walking on it." Her mother leaned against the door jamb and began crying.

"I'm sorry, we haven't seen him," the woman said. "I can come with you? Let me ... let me get my jacket. Should we take the car?"

They got in the neighbour woman's car. Mira sat in back with her mother and looked out the window. They drove very slowly around the small streets and then went out on to Elgin Mills and Yonge. People were in flux here, moving along on the shiny streets — it had freshly rained and the car lights narrowed and widened as they drove past. People waited for buses, climbed on the buses and hooked their hands into the rubber loops on the bus ceilings; people entered and exited video stores with the flat plastic DVD boxes under their arms; people coughed as they walked into and out of walk-in clinics, tucked their keys into pockets and purses as they ran up to and through the automatic doors of convenience stores. It was like *Where's Waldo?* Mira had one of the books at home and had looked through the others at the dentist's office. Like a spread in *Where's Waldo?*, the people faced in every direction, each concerned with only himself, engaging in his own hilarity or tragedy. Those scenes were chaos — colourful and chaotic, with distant, small faces, items spilled. Everybody looked like

Waldo and everybody looked like Ravi. She wished there weren't so many Indian people in Richmond Hill. "There he is!" she said, pointing, but it turned out to be a grown man.

In the Tim Hortons parking lot, high school students stood in groups, eating out of paper bags and kicking garbage around. Mira's mother asked the neighbour woman to stop the car in the lot, and then she took a photo of Ravi from her purse and went to show it around. She was still wearing her work clothes — a light grey skirt suit with a green Indian-style blouse inside — but she had changed her shoes to sneakers. She shivered next to the teenagers in their black jackets; she waved the photo in front of them. How could she hope for them to recognize Ravi if she didn't hold the photo still?

Mira's mother got back in the car. "Should we go back and call the police?" asked Lala Aunty's husband, gently. The neighbour woman dropped them back to their house.

"You'll find him. I'm sure he's just gone to a friend's house," she said. The woman had no idea about Ravi, Mira thought.

"I told you, should have called the police right as soon as you found him missing," said Lala Aunty said when they went in the house.

Found him missing, the phrase echoed at Mira and she catalogued it for later. She sat on the shadowy ledge of carpet that curved above the staircase and swung her legs until her legs got tired. They waited. Eventually the doorbell rang.

"Is your son Ravi?" she asked Mira's mother, who had removed her blazer and was clutching her own shoulders in the cool air that came through the doorway. "I have him — he's in the car. He came to my house and we tried calling the number he gave —" Mira jumped off her ledge and hopped down the stairs and peered around her mother. Ravi was in the car. He got out when he saw Mira and her mother, and came up slowly. He knew he was in trouble.

"Oh, he must have inverted the digits," said Mira's mother, making an absent inverting motion with her hands, then pulling Ravi against her, tightly petting his hair.

"Well, glad he got home safe ..." the woman trailed off.

"Come and have coffee," called Lala Aunty over all of their heads, but the woman politely declined and headed back to her car.

"Why did the stupid woman take so long to ask him where he lived?" Lala Aunty asked after the woman was gone.

Then they ate ice cream as though it were a birthday party. Mira didn't want the ice cream, but she took it anyway, letting it melt before she ate it, so it became the consistency of milk, and so it was more like a punishment.

"You can show your drawings tomorrow," their mother said to Ravi. He shook his head.

"No?"

"No," he said, not meeting her eyes.

She went to his backpack and unzipped it. She pulled out the portfolio and looked at it, turning it over slowly. The papers were streaked with dried mud, the colours smeared. Some of the pages were torn and still damp.

"Did that boy do this?" their mother asked Ravi. She turned to Mira, her mouth contorting, about to speak, but she didn't say anything.

"BEES ARE ATTRACTED to applesauce," said Lucy Chin.

Mira knew only to be afraid.

"And perfume," the girl continued. "Are you wearing perfume?"

"No, I never wear perfume," said Mira. It was a lie, because her mother sprayed *Charlie White* on her almost every morning, and brushed it into her hair. Lucy Chin was the bus driver's daughter, and Mira had decided to keep as many secrets from her as possible.

Mira had been there when the conversation took place between her mother and Lucy Chin's mother, the bus stopped at the bus stop, her mother inside the bus leaning forward on one heeled foot, the driver sitting in her seat, her hand waiting to shift gears, thirty kids, the engine running under them all.

"Will you keep an eye on that awful boy?" her mother had said to the bus driver. *Awful*, was that what he was? It was unusual to see her mother in the context of the bus.

"Sure of course, I didn't realize anything like that was going on." There was a line of cars behind them, stopped for the bus's stop sign. The driver waved them around.

"It's that I can't keep being late in the mornings, and I don't get home til five." Boring, boring Mom-talk.

"What about their babysitter?"

"No babysitter, they take care of themselves." Like cacti. Like self-cleaning ovens. Why did her mother say that? Didn't she know they were too young to stay at home alone?

"They're a little young for that, aren't they? You know, I can watch them, if they stay on the bus with me until the end of the route. Lucy will be there, too, that's my daughter." No, no, Mira thought, and this was before she even knew Lucy Chin. It might have been the first time she'd heard words and felt dread, the first inkling that a single sentence from her mother or another mother could so drastically change her routine. After school was when she searched the kitchen for the most delicious foods, when she ate Joe Louis cream-filled cakes right from their wrappers without even using a plate. After school, she hammered together old paint stir sticks, with the smallest nails from her father's kit, to construct fantastic wooden alligators. After school, she went on cleaning binges, folded all the towels in the hallway closet and organized them by colour, and then said nothing about them, hoping to witness the moment when her mother opened the closet door.

And now, nearly a year later, she didn't find it easy keeping secrets from Lucy Chin because she attended school with her, and Brownie meetings, took morning and afternoon bus rides with her, ate lunch and dinner with her. Mira began to eat strange breakfasts, asking her mother for Indian foods with names Lucy wouldn't be able to pronounce. Lucy had slept over at Mira's house one time, and had inspected what Mira kept under her bed (*The Monster at the End of This Book*, an extra blanket, pipe cleaners, wooden alligators), and peered under the comforter to note the colour of her sheets (blue). After that, Mira changed the sheets and put more things under the bed, so if Lucy ever told anybody about these intimate details of Mira's life, she would be wrong.

"Let's do a test," suggested Lucy Chin. Morning recess had just started. Children still streamed out of the steel double doors, wearing baseball gloves and holding skipping ropes. The two girls crouched together on the four-by-fours that bordered the playground sand. Mira wished she had eaten her applesauce faster.

"I don't know if we have time," said Mira, not curious

about the test's design. She scanned the school property for teachers. If she saw a yard monitor holding a garbage bag, she would run to help clean up. She would claim she wanted to win more class points for the monthly school prize. Lucy would abandon her for the playground, to swing on the monkey bars or the rings, her legs bending like hinges, the ground beneath her sharp and white with small pebbles, her face as cold as the metal under her curled hands. Mira would pick up trash at the teacher's side, even the grape juice boxes that leaked over her and whose smell made her want to retch.

"There's time," said Lucy, taking Mira's applesauce from her. "Hold your arms out."

Mira extended her arms and rolled up her sleeves as Lucy instructed. Lucy took the plastic spoon and began to spread a thin layer of applesauce over Mira's arms. It formed sticky stripes over the soft hairs. She put more on Mira's neck and then on her face.

"Go stand over there," said Lucy, pointing at a secluded area under where the school building's roof jutted out. The bee corner. There must have been a hidden hive under the roof that the janitors had not yet removed, because bees waited there, as if for a secret meeting, forming palpable electricity in the surrounding air.

"Are those really bees, or are they yellow jackets, or wasps?" Mira asked, stalling. Four of the fifteen recess minutes had passed.

"I told you they were bees," said Lucy. She placed one hand on Mira's back, careful not to get applesauce on herself, and pushed Mira hard towards the bees.

Mira looked around again for the teacher, but he must have

been confiscating a tennis ball or blowing a whistle at somebody or clearing up a traffic jam on the slide. The area was deserted; all the other children had disappeared to the playground or the back field. She dragged herself over to the shady corner, slowly, careful not to jostle the bees that socialized on the wall ledge, careful not to open her mouth. When the bees began to land on her, Mira tried to think of what it felt like — marbles rolling over her skin, or a roaming cat's paw. By thinking of these, of the visceral, immediate feelings, she could almost ignore her fear. She considered how she must look, standing alone there. If enough bees covered her body, colouring her in a constant moving pattern of opaque black and yellow, she might look like a campfire, with a girl instead of kindling. For a moment, she felt a terrible urge to stop, drop, and roll. Logic kept her from doing this. She didn't want the bee bodies crushed under her, into her. So she stood there, waiting the eleven interminable minutes for the recess bell to ring, standing and waiting, like a girl on fire, a girl aflame, watching Lucy Chin watching her, watching Lucy Chin licking the applesauce spoon.

UNTIL SHE MET Lucy Chin, Mira thought bullies had to be boys. They needed to be taller than you, so you'd have to stand on your toes to spit in their eyes. After meeting Lucy Chin, she practised the spitting while brushing her teeth, but in the times when she was close enough to Lucy's face, her saliva failed her. She knew that after spitting, there wouldn't be anywhere to run where Lucy Chin couldn't find her. Even if she made it out of the classroom or the school grounds or Lucy's house and somehow into her own house, locking all the doors behind her, she would still have to see her the next day. Lucy Chin's mother held four part-time jobs, including driving the school bus. Lucy always sat two seats from the front, where her mother couldn't hear what she whispered to Mira, but could still offer a certain protection.

In books Mira read later, she came across bullies whose motives arose from being richer or dumber or somehow insecure. She read these books and contemplated what Lucy's motives might have been. There were girl bullies in those books, girls with charisma, who delivered sharp, quotable dialogue to their tragic girlfriend minions. They were beautiful; they had original thoughts. Mira tried to picture Lucy Chin with a sizzling personality, but it was impossible. Her only creativity came out in the various punishments she thought up.

"I'M LUCY CHIN," Lucy Chin had said on the first day they met, patting Mira jovially on the shoulder, like a colleague. She always used her full name, but later Mira began calling her just Lucy in her head, in silent rebellion.

They lived on the same street, and before they met they had orbited around each other — in different kindergarten and first grade classes, different after-school activities. They had probably passed each other on bicycles, Mira thought, initially pleased with this idea, to have found a potential friend, so close. This must mean there were other people and things she hadn't discovered in her small universe, an infinite number perhaps. It was like the time she'd lifted a rock in her front yard and found an oblong beetle and then couldn't identify it in her book of insects and thought she'd discovered a new species.

That first time at Lucy's house, she noticed it had a yeasty smell, as though organisms grew anaerobically out of the carpet. Not that it wasn't clean — the trinket display was absent of dust and a lower step held a basket of folded laundry — but the windows seemed as though they'd never been opened and the walls seemed to take up more space than in other houses, overstepping their boundaries and bulging with gratuitous corners. After about ten minutes of drinking orange juice in the kitchen while the mothers worked out a babysitting schedule and Ravi opened and closed all the cupboard doors, Mira asked to use the bathroom. Lucy Chin led her down the hall. They passed a small living room where Mr. Chin read the newspaper, sunk into a suede loveseat. He hadn't said hello. Behind him was a shelf lined with jars that looked like they were full of somebody's tonsils. She never found out if that was what they were. In the bathroom, after washing her hands with the green shell-shaped soap and drying them on flowered paper towel, Mira tried to open the door but couldn't. She worried that the walls had grown too close to the door edges, their paint sticking against each other and sealing, and that she would be trapped forever in this square, airless room. At least she had drinking water, she thought, looking at the faucet.

She tried the door again, aiming not to make too loud a sound. The lock looked easy enough, the same as at her house. She yanked at the door. She said "Mom?" quietly, knowing she wouldn't be heard. "Ravi?" she said, banking on her brother's superhuman hearing. She thought about calling Lucy's dad, since he was closest, but hesitated at saying "Mr. Chin" aloud. Then the door opened, suddenly and easily, and Lucy stood outside of it.

"The door was stuck," said Mira.

"It's never been stuck before," the girl replied, in a voice that refused to fluctuate in tone. But then she smiled and took Mira's hand and pulled her into the kitchen, where their mothers had finalized the arrangements.

"I'M THE BOSS of you," Lucy said to her in the back of the classroom while they cut fake leaves out of construction paper to glue on to the fake autumn tree on the wall. When second grade started, they'd been put in the same class for the first time.

"What do you mean?" asked Mira, pausing in her task.

"I tell you what to do and you do it," explained Lucy almost patiently, her safety scissors open and ready.

"You mean like a game?" she asked, and Lucy shook her head.

The teacher came by and collected their leaves.

The boss of you. It reminded her of robots, boxes of galvanized metal arranged on top of each other, filled with a tangle of red wires, square faces blinking with lights, walking and talking and operated by remote control, programmed to make breakfast but not to eat it, saying pre-recorded robot words in electronic voices. To really have somebody be your boss, she figured, you'd have to have almost no brain. You had to be detached, or have a wire loose somewhere. Even robots rebelled, in movies. You had to have enough of a brain to do things but not to think about them.

Like those kids in 314, where her brother was now. They kept one kid in that class on a leash though he must have been twelve years old, a squiggly phone cord leash that tied his wrist to the teacher's when they ventured into the hallways. One time, Mira had peered through the classroom window and watched the teacher grasp Ravi's hand, which was holding a pencil, and guide it pointlessly over a piece of notebook paper.

"GO OVER THERE," said Lucy Chin.

There meant Fantasia, the pink brick building across the street from the McConnaghey Centre, where they had their Brownie meetings, in downtown Richmond Hill. After the Brownie meeting, if Mira's mother was late to pick them up, Mira and Lucy stood and observed the women who lingered outside its doors in their costumes, slender and fragile as insects, smoking cigarettes and laughing into each other.

"Why would I go over there?"

"Just do it. Go inside," Lucy said.

Mira wouldn't mind going inside. A hundred times she'd passed by that building with her mother, on the way to the library, and every time her mother made a clicking noise with her tongue and hurried her along. In daylight, the building reminded her of discarded bubblegum wrappers — not only the colour, but the way the brick looked crumpled. Now, at night, lit up with pot lights under the roof, Mira thought the colour was more fuchsia or magenta, colours she'd only just discovered. The inside, she imagined, would be like nothing else in Richmond Hill. The building appeared small from the outside, only one storey high, with a flat, shingled roof, but she pictured the inside as cavernous, with multiple lower levels opening into the ground like the open pit mines she'd seen pictures of at school. She imagined the walls painted black, floors in slippery gold, but nobody would ever slip. The women would mingle, their elbows rubbing against each other as they made clever, biting remarks, as men in suits brought them drinks — fuchsia/magenta drinks in clean glasses with hip-shaped curves. Her mother owned a few glasses like that. On Sunday afternoons, Mira, her mother, and Ravi made mango milkshakes in the blender and poured them into the glasses, drinking from straws almost too narrow to carry the dense liquid to their mouths. Mira thought the inside of Fantasia would be as perfect as mango milkshakes in lovely glasses when her mother was in a good mood and Ravi was almost normal, only amplified with lights and colour and sound.

"I think only older people are allowed to go in there," said Mira, wishing it weren't true.

"*Obviously*. You'll go in, they'll tell you to get out. Just go in for a second."

"Aren't you going to come too?" It seemed to Mira like the sort of fun adventure girls might have, sneaking into a place and solidifying their friendship; she still thought they might be friends.

"No, I'll stay here." Lucy stared at her, angry. Mira couldn't figure out why she would be angry, but she stepped forward to the curb, looking both ways at the fast yellow lights of cars speeding down that congested, narrow area of Yonge Street.

The women looked down at her as she passed, but only smiled and exchanged looks. Mira opened the pink wooden door and went inside. It was as dark as outside, and she couldn't see much, because a partition blocked her view. Lines of coloured light flickered over the wall, and music played, quieter than she'd expected. A tall man in a black T-shirt sold admission and Mira thought of slipping past his knees unnoticed, but then a customer plucked the back of her brown Brownie uniform dress.

"Where are you headed?" he asked.

"My dad's inside," she lied.

"How about I go get him for you," the man said.

Mira wondered if there was an Indian man inside who would pass as her father. She thought of Lucy waiting on the other side of the road, and of her mother coming to pick her up. The man looked at her with impatience. A girl's leg flashed behind him and she observed it, knowing she was too self-contained to run around the man and make her way inside the place. "I'll wait for him outside," she said, and jerked out of his grip, turned and left, the man and the other man laughing and laughing. *Her dad's here while the kid's at the Girl Scout meeting!*, they laughed. She had disgraced her father's name, she thought, before she deleted the memory of the too-soft music and the men she'd seen — dressed not in black blazers but in wrinkled, cotton blends — and kept her old imagined image of Fantasia brilliant and intact. In the car on the way home, Lucy pinched her arm, digging in her fingernails. Neither her mother nor Ravi saw. She thought about how people pinched each other or themselves to prove they weren't dreaming, to prove they were really there. They dropped Lucy off at her house, waiting for her to open the door, turn and smile and wave, her hair turning with her like a scuttling beetle, round and shiny and black.

"WAIT AT THE other bus stop," Lucy told her, indicating the next stop on the bus route, about six blocks away.

Mira barely noticed that, waiting for the bus each morning, she'd been crossing her fingers and praying not to see Lucy's pale face in the window. What Lucy wanted her to do was walk the six blocks from this stop to the next, after her mother dropped her off. She didn't mind the walk, because she passed houses she didn't normally notice, and she liked to see who matched which garage door colours with which bricks. It delighted her to see a cream-coloured house with a bright turquoise garage. She didn't even worry about being abducted. The problem arose in that her mother sometimes dropped her off at the stop only a couple of minutes before the bus arrived, which didn't leave much time to get to the other stop. She'd first wait until her mother had driven away, and then check her pink velco-strapped watch, which she'd synchronized with the school clocks. If she had fewer than five minutes, she'd run, feeling the heavy thermos inside her backpack hitting her back as she ran.

The actual bus ride held other stresses. Lucy and Mira shared a seat and Lucy shared her thoughts, for example that the teacher only liked Mira because she was the only Indian in the class (Mira questioned if this was true and if it mattered), that Mira had too-long hair and should cut it short (but Mira loved her hair, loved hiding under it and twirling it around and pretending she had the inky tentacles of an octopus), that Mira was ugly, hideous even, and didn't smile enough, and didn't talk enough (strange, since Lucy Chin also fell into the quiet category), that she needed to improve herself, her posture, needed to do better on math quizzes (according to Lucy, Mr. Chin said spelling never got anybody anywhere), and if she didn't make these improvements, boys would never like her (Mira found boys completely irrelevant, except in comparison to girls, the gender she might forever distrust).

Lucy Chin traded stickers unfairly, gave Mira a single used scratch and sniff sticker, in the shape of a pear, for a whole package of shiny zoo animal stickers. Mira gave the sticker to Ravi, who stuck it on a piece of blank paper and then drew other pears, exactly like it, in even rows across the page.

Lucy Chin made her push a bird's nest off her second storey bedroom window ledge, her reasoning being that it obscured the view of the backyard. The nest had three blue eggs in it, like Cadbury eggs. They cracked when they landed in the grass. On days with nicer weather, Lucy Chin's mom took them to Mill Pond and they fed the swans and geese the crumbled ends of bread. When *The Liberal* reported dead swans found, one-by-one, with twisted, broken necks, scattered here and there, wings spread wide along the Mill Pond walkways, Mira knew Lucy hadn't done it — the crimes had happened at night, and the birds were too big — but she still pictured her thin, eight-year-old friend standing by the dark water with her arms around a huge, white, struggling bird.

Lucy Chin attended Mira's birthday party, along with six girls — chosen randomly. They went to the newly opened Richmond Hill wave pool. The pool alternated between periods of waves and calm. During one of the wave periods, Lucy held Mira's head underwater for a stretch of time. Mira carved the water with her hands, trying to push away Lucy's slippery arms. Back at Mira's house, before Mira opened her presents, Lucy whispered, "You can open mine, but don't take it out of the packaging. I want it back tomorrow." Ravi ate pizza next to them, playing with the melted cheese. Mira's mother took pictures. One of the other girls, Cynthia, hugged Mira, big and genuine, after Mira gave her a loot bag. Mira shrank for a second and then hugged her back. Cynthia smelled like cake frosting, and Mira didn't want to let go.

Lucy Chin's present turned out to be a ceramic doll, its head tilted coyly downwards. Its skin had the iridescence of carnival glass. Instead of returning it, Mira wanted to smash it with a cloth-covered hammer, like she'd seen in a craft book at the library, and cement it into a mosaic plate, and eat odd and lovely things from it, things Lucy Chin could never guess at — frozen red grapes, clumps of brown sugar, white overgrown cucumber seeds.

Every day after school, they walked from the afternoon bus stop to Lucy's house. Lucy made Mira walk ahead of her. She kicked the backs of Mira's knees until they ached. Mira longed to spring away, but needed some invisible flare gun to loosen her legs. She watched the ground, counting the sidewalk squares and the shadows of trees, angling in the afternoon light. She created games with illogical rules. If she avoided stepping on all the lines on the ground, Lucy Chin would move away to a foreign land. At night, Mira felt her legs throbbing to the phantom rhythm of Lucy's steps. She hid most of the bruises from her mother by being more private with her bathing and dressing rituals. Still, her mother must have thought her exceedingly clumsy, to accept not only the bruises, but the occasional bite, and several paper cuts, where Lucy had tested the sharpness of paper across Mira's arms.

She told her brother once. He was sitting on the carpet in front of the television at home, watching an educational show, swinging his head back and forth, singing along to a song, with incorrect lyrics. "Lucy Chin might be a bad person," she said. She listed some of the things Lucy had done. She imagined him finding her and beating her up, like a brother should.

Her brother nodded.

"Lucy Chin is mean," she said.

"People should always be nice," her brother said.

One day, Mira got on the bus and Lucy wasn't there.

"Lucy's at home sick today," Lucy's mother told her.

The seat next to Mira remained empty throughout the drive to school. The amount of extra space was overwhelming. *I could keep my backpack here next to me*, she thought, and moved it from her lap to the seat. *I could stretch my legs out*, she thought, but wasn't sure if it was safe to sit sideways, or if Lucy's mom would yell. She didn't yell often, only once in a while at her house after school, when she'd yell at Lucy's brother in Chinese and then he would scoot to emptying the dishwasher. Lucy's mother was kind to a fault, so Mira assumed she had gotten it from Mr. Chin, with whom Mira had interacted only minimally. On the occasions when she had seen him, he had spoken only of newspaper articles.

In class, Mira went through lessons as usual. She worked on a craft project, taped feathers to corrugated cardboard and stapled paper to paper, solved math problems, and leaned sleepily against a chair while the teacher read aloud. During the first recess, Mira played by herself, removing a loose button from her sweater and burying it, then searching to retrieve it again. Scooping the sand, and even letting grains fly back in her face was mildly pleasing because Lucy wasn't there. By lunch, Mira felt three feelings. One was the ache she had on Sunday nights, knowing she would have to get back on the bus with Lucy the next morning. The second was loneliness. The third resulted from the first two, and had a hint of strategy in it — if she could align herself with other girls, make other friends, it might be her way out. Lucy Chin would return to school but Mira would have moved on. Mira would walk right by her on the bus and link arms with a different classmate, whose mother could probably take over as babysitter.

At lunch, Mira clutched a granola bar and stood at the edge of the yard, considering her options. There were several groups of girls from her class, huddled outside portable classrooms and in the playground. She ruled out the bigger groups, not sure she could speak loudly enough to join them. A few of the smaller groups were eliminated based on members (intimidating) or activities (Cops and Robbers). Finally, she decided on a group of three girls — one was birthday party Cynthia — talking quietly on a low bench that faced away from her. Their hair appealed to her, one girl's climbing the air with static, another's ponytailed, the third's swirling to her shoulders. Her own hair would make a reasonable fourth. All three of them were pulling the tips of their shoes (sneakers, Mary Janes, out-of-season sandals) through the gravel at their feet. Maybe they were talking about their shoes, comparing them, or maybe about the gravel, the grating sound it made as it moved.

She approached, opening her granola bar and chewing it, to seem more casual.

"Hi," she said, but wasn't close enough yet, so they didn't hear her. "Hi," she said again, stepping closer to the side of the bench, and this time it was startlingly loud.

"Hi Mira," said Cynthia. "Where's Lucy today?"

"She has a cold so she stayed home."

"Oh." The three girls looked at her.

"What are you guys doing?" Mira asked.

"Nothing," static-hair girl said. "What are you doing?"

"Not much. Eating a granola bar because I didn't have time to finish it inside." Mira thought it sounded like one of her mother's phone conversations with Lala Aunty.

"Yeah we would go on the playground but it's so crowded we might fall off and get killed," Cynthia said. Mira liked the exaggeration of this.

"And Cops and Robbers is such an idiotic game," static-hair girl said.

"And what are you supposed to *do* with stickers once you've collected them?" said ponytail. "You look at them, and then what? You can't even stick them on anything, because then they decrease in value."

"Her dad is a stock broker," said Cynthia.

Mira agreed with them, and tried to think of a matching apt comment of her own. "What about jumping rope? I know it's pretty foolish," she added quickly, quoting Lala Aunty, who called everything foolish.

"Yeah but it's good exercise," rationalized Cynthia.

Unfortunately, none of them had a rope, so Mira couldn't figure out what to say next. The girls kept looking at her, perhaps waiting for her to leave so they could resume confiding in one another about their families and secrets and ambitions. "Well, I should go," Mira said, remembering how Lala Aunty said one should not overstay one's welcome.

The girls seemed surprised, and then Mira regretted saying goodbye. The bell rang as she was leaving them, and the three girls went back together to the school entrance. Mira followed just behind them, matching their pace, pretending to be a fourth in their little group, until all of the students in their class formed a line for the teacher to direct inside.

Lucy returned the next day, though Mira had hoped she might have tuberculosis. At recess, she saw Cynthia looking at her, and she said to Lucy Chin that maybe they should go over there. Lucy glared, and they stayed where they were.

"YOU HAVE THE longest hair out of all the girls in the class," said Lucy, but she didn't mean it as a compliment. Bending her head to touch Mira's like they were dear friends or co-conspirators, she compared her own hair, short and straight, to Mira's, long and tangled.

"It's not that long," said Mira, willing her hair to seem shorter than it was.

"You better not get on the bus tomorrow with that hair," she said. "It should be shorter than mine. Otherwise, my brother will kill you."

Lucy's elusive brother was older, in ninth grade at least, and Lucy often used him as a threat. Mira was uncertain about what "kill" meant in this case. Whenever Mira saw him, she would try and judge if he were the type of person who might attack a little girl. He must be. Mira never knew what to think about other people's brothers, who acted cool and argued and said funny things.

So Mira went home and got the scissors from the kitchen drawer. In her mother's bathroom, she climbed up on the counter to see better, and rested her bare feet in the sink. She marvelled at Lucy's care in not cutting the hair herself, not letting the evidence accumulate on the floor of her own house. She whispered goodbye to her hair, silly but necessary, and held the scissors up. She cut bangs first, a straight line across her forehead, thinking they might look okay, but they didn't. So she cut them shorter, and then moved the scissors around to the back, first just shortening the pieces an inch at a time. She had never had her hair really cut before, except for trims her mother did herself. Finally, she took a fistful of it and closed her eyes and snipped until there was nothing left to snip. When she opened her eyes, her hair stood out from her head like a boy's, except where a few long pieces hung off her scalp, but worse than that, her mother had opened the door and come in, silent in her shock, rushing forward to take the scissors away.

"What are you doing? Why would you do that?" She shook Mira's arms until her whole body shook, and picked her up off the counter and stood her in front of her. She put her fingers through Mira's hair. "Mira! You look ugly! You know that? Why would you do that?"

And Mira started to cry, and almost, *almost*, told, but she couldn't, not just because of Lucy's brother, but because she didn't want her mother to know how stupid she was, how brainless. Now she was stuck, and maybe it would go on forever. She should have been smarter. "Don't cry," her mother said, looking surprised at the outburst. Her mother sat down on the closed toilet lid and sighed and hugged her, and said reassuringly that it would grow out, but that really she should have just asked if she wanted a haircut and they could have gone to a hairdresser. She pressed her face to Mira's as though to share her tears, and bits of hair stuck to her cheeks where the tears made them wet.

When Mira came home with multiple bee stings on her face and arms, she told her mother she'd gone over to the bee corner to retrieve a stray tennis ball and had stumbled across a hive. It was the same story she'd told the recess monitor. Before telling anybody, she'd gone to the bathroom and rinsed off the applesauce. When the teacher asked her to point out the hive so the janitors could remove it, Mira had started crying — she was turning into a crier — and he had let it go unanswered, deciding aloud that with so many bees, the hive couldn't be too hard to find.

Her mother put hydrocortisone on the stings, and gave her a swig of Benadryl, but it still took a long time for Mira to fall asleep. She wondered if she'd die like Macaulay Culkin in *My Girl*. She kept thinking she heard bees in the room. The heat from the air vents sounded like buzzing, and the blankets on her felt like millions of tiny, landing legs.

The next day was the weekend, and Mira's mother took Mira and Ravi to Hillcrest Mall because Ravi needed shoes. They took the movie theatre entrance, the hallway of which was decorated with movie posters, framed in glass. One of the posters had, in its centre, a large brown eye with dark lashes, and faint red veins surrounding the pupil. The pupil revealed the shadow of a menacing man, which Mira disregarded. A bee perched at the edge of the eye, where the skin touched the eyeball. Enlarged in the poster, the bee was about the size of Mira's fist, so large you could see strands of its fur, amber-coloured, matching its translucent wings. Its legs looked almost metallic, golden in the light, and sharp; its front legs literally touched the eye, as though the bee were trying to enter it.

Mira couldn't make herself walk past it. Her mother and Ravi had gone a few feet ahead before realizing that she had stopped.

"It's just a picture, Miru," said her mother, but Mira barely heard her. She was remembering the bees and how they had congregated on her face, and how she had wanted to brush them away but more bees had gathered on her hands. Her eyes had closed automatically, even more terrifying, because she could only hear them, flitting at her ears. Was a bee like an earwig? Would it go inside an ear? Easily, it could burrow its way inside, choose to live inside her, turn her body into a hive. Her body would sound constantly of buzzing; she would hear it and try to find it, to eliminate the source. They'd sculpt their hexagonal honeycombs in stacks down her throat. When she spoke or breathed, it would be through honeycomb, which sounded sweet or pretty, but wasn't. She had eaten honeycomb before, but took too big a bite at once, so she struggled to chew on the wax and nearly choked on the cloying, too-intense flavour.

She stayed a few feet away from the poster, took it in, but had a worry — one she knew was irrational — that the bee would come out of the picture, and that more would follow.

"Mira, come on inside," her mother said. She picked Mira up and carried her, facing her away from the poster, down the hallway into the mall.

IT ENDED WHEN Lucy Chin grew out of it. One recess near the end of second grade, Lucy Chin joined a game of Cops and Robbers and left Mira alone in the grass, where she sat and made chains of dandelions. Another recess, Lucy Chin went to play handball with a group of boys; for five minutes, Mira watched her dashing here and there in her bicycle shorts, which everybody was wearing those days but made Lucy Chin look like she was trying too hard, and then Mira got up and invited herself to skip rope with her three desired friends, and though she kept looking over at Lucy Chin, she never saw Lucy look back at her. They didn't sit together in class after that recess, and when they went to Lucy's house after school, they watched television silently until Mira lied and said her mother was coming home early that day, and walked home, using the key she still kept around her neck to enter the house, and ate potato chips she found in one of the kitchen's hiding places. When her mother came home, Mira declared that she did not need a babysitter anymore.

On the second-last day of school, Lucy Chin stood up in class and announced that she was moving to Vancouver, where her father had found a new job. The teacher insisted Lucy exchange addresses with everybody in the class, to keep in touch. In July, Mira received a letter from her, on unicorn stationery. It had ordinary sentences in round letters; she couldn't believe Lucy Chin had written it. "How are you? I am fine. Our new house is big." She didn't answer it. Years later, cleaning out her desk, she found the address and paused her cleaning to write Lucy Chin a letter. She began the letter as ordinarily as Lucy's, then deleted it, then wrote in some questions, some accusations, demanding to know why, why her, why at all, then started listing all the tortures she could remember, then thought maybe they weren't so horrible after all — stickers, birthday presents, birds? — then she worried that Lucy Chin might not even remember her, and deleted the letter entirely. She composed a new letter, giving an update on herself and changes in the town. The letter was posted with her mother's bill payments, but Mira never received a response. In college, she typed in Lucy's name on the internet and found a dozen Lucy Chins, said to herself, haha, she has multiplied. The search yielded one photo that might have been her — a girl with long, black hair that had been tinted red. She stood with two other girls, whose demeanours Mira checked for signs of abuse. There was *affection* in their body language, in their faces, and Mira tried to conjure up a memory of laughing with Lucy Chin, but this proved impossible.

IT WAS IN the spring before Lucy Chin had left — March, Mira remembered, because they'd just returned from a week of break, which hadn't really been a break for her because she had spent it at Lucy's house — when Mira's mother drove Mira and Ravi to their bus stop, and they spotted a boy out the window.

"Isn't that the bully?" their mother asked. Mira thought she meant Lucy Chin at first, and was surprised to see the swaggering, red-haired boy who had chased Ravi. The chasing had dwindled somewhat under the eye of Mrs. Chin, but it still happened when both Ravi and the bully were at the bus stop early enough. Months ago, Mira's mother had asked Mira to point out the boy in the school record, which had pictures of all the kids from kindergarten to eighth grade. "That's him?" her mother had asked. "He's so small." In the pictures, everybody looked small, thought Mira. The record was printed in black and white and laminated. The faces were bleached out under the gleaming plastic. Lucy Chin looked like a picture that went along with an obituary in the paper, ghostly, from another time.

Mira was surprised when her mother recognized the boy now, and surprised again when her mother dropped them off and parked her car around the corner. Mira noticed, but the boy must not have, because he immediately started chasing after Ravi. Ravi began to run, his arms lifted as though he thought he could fly. Mira stood at the bus stop and felt her irrelevance, felt herself become smaller in the distance as her brother ran farther away, and for a second, she saw how her mother must have seen him — with a clutching pride that he could run so elegantly, his legs beating through the air. He whipped over the pavement and only at the end of the street, where the pond began, did the boy catch up, because there was nowhere left for Ravi to run. He shoved Ravi once, hard, and retreated, began his swagger back up the street.

At the shove, Mira saw her mother's car begin to move. She saw her mother roll up the sleeves of her shirt and accelerate over the concrete towards the boy. He waited for the car to stop, but it didn't. The car headed straight at him, much faster than Mira had ever seen cars go on the neighbourhood road, and the boy jumped, his legs nearly buckling under him. He stumblingly switched directions and ran away from the car — too stupid, Mira thought, to run sideways onto the lawn where the car couldn't go, or maybe he thought she'd drive right up there after him, crush him under the wheels with the lawn ornaments and discarded tricycles. She wished wistfully that Lucy Chin were the one running. But even if she told her mother, it wasn't like her mother could run down Lucy with her car. Lucy Chin would never place herself vulnerably in the middle of a road. Even if, by chance, she did, and Mira's mother began to drive the car towards her, Lucy Chin wouldn't move. She'd stand her ground and get run over, and then Mira's mother would be in trouble, though probably not for murder, since Lucy Chin was the type of girl who would be run over by a car and still survive.

Mira's mother chased the boy almost to the end of the road before the boy regained his senses and turned onto a house driveway. Mira's mother swerved the car right up to the garage door, followed until she was inches from his legs — she was going to run over him, Mira thought, knees first — and then the car stopped. The boy was gasping, his face pink and chest pulsing, as Mira's mother backed up the car.

"I'll drive you to school," she told Ravi and Mira once they were both in the car. The other kids at the stop spoke inaudibly. The car door shut; their mother started driving. And then Ravi started laughing, his cheeks round, his mouth wide and exposing his miniature teeth. Mira wondered if her mother would get angry, but, as Mira watched with disbelief, her mother began laughing too, squinting so she could still keep track of the road, and then Mira was laughing, falling back to her seat and touching one cheek to the glass of the window, their laughter electric and volatile and wild and piercing.

Breaking

"I'M THE BOSS of you," Mira said to Ravi.

It was the fall after Lucy had left. Mira and Ravi and their mother had large pieces of paper in front of them on the dining table. Mira was reconstructing Pangaea on hers for a school project. She'd found a tall, floppy Atlas at the library, and the librarian helped her photocopy its pages, lifting the lid of the copier and placing the book down carefully on the glass. Mira used scissors to cut carefully around the edges of South America, then held it up next to the other continents. She was confused; she couldn't remember which country went where, and the edges didn't match exactly like a puzzle, as her teacher had said they would.

"Which one goes where?" she had asked her mother, holding up Africa and Australia. Her mother took them from her and moved the pieces of paper this way and that way in the air.

"Let me run and get the globe," her mother said, and jumped up from her chair.

Mira waited, closed the scissors, and put them back in her

pencil case. She looked over at Ravi's piece of paper. It had a sort of map on it, too, and the ocean was covered with wavy stripes of different blues. "What is that supposed to be?" she asked him.

"It's countries," said Ravi.

"Those aren't even real countries," said Mira. She sat up on her knees in the chair to get a better look. "You should look at the map and do it. Or no, you could try inventing your own world — with new countries! What do you want to name them?"

"Oh, I don't know," said Ravi, as though she'd asked him what he wanted to drink.

"You can name them after people we know, maybe?"

"That's okay," said Ravi.

He never wanted to do anything. She glared at him.

"I'm the boss of you," she said. "If I tell you something, you have to do it."

"No you're not!" said Ravi, shoving her.

He was smarter than she was. She narrowed her eyes at him, and then, in a voice so angry it was out of breath, said, "I am. Go get me a glass of water."

Ravi squealed and hit his hands against the table, dropping the crayon he was holding. But then he went and got the water, brought it back.

"Thanks, Ravi," Mira said, forgetting that Lucy Chin had never thanked anybody. She glowered at him again to make up for it.

"What?" he asked.

Their mother came back with the globe, popping it from hand to hand like a basketball. "All right, I've figured it out …" she started to say.

"What?" said Ravi again, widening his eyes at Mira.

"What is it, Rav?" their mother asked. She was facing away from Mira, so Mira held her finger up to her face and silently shhhed him, turning her head slowly from side to side, like how she imagined a stranger would when offering candy.

"Mira's bothering me," he said.

"Mira, stop it," her mother said.

Mira stopped it, but glared at Ravi again when her mother looked away. She called up the cruel image of Lucy Chin like some kind of spirit guide, as she would call it up again in the future, pale and indefinite in her memory, hoping it might give her the capacity to be mean.

THAT SAME EVENING, Mira had to go to the basement to complete her chore of vacuuming the prayer room. She had never fretted about this chore before, had never worried much about insects before Lucy, had picked up ladybugs and let them wander over her clothing as she admired their backs, smooth and glossy as jelly beans, had collected crickets in open-topped boxes, tenderly encouraging them to vault over the cardboard walls. Spiders guarded corners, not fat hairy spiders, but slender ones, with speck-sized bodies and legs like the women at Fantasia. They pulled thin webs across the blue walls, and were barely noticeable until you aimed at them with the vacuum cleaner, and then the spiders would begin to run, fighting against the suction, their webs shaking under them and casting tremulous grey shadows.

Despite its seeming sacrilegious to murder the tiny creatures while the many visages of gods looked on from paintings and sculptures and statues, Mira had loved this task. The gods lined the prayer room walls with their placid faces, sitting on lotus petals or tigers, holding out palms for blessings, as if they approved.

She brought the vacuum cleaner down from upstairs, hoisting the cord over her shoulders, bracing the appliance's weight against her body. She went to plug it in, but there was a spider waiting on top of the electric socket.

Another spider appeared from under an electric brass lamp, coming purposefully towards her, and she screamed. She couldn't remember the last time she'd heard her voice so loud, and was embarrassed by it, but secretly pleased. And anyway, the basement was soundproofed. The spider actually skittered away. She screamed again, first at that single spider, then at all spiders. The sound rolled around the corners of the room. Mira screamed unintelligible words, and then curse words that she had heard before, which seemed to be waiting inside her. She felt foolish, too loud, but ignored it, hoping some entity in the room would understand her and carry the message across the country to Vancouver, to Lucy Chin, who had never heard Mira's voice above its shallow whisper.

THE NEXT WEEK, when she went to the basement, she broke something on purpose. On the curved edge of the wooden shelf of gods, there stood a blue porcelain urn. Her father had built the shelf when he was alive, had sawed it and attached the swooping brackets in the basement, before the basement was finished — she imagined him with a workshop set up in one corner, sanding lovingly, sawdust suspended in air. He'd bought the urn, too.

She'd come down to the basement not to clean it, but because her mother had sent her to get the money that was inside this urn, and bring it back upstairs. "I'm pretty sure there's money in there, there should be," her mother said. But when Mira opened it, there was only a piece of paper that said "IOU $463." *I owe you.* An IOU to God. *I owe you, God.* This was the jar where they put their offerings to God, a dollar or two, every time they prayed. It had been her father's idea, to collect it over time and donate it to the temple, though the temple had its own urns, more like filing cabinets, with rectangular slots for coins. When they went to the temple — not often, once every couple months — her mother would reach into her black swoop of a purse and pull out quarters, giving them to Mira and Ravi to deposit. Mira always listened for the clink, estimating how much money was inside by this sound. She wondered if one of the priests was assigned to open it, and if he ever took any for himself. Or maybe all the priests sat together on the floor and rolled the coins into paper for the bank, and then they all went to the bank together, swathed only in white cotton, each of their wire-haired potato chests covered only by a diagonal sash.

She supposed there were obligations you had to God; she could guess this from the religious stories her mother told her. You were obligated to be good, to be honest, to respect others, to treat people fairly — there was a lot of overlap, it seemed, with the pointedly secular discussions of character and values they had at school. "We must learn to respect others," the teacher had said, and one boy who nobody liked had raised his hand and asked, "Why?" and then "Why?" again at her response, and he whyed approximately a million times at everything the teacher said, and though her class was annoyed with the boy, and though it was only a class full of nine-year-olds, even they could see that the teacher couldn't think of a good answer.

But to owe good behaviour to God made more sense. God had given you basically everything — life, your family, good weather — probably God was the one who had made Lucy Chin move away. She had certainly prayed for it. It was okay with her if being good was a favour, if everything good that happened was a debt to be repaid. But if bad things happened — here was where it became complicated — didn't she owe God less? Every time her brother started laughing uncontrollably at the dinner table, every time Lucy Chin bruised her calves, was it not a deposit back into her bank, a reduction in her loan, one fewer occasion where goodness was expected of her? Her mother owed God four hundred and sixty-three dollars. She would have to be better, now, or find the money somewhere. It had probably gone to her brother's therapy group.

The porcelain urn had taken on the cold temperature of the basement. She felt it in her hands and then she didn't, because she had thrown the urn on the floor. It broke beautifully. And she had never heard such a satisfying sound as that smash. The pieces were blue on their surface — a dark, glazed, kiln-developed blue — but white on their insides, unfinished and dry. Immediately, she went for the dustpan and bent to sweep, and even that was satisfying, picking the big pieces out first and then brushing up the small ones, catching stray lint along with them.

It was the first time she'd ever intentionally ruined anything, a sort of coming-of-age. And even so, it wasn't like she'd planned it, or that her intention had been the ruining. There was a smooth, solid mass of porcelain in her hands, and then there wasn't, then it was sharp pieces on the floor. It was a transformation. What she had intended had been only to let go of it, to feel that instant of something to nothing.

"How much was in there?" her mother asked her when she came upstairs. Her mother was folding laundry with the television on.

"I couldn't find it," said Mira, and her mother said it must be behind one of the God statues, or moved into a cupboard, and that she would look for it herself later.

MIRA KNEW HER family didn't have any money. It had been a surprise when, two weeks ago, her mother had arrived home from work with a stack of flattened boxes tied to the top of her car. She took them down and asked Ravi to help her carry them into the house, which he did, bending at the waist and balancing them on his back, so that he looked like an airplane.

Inside, they began assembling the boxes, and Mira whispered, "What are they for?" She wanted to think her mother had brought them home for a game, for building cardboard cities in the basement or backyard — they could paint black silhouettes of skyscrapers over the boxes, the windows yellow Post-it squares, and a background of blue night sky, with a slim moon and a sparse spatter of stars, and she could turn off all the lights and go inside and take a bag of potato chips and eat them slowly, crunching and letting her tongue absorb the salt and wondering if anybody knew where she was — but these boxes were brand new, not old supermarket boxes, and her mother wouldn't have spent money for no reason, and she was nine now, she'd known people who'd moved.

Later that week, her mother drove them to see the new house, just the outside of it, because there were people still living there. It was in their neighbourhood, basically, not far. "Look, a brick driveway, Ravi," her mother said. The house was inoffensive — a brick driveway, one young tree, a vague rock garden in a kidney shape — but it looked like a miniature house. Their house now had rooms that nobody slept in and closets full of her father's engineering textbooks. Where would the textbooks go?

The living room Persian rug stretched to a full three times Mira's height. During house cleaning, she and Ravi would each take an end and roll it up so her mother could sweep the hardwood — the rug was heavy and they breathed hard with the effort, and rolling it revealed the satiny label sewn on back that said BLUE TABRIZ and EATON'S. It had a gorgeous fringe that her mother scolded her once for braiding. She lay on it sometimes and counted the hidden creatures in its pale blue and red and black and amber patterns; there were leaping horses and morose lions, mountain goats and strange flowers and leafy branches, arranged symmetrically between its intricate borders. There could not be a room in the new house that was big enough for this rug. She confirmed this with her mother, who said, hesitantly, "Well, maybe we'll roll it up at one end and hide it behind the sofa."

In a miniature house, she didn't think they'd all be able to avoid each other when they wanted to. If she cried in her room, everyone would hear her and come running. When Lala Aunty came over, she'd be unable to escape her voice. Other than houses, what else of their possessions might be traded in for miniature? Maybe they would drink from smaller mugs and eat from smaller bowls, to make room in the cupboard. They'd roll the rugs in half, saw the furniture down until it fit against the narrow walls. She would have to stop eating potato chips, to keep from taking up more room.

Mira's mother gave Mira and Ravi each a large box and told them to pack up their rooms. First Ravi tried to put the comforter from his bed in his box (he didn't even try to fold it, Mira observed, just piled it in and punched it down with his hands, but it rose back up like pizza dough), but their mother saw him and laughed for the first time all week and said, "Just focus on the toys and clothes for now, Rav."

Mira put her many collections of erasers and stickers and My Little Ponies into the donation box. She kept her rock collection, though she'd lost some interest when, to save money, she'd stopped buying those mini chunks of pyrite and mica at the store and now picked her rocks off the street (it was stupid, she knew, because they all looked the same). She folded her clothes up into neat small bundles, except for her T-shirts, which she used to wrap up each of her more breakable possessions — ceramic cats from the dollar store, a hanging mobile of papier-mâché butterflies she'd made — and she put the plushest toys on top, though she was growing out of them, and doubted if there would be room in the new house. There wouldn't be room for any of their family's silly collections. The miniature walls would not have shelves built by her father, to line with Ravi's Hot Wheels cars. It would help them out a little, if they opened up the box marked "Norman Rockwell Decorative Plates," and found all the contents broken.

THE FIRST INDICATOR that they needed money had been when she'd overheard her mother tell Lala Aunty that Mira's father hadn't had any life insurance. Obviously, Mira had thought, since he had died. "You paid everything out of pocket?" Lala Aunty had asked.

"At least cremation was cheaper than burial," her mother had responded, monotone, before dropping her head into the pile of receipts on the kitchen table.

She wasn't completely sure what life insurance was, but funeral costs, Mira realized, must have been expensive. She had been too young to remember the funeral, but knew there had been two hundred people present ("So many people loved your dad," Lala Aunty had said to her once) and knew that food cost money and that even the temple charged for use of their hall. But the funeral had been several years ago; they must have paid it off by now.

Since then, Mira had kept track of the other costs — the house, the car, the phone, the electricity, the water. When Mira turned the faucet on to fill the bathtub or to rinse a dish, she considered how much the water was worth. She paused the water when she brushed her teeth. How did they measure how much water she was using? she wondered, unsettled by the idea she had of a large basin in the sewers below her house, collecting what went into their drain. She imagined this basin with markings on the side, like a big measuring cup, collecting and measuring every time she rinsed and spat, every time she peed. Was the amount of water that came out when you peed the same as the amount of water you drank? How did they discount the times when you drank juice, or had water at somebody else's house, or used somebody else's bathroom? She sensed that there were gaps in her knowledge, and sought to fill them. She wanted to know the price of electricity; she wanted to know why the numbers on the signs outside of gas stations changed so often, and how much it cost to drive from here to her school or from here to the Science Centre, to explain why it was that her mother took the car out late at night sometimes to fill the tank — "I have to get it while it's cheap!" her mother would say, grabbing the keys off the elephant-shaped key rack on the wall, gone for fifteen minutes and then back, the car humming and full.

What else cost money? Her brother's therapy group, which met once a week, her brother's drawings lessons (Mira had discontinued), Mira's piano lessons, Mira's school trip to the Science Centre, Mira's clothes (she was shooting up), Ravi's clothes (he was picky about clothes), the food they ate, which was always plentiful but always what she knew to be cheap because she saw her mother compare labels at the grocery store. Luckily, South Indians generally ate rice and lentils. It was the granola bars that her mother fretted over, the cookies and the potato chips and the imported fruit (they all preferred mangoes to apples), which disappeared so quickly from their house. Sometimes Mira and her mother spent an hour and a half at the grocery store. They would put an item in their cart and then halfway to the other end of the store, her mother would decide they didn't need it, so she would walk back to return it or get a different brand, or she would decide the sale was so good that she would go and get three more. Then Mira waited with her just next to the row of checkout lines, while her mother went through the cart, pointing pointing pointing at each thing, double-checking her coupons and adding the prices quietly in Kannada, the language they spoke at home. Mira liked that, how her mother did her math in another language.

Her mother mowed the lawn herself, waving away the boy going door-to-door. The mail was always bad news. They threw the catalogs out to avoid temptation. The bills were sorted and sorted again. Her mother only called India once a month on Sundays, chatting in a fake cheery voice, and afterwards she would sit in the family room alone and watch a Hindi movie on TV, and even Ravi knew not to bother her for those three or four hours. And then they had cancelled the cable and lost the Asian Television Network, so her mother flipped through their few channels, sighing and saying that there was nothing to watch.

ONE MORNING, FOUR days before they were to move out, Mira had woken up on her twin mattress — which her mother had placed on the floor after dismantling the bed frame — and looked up to towers of boxes on each side of her, which had been shoved into Mira's room to make space elsewhere, and, still half-asleep, she thought she saw them shift. They hadn't been careful about placement, and the boxes surrounded her, like the city she had imagined building when the boxes first arrived, except precarious, and full of heavy things. She must have kicked one in her sleep. She was awake now, and sure the box had moved — it *had* moved, in fact, was moving now. Mira darted, feet tangled in the blankets and then bless-edly free, while the boxes fell, toppling and crashing over the bed, like toy blocks, like life-sized Jenga pieces.

"Oh my god," her mother said, in the doorway suddenly, in her pyjamas.

Mira was fine, but in the other room, Ravi, frightened by the sound of the crash, screamed and twisted in his blankets, pressed his eyes together until their lids made a crescent shape, held his hands to his ears.

AT BREAKFAST, RAVI was still upset. He slapped his hands on the table and Mira's cereal shook in its bowl. "Why did the boxes fall?" he asked. "WHY DID THEY FALL?"

"They fell because we didn't stack them properly," said Mira's mother. "From now on, we'll be more careful. We'll keep them away from the beds."

"We'll be more careful," said Ravi.

"Yes," said their mother. She was making lunches, putting chicken nuggets in a red thermos.

"But why did they fall?"

"They weren't balanced," said their mother.

"But will the other boxes fall, too?"

"No, we'll keep them balanced," said their mother. She stared off for a minute. "Balanced like a good breakfast," she said.

"But couldn't they still fall?" Ravi said.

"STOP IT!" shouted Mira. "Stop asking about it!"

"Mira," her mother said sharply.

Ravi put his hands to his ears again, his elbows two triangles.

"STOP IT!" Mira shouted again, and stood up quickly, leaving her cereal. She stomped up the stairs, but couldn't stomp very loudly, because there were boxes and bags and a stack of magazines blocking her way. Her mother was coming after her, and Mira went faster, leaping over a radio, sidestepping a basket of laundry.

"Mira, we don't have time for this!"

Mira chose the bathroom instead of her own room, because the bathroom door had a lock. She stomped in and locked the door and turned around. She was seething. How dare he act as though the boxes had fallen on him, as though he were the one who had awakened to near-death? It was she who had scrambled from her bed, to desperately find footing in a half-dream world where everything seemed to be falling. She took her fists now and squeezed them and looked around the room and spotted the orchid plant, in a slim green pot, which she picked up and threw as hard as she could on to the floor. As she threw the orchid, she let out a noise, a "rrraaaa" sort of noise. Her mother kept rattling the door handle.

On the bathroom floor, the orchid's soil had dirtied the grout of the tile. The orchid itself was intact, but its roots had been exposed, and stuck out hideously from the base of the stem. The pot was shattered, and under it, one of the bathroom floor tiles had broken in four pieces. Mira covered the broken tile with the bathroom rug and unlocked the door.

THE BEST, MOST well-behaved child Mira could think of was Prahalad, who wasn't somebody she knew personally, but rather a boy from a myth, the son of a king. "King Hiranyakaship was a terrible man and a terrible king. He hated God. He committed atrocities," he mother told her. Her mother told Mira and Ravi this story when they had committed their own atrocities. *Atrocities*, Mira loved the word, simultaneously space-age and ancient, chemical and dark; she wanted to brew atrocities in a laboratory, build atrocities on the moon. Lord Brahma, whose three crowned, white-bearded heads Mira could picture vividly because she had seen his character on the long-running Mahabharat television series, had granted King Hiranyakaship the boon of near-immortality. "All living beings must face death," Mira's mother said Lord Brahma had told the king, when he had asked to live forever. So instead Brahma had given him the choice of *how* he would die, and the king, cleverer than most villains, chose the finest and narrowest of death moments, deciding he would be killed by someone who was neither man nor beast, in a place neither inside nor outside, at a time neither day nor night.

Imagine how perplexed a villain would be to have a child as pious as Prahalad, a boy who worshipped Vishnu with a devotion equal to Hiranyakaship's villainy. When Mira's mother pointed this out, Mira, too, became perplexed. Where would a boy pick up a hobby like worshipping Vishnu? She was expected to believe that he spent as many hours a day praying, cross-legged in a grove of trees, as she did attending school, or sleeping. Prahalad was not only good, but unbelievably good, the epitome of goodness, and it rattled her that children like him had existed, in some alternate, mythical world. She remembered, too, the stories her mother had told her about her own childhood, of jumping in burning leaves, of childish vandalism, of the time her younger sister had a ring stuck on her finger and she banged it with a stone to try and loosen it, stories of foolishness and adventure and danger, conflicting messages that made her wonder if her mother wanted her to take those same lively risks.

"Vishnu is everywhere, is in everything," Prahalad told his father. It must have infuriated the king, Mira imagined, to see his child — solemn-faced, or maybe with a small smile —

speak so oppositely to his own beliefs. They stood in the palace foyer, she imagined, where even the ceilings were engraved with indecipherable patterns, and the marble floors gleamed cool as air conditioning in the oppressive Indian heat. Outside the mahogany doors, carved with dancers and plant vines entwined, the sky turned magenta and orange.

"Where is Vishnu to protect you now?" Hiranyakaship said. He pulled out his sword. He threatened his own son with death. "Is he in here?" he gestured at a pillar and Prahalad quietly observed the white plaster, the loveliness of its imperfections, and knew that it contained God. He nodded, and the king slashed at it until the plaster crumbled, dust fogging the air. "Is he in here?" he pointed with his sword and another pillar and Prahalad nodded again while his father destroyed it, and the ceiling began to fall.

It was out of the third pillar, which Hiranyakaship sliced mercilessly in half, that Vishnu emerged, not in his usual form, but in the shape of Narasimha, a half-man half-lion incarnation ("*Nara* means man and *simha* means lion," Mira's mother said) known for protecting his devotees. He leapt from the pillar, lion head blended seamlessly into human torso, lion claws extended smoothly out of human hands. Narasimha took the king in his claws and carried him to the threshold of the palace; he pierced his claws deeply into the king's stomach and tore his flesh while the king screamed, his back arching, arms flung wide. Narasimha, a form neither man nor beast, held the king down on the threshold of the palace, neither inside nor outside, as the sky turned from magenta to black, neither day nor night; he killed Hiranyakaship, under a rain of marble and plaster.

Mira's family had driven once to a temple outside Pittsburgh, unlike any temple she'd ever been to. They sat in wood pews, behind the congregation, rows and rows of worshippers of Narasimha. The people sang, in monotone, "You killed Hiranyakaship, You killed Hiranyakaship …," the only words of the prayer song Mira could recall — she shuddered when she remembered it, thinking not of the incredible power of the form who had killed the king, who had, after all, saved Prahalad from death, but of Prahalad watching his father murdered by the hand of a god to whom he had prayed devotedly, on whose idol he had placed the petals of lotus flowers, whose name he had chanted before sleeping and upon waking. When Hiranyakaship slashed the pillars, had Prahalad prayed for God to kill his father? It was this image that stayed with Mira: Prahalad, dressed in simple cloth, gold around his ankles and wrists — he was a prince, after all — holding a garland of flowers to place on his god, looking upon his own family and seeing something different, something cruel.

MIRA VOWED TO be good, and being good meant blind faith and being nice to your brother and perhaps even contributing to the household finances. She'd buy a new money jar for God and fill it with money — maybe even more than what was owed — and her mother would enter the God room and see the new jar sitting there, maybe a red jar this time. She would pick it up and feel its weight, and she might not even remember the IOU note (she hadn't before, after all). Perhaps she would only recognize that the jar had changed.

All morning, after she'd smashed the orchid, Mira thought up ways to be good, ways to make money. On the school bus,

Mira stared at the back of the bus driver's head and considered lemonade stands, bake sales, garage sales — she could sell all their junk, make room before they moved. October was too late in the season for lemonade, and anyhow lemonade smacked of childishness; she would sell apple cider, buy jugs from the supermarket and heat it in a big steel pot with floating cinnamon sticks. Neighbours out pulling rakes through beds of leaves would smell the cinnamon and drop their rakes to come to Mira's driveway, where they would drink apple cider in mismatched mugs — "The mugs are included in the price," Mira would say — and hunt through sale items she would place neatly on tables with price labels marking each category. They would walk away with appliances under their arms, bags of toys dangling from their free hands.

That morning at school, her teacher drew fractions on the board while Mira copied them in her notebook and thought of the little notebook she would use to keep track of her earnings. The class moved on to current events; they read an article about the prime minister from the *Toronto Star*, and Mira thought of starting her own newspaper, a neighbourhood newspaper. In the margins of her schoolwork, she wrote down what to include: a crossword puzzle with the street names as answers, a list of houses for sale in the area, birthdays of residents. Perhaps she could even sell advertisements — for people selling cars or barbecues or offering swimming lessons in their backyard pools, or for people who wanted to announce their weddings.

Mira was thinking about how she would have her mother photocopy the newspaper at work, on a different colour of paper each week, when she realized it was noon already and her classmates were standing up and clamouring over something. She stood up herself and noticed the pizza boxes arranged on the front few desks. So it was Pizza Day, the first Pizza Day of the school year; she tried to remember if her mother had filled out the form and sent in the envelope with money. The teacher had left for her own lunch break and the monitor hadn't yet arrived so she couldn't ask them to check if her name were on the list. The student in charge of Pizza Day hadn't started calling out the names yet — his task was to call out each name and one by one the students would go up and receive their pizza on a paper plate, along with a plastic juice carton sealed with a foil lid, and a glazed donut wrapped in a square of cellophane.

The same boy, Nathaniel Craig, had been in charge of pizza last year, and had acquired an expertise. He called the names out alphabetically, but, to be fair, he'd sometimes start from the other end of the alphabet. He did this today, and Mira, since her last name was Acharya, felt a terrible inward sigh. The waiting was somehow worse than any other waiting. The Zimmermans and Wongs were chomping away, crust-first or crust-avoiding, saving the donut for last or alternating bites of donut with bites of pizza then glugging down the juice. Mira could almost taste the foil of the juice wrapper, sharp against her lip, matching the acidity of the apple, and that donut, not airy and yeasty like ordinary donuts, but dense as gingerbread and slightly damp with frosting and from the condensation in the package. Nathaniel was proud of himself, Mira could see, of the loud *Price Is Right* announcer's voice he used to name each student — "Come on down!" he yelled, drum-rolling on the desk, whooping when somebody had ordered two slices instead of one. He was a ham who'd been given responsibility, and was proud, too, of the martyrdom in accepting his own pizza last. By the time Nathaniel called her name, nearly everyone else would have finished their food, and Nathaniel himself would gulp his down, or go to recess with a donut in one hand and pizza in the other, but Mira was a slow eater. She wanted to taste everything, and she didn't want to eat alone. Imagine if the school monitor came and saw her there, a girl in a dark, empty classroom, savouring a donut.

But worse, she didn't even know if she should wait. She might not be getting pizza at all. And then he'd reach the end of the list of names and see her waiting there, and tell her that her mother hadn't paid for her pizza after all. He'd say it regretfully, but also with disbelief — how could she not even know? She should start eating the lunch she'd brought, probably chicken nuggets again, lukewarm in the thermos, or maybe a bagel, the texture changed five hours after being toasted and spread with cream cheese, but if she ate her bagel/nuggets and then her name *was* called … she couldn't eat both. People would see her. Boys in the class would assume she couldn't eat that much and offer to take the pizza off her hands; she had seen similar things happen to other girls — "You can't finish all that, can you?" a boy would ask a girl with a larger than average packet of chips and she'd look down at them, at her oily, crumby fingers, and pass the bag over.

When Nathaniel paused to count the juice cartons, Mira seized her opportunity. "Nathaniel," she said quietly, coming up next to him, "am I on the list?"

He looked back at her, brushed the flop of hair from his face. He was a nice-looking boy, Mira thought. "Are you … I

… let me check," he flipped back to the first page of names on his clipboard.

"Eyy, what's the hold-up?" said John Ferguson.

"No cutting, Mira," said Eugene Chao.

"Who's cutting?" asked Allison Miller, from the back of the crowd.

"I just want to know if —" Mira started saying, but John Ferguson had taken the clipboard from Nathaniel.

"Hmmm," said John. "Let's see, let's see. Well I see your name here, Mira Acharya," he said her last name wrong, the *ch* sounding like a *k*. "But the question remains: did you order pizza?"

Mira waited patiently.

"Payment required," he said. John had a pudgy face and a thin body. Mira thought there might be a blockage in his esophagus that prevented the food from travelling down. The class watched.

"Oh, John, just tell her if she's on it," said Cynthia Martin, who Mira secretly liked a lot and imagined riding bicycles with, if only she could figure out how to cross the barrier into friendship.

"I'll tell her," said John. "But first, she has to do a dare." The class had recently taken up games of truth or dare. Mira rarely participated, but had lingered at the periphery of such games and watched as girls and boys were made to slow dance, music-less, in the centre of a ring of onlookers counting down from ten or fifteen. For the Truth portion, girls usually asked people the identities of their crushes — once, Cynthia had asked a boy to name his crush and he'd named her, and they had dated for one week and even kissed publicly on the wooden porch of a portable classroom. Boys who requested truths usually asked each other whether or not they masturbated. According to the results of the game, none of Mira's classmates had ever masturbated, or peed themselves, and all had known all along that Santa Claus was fiction.

"I dare you …," said John, thinking and thinking, though probably he already knew what he was going to ask. He was milking the attention. Maybe he would ask her to kiss Nathaniel. She wouldn't mind it. She might even push his hair from his forehead first. For a second, she was glad she hadn't yet eaten any pizza. Even slow dancing would be nice, arms on shoulders and waists, and nowhere to look but at each other. The class had a recent obsession with slow dancing because there was a Halloween dance coming up. It occurred during the last period of the Friday before Halloween, in the gymnasium, where the organizers would turn off the lights to mimic nighttime and all the cool kids would leave the gym in protest when Mariah Carey was played.

"I dare you," said John, "to throw a donut at the clock." Everyone's head swivelled to look at the classroom clock. It sat high on the wall behind the teacher's desk, big-numbered and plain, ticking slower than usual.

"Yeah, but whose donut?" asked Eugene.

"I volunteer my donut," said Adam. "I can still eat it after, right? Like, keep the wrapper on." He wanted to be a part of things, thought Mira.

"She won't even be able to hit it," said Eugene, with disgust.

"I can hit it," said Mira. Mira knew she had excellent aim. Cynthia started laughing. "Ha!" Cynthia said to John.

Mira often spent whole afternoons throwing a tennis ball at

the side of her house, aiming for particular bricks. They had a basketball hoop over their driveway, drooping a little because her father had installed it before she was born, but still, she'd had practice, she knew she could throw a donut and hit the clock, especially a donut as dense as these. She could throw a donut and hit John's head, if she wanted to. She smiled to herself. What a pleasant thud the donut would make.

Donut in hand, Mira positioned herself to face the clock. Cynthia started to chant, "Mira! Mira!" and the class joined in. Mira stretched her arm a couple of times — not too many times, lest anyone think she was posturing — she wound up, aimed, and threw. She knew the donut would reach its target, and she knew, too, that the cheap clock on the wall would not withstand the attack. The packaged donut travelled through the air with hardly a rustle and hit the clock. The clock slid down the wall and clattered on to the floor, batteries skittering and rolling away. Adam ran to the clock and picked it up and held it above his head so everyone could see its cracked face.

The class was quiet and then it started cheering. John slapped Mira's back with his hand — she wished it were Adam — and the class exited en masse for recess. Mira realized only later that she'd never discovered at all whether her name was on the list, but she didn't care. She ate her bagel and didn't mind it, sitting on the edge of the portable porch, with Cynthia sitting next to her, still laughing — "Nothing this year will be better than that," said Cynthia.

WHEN THE TEACHER found the clock later, nobody admitted anything. After all, they all shared the guilt. All had witnessed the daring, the throwing, the clock-breaking. The teacher assumed the clock had fallen of its own accord. At the end of the day, taking her coat from her locker, Mira made the mistake of looking the wrong way and catching the eye of Ravi's old bully — she still didn't know his name. "*What?*" he said, and opened his eyes wide at her. She didn't feel afraid. He had never even told any authorities about what her mother had done. You could get away with anything if you had no witnesses or the right witnesses, she saw that now. You could get away with throwing donuts at clocks, or with cruelty, or with chasing people down with your car. You could break things — urns, plant pots, clocks — and no one would even really miss them, and no god would jump out from the broken pieces, wanting vengeance, baring his godly teeth. If God existed now, he stayed in hiding.

By the end of the week, they had a new clock on the wall, identical to the old one.

YOU COULD MOVE to a small house if there was nobody there to stop it from happening. Before they packed the globe, Mira looked at the spot where Richmond Hill must be, a little north of Toronto. It wasn't even marked, so if she pointed her finger at her old house and new house, she didn't even have to move her finger. They taped up the last boxes and her mother mopped the floor with an old towel one last time. On the night they moved, her mother went out early to run errands, to pick up the new house keys and drive a carload of their belongings over, things they'd kept unpacked so they could access them quickly. She left Mira in charge of cooking dinner out of the few items they'd kept behind. Mira boiled a pot of pasta for herself and Ravi, and heated up sauce in the microwave, then mixed the two together. Mira was carrying the pasta to where Ravi sat on the kitchen floor, waiting — the movers had already taken the table and chairs. Ravi twitched and smiled, held his knees with his hands and rocked forwards and backwards. He looked at her sideways. "*What?*" she said, and opened her eyes wide at him, her hands on the sides of the CorningWare to which she'd transferred the pasta. He made a high-pitched sound and she threw the dish of pasta on to the floor at his feet. The sauce splattered on to Ravi's socks and he pulled his legs up to his chair.

"Hey," he said, "hey."

"Shut up," she said. "You clean it." She was shaking; she was angry and she didn't know why. Her brother started to pick up the pasta with his hands, scooping it and placing it back in the dish, which was smeared with sauce across its side but which hadn't broken.

Mira went downstairs to the empty God room, repainted white now. She screamed at the spiders, though there weren't any. When she went back upstairs, she found her brother at the table, eating the pasta from a paper plate. He'd attempted to clean the floor but had left semi-circular streaks of sauce. Mira found the towel her mother had used earlier and soaked it in soapy water, then mopped the floor properly before her mother came home.

Her mother didn't notice a thing. She washed the steel pot and the CorningWare dish and the spoon or two that remained and dried them and put them into one last small box. Mira and Ravi put on their backpacks, each of which contained a toothbrush, pyjamas, a towel, and clothing for the next day. They helped their mother check the house for anything they had missed, and then got into the car. The car murmured while its headlights illuminated the house's double doors. It was eight p.m. and the sky was dark blue, and moths alighted on the outside front light fixture before Mira's mother turned it off and locked the front door. As the light went black, the moths flew away, but Mira could see them, their swiftly moving wings, and to her they looked like pieces shattering, though they moved of their own accord.

Another Dinner Party

MIRA'S FATHER HAD always kept a pen and notebook in his pocket, or if not a notebook, then an assortment of papers picked up here and there — folded-up flyers and torn newspaper ads, car wash receipts and to-do lists — and when the family went to dinner parties, if Mira had no company, her father would take pen and paper from his pocket and they'd play a game of dots and squares. "Dots-and-squares, dots-and-squares …" he'd chant rhythmically as he watched Mira draw a grid pattern of dots all over the back of a five-cent bill of Canadian Tire money. She drew the dots in even rows, like holes on a pegboard. The game went: Mira drew a line connecting two dots; her father drew a line connecting a different two dots. All lines were parallel or perpendicular, and formed the sides of potential squares. Each player tried to make a square, while simultaneously preventing the other from making a square. It wasn't a difficult game, but there was comfort in its patterns — she drew a line and he drew a line and she drew a line and he drew a line and oh-a-square! And so it continued until the paper was filled, a pleasing tessellation.

If Mira hadn't drawn the initial dots neatly enough, or if they found no coffee table nearby and while playing had to balance the paper on Mira's father's wobbling leg, the squares took on the distorted look of longitude and latitude lines on a globe, narrowing and widening from one end of the page to the other. "A Mercator projection," her father said once, and drew a world map on their finished grid lines, raggedy islands up top. He drew India as a rough-edged diamond. Mira asked him if he would spend the five-cent bill afterwards, and he said he would, "On a lawnmower," but added, "unless you want it," but Mira said no, because she liked the idea of his spending it, of handing the bill over to the cashier, who would smile and accept it into the circulation of bills — or did Canadian Tire money get reused? She wasn't sure, but imagined it passing from hand to hand, each person adding another island, another lake, another provincial boundary.

It wasn't rude, exactly, to play this game at dinner parties, since they played while Mira's mother carried the conversation, or while the husband of the hosting couple was off getting paper plates or when there were so many people in attendance that Mira's father didn't have any conversational obligation. And anyway, they attended many dinner parties, as many as two a weekend, with sometimes a lunch party in between. The parties were casual affairs — buffet-style, children invited. Her father did sometimes have to pause the game for later when the conversation took off and he opined intensely about whatever was happening then — the Gulf War, Roberta Bondar in space — and Mira would use that time to draw more dots. For his birthday the year she was five, she had taken a sheet of large-sized chart paper and marked it with hundreds of dots in different colours of marker. Her mother helped her spell "Ultimate Dots and Squares" at the top. She presented it to him on the morning of his birthday and he pretended to faint at the sheer volume of dots, and the mere thought of having to fill it, and she could tell that, under his pretending, he really was surprised. She overheard him tell her mother that it must have taken forever to draw those dots — "She's so diligent," he'd said, and she'd known diligent meant something good. Her father had died before they had used up all the dots and drawn up all the squares.

One of her father's favourite shirts to wear to dinner parties actually had a grid pattern on it, like a sheet of graph paper, a wonderful coincidence, and after he died she found it in the laundry, a pen still in the pocket, and she'd taken the pen and coloured in exactly one square near the hem. After the funeral, Lala Aunty came and did all their laundry, and when Mira checked afterward, she saw that the square had stayed, faded, bleeding at the corners, but its shape otherwise intact.

HERE THEY WERE now, at another dinner party; it had been five years since the last. Lala Aunty had invited them, though their mother had tried to decline, the way she'd declined every dinner party since her husband's death,

"Have one samosa, one at least," said Lala Aunty, holding out the plate as she tipped her body in a cartoonish bow.

"One samosa? I could eat ten samosas!" said Baskar, the man lounging next to Mira's mother on the couch, but he only took one.

Mira didn't think anybody could eat ten samosas, especially

not these ones made by Lala Aunty. (Lala Aunty's real name was Lalitha Aurora, but she insisted on the nickname. "La, la, la! like a song," she would say.) Mira took a samosa just to see Lala's face light up at the lighter plate.

Unlike most aunties, Lala couldn't cook at all. She thought she could, and it would have made more sense if she could have, since she hosted an Indian healthy cooking radio show called *Eating with Aunty.* The problem was that she liked to improvise. When Mira's family first arrived at Lala's house, the aunty had sat them down in the living room — Mira's mother next to the man named Baskar and Mira in the chair across from them, while Ravi contentedly chose a cushion on the carpet — and she described the recipe to them all in great detail. This time, she had baked the samosas rather than frying them and she'd replaced the usual potato filling with a puree of vegetables she declared more nutritional, such as Swiss chard and broccoli, which, after being swirled in the food processor, had become too watery to hold up the samosa's triangular shape.

Mira heard Baskar's teeth crunch over something as he chewed and she hoped it was cumin. Her family and Baskar were the only guests so far, although the party had technically started an hour earlier. Mira saw Lala's husband hover roundly in the background, waiting for a good time to say hello, even though any time would have been fine. He peered out at them and smiled from various doorways, and eventually came out and said hello.

"Hello!" he said, "I am Lala's husband!" He spoke to Baskar, whom he hadn't yet met.

Uncle beamed at Baskar. He bowed exactly as his wife had and took Mira's mother's hand and then Mira's own hand, kissing each lightly and off-centre, then darted away like a woodland creature.

THE REASON MIRA and her family came was that they had spent approximately three months in their new house, but had still barely unpacked anything. The kitchen was furthest along due to necessity; the toaster came out one day when Ravi wanted an English muffin, and Lala had unpacked the rice cooker for them, along with other small appliances, cutlery, trivets.

"Come help me, Shilpi," Lala Aunty had said to Mira's mother, tilting her head and beckoning like a movie heroine. "How am I to know where you want all this-that things kept?" Mira's mother had responded by putting a cup or two on the shelves.

The fridge door had no magnets on it and the linen closet had only one towel per person. The rest of the towels, along with the extra bedsheets and pillow cases, remained neatly folded, bars of Mysore sandalwood soap tucked between them for freshness, inside one of the many boxes that crowded their new, shrunken home.

They had come to the party for a break from boxes and bare walls, and to please Aunty, who had known Mira's father for several years. He had been a chemical engineer, and she had interviewed him once on her show. Lala Aunty never lost contact with a single person she had a conversation with. She invited bank tellers out to lunch with her and, after meeting the Canadian prime minister's wife once at a cultural conference, had obtained her home phone number.

Mira had never been to Lala Aunty's house, though her

mother had. The home's decor seemed to mimic the decor of Aunty's favourite South Indian restaurant, Udupi Palace, which served the exact same dishes Mira's mother made at home every day. (She still cooked them dinner; it wasn't like she'd abandoned them. But she cooked with one strange, small frying pan, without hunting for pans of a more appropriate size.) On Lala Aunty's wall someone had placed ornate plaster carvings that looked heavy but probably weren't, portraying Bharatanatyam dancers with imprecise faces, noses placed too high and mouths that smirked too readily. Stainless steel dishware crowded into glass shelves around the room, underlit with neon pink light. A pewter salt-and-pepper set in the corner nearest to Mira identically matched the shakers at Udupi Palace. There was also an oil painting of a warped bowl of fruit, which Lala Aunty told them she had done herself. It was so tall and so wide that, rather than hanging it, she had stood the painting on the floor, after pushing aside the red IKEA furniture to make room.

Predicting the absence of children her age, Mira had brought a book with her, a book of ghost stories and urban legends, tales of chicken-fried rats and oven-baked babies which she read dutifully along with the ones she liked better — the one about a woman's neck held on by ribbon (how could a ribbon secure a neck?), the one about the boy whose skillful hiding in a game of hide-and-seek got him trapped in an airtight chest in the attic. She propped the book on the fat arm of the chair, so during the occasional boring passage she could glance over it at her mother.

Gradually, more guests started to arrive. Lala Aunty offered to take their coats even though it was summer and nobody had any coats. "May I take your jacket?" she asked one woman in a fitted sleeveless selwar kameez.

"Ohhh, Lala, you and your jokes!" the woman said.

A few of the guests were radio folk and some were neighbours, others colleagues of Uncle, who taught Hindi classes at the university. Some guests seemed entirely arbitrary, like Baskar, who turned out to be a manager at a factory that made computer ink, and couldn't remember how he had met the Lalas at all. "Here or there," he said to Mira's mother when she asked. Baskar balanced his quarter-eaten samosa on his napkin, almost dropping it when Mira's mother explained that she'd met Lala Aunty at her husband's funeral. "Oh, I'm very sorry," said Baskar, and moved exactly one centimetre away from her on the sofa, so their legs no longer touched. Baskar wore appalling, frayed, bulky jeans that caused Mira to remember her father's perfectly ironed pants and how he'd once demonstrated to her his sitting-down test to make sure his hems didn't rise and reveal too much of his socks.

Maybe twenty people had arrived, and more kept coming.

"It has been a thousand-million years since we have seen one another!" exclaimed Lala to one extremely thin woman. Lala Aunty had a habit of hyperbolizing time, of exaggerating a few days into millions of years, and this habit gave such greetings and many of her anecdotes a fairytale beauty. Lala Aunty embraced the woman, whose elbows pointed out like warped branches.

Shoes piled up near the entrance and two or three industrious five-year-olds began moving the surplus to the laundry room. Ravi helped them, too, though he was almost thirteen now.

"Not mine!" said one old man, shaking his head amiably at Ravi, who had tried to nab his loafers before he'd even removed them. "I need the support of my orthotics." Ravi moved on to the next pair and the man wore his shoes for the rest of the evening, happily trampling many other people's feet, socked and bare.

"Sit down, sit down," said Lala Aunty, guiding the ladies and men into the living room. Two more people crammed on to the sofa with Mira's mother and Baskar — suddenly their legs were touching again — and four more pulled chairs from the dining room and arranged them nearby. A scattered assortment of candy-coloured cushions lay around the floor as extra seating. The guests crossed their legs or pulled their knees to their chests or searched the other rooms for chairs (depending on whether they'd worn skirts or pants or Indian clothes), and some stood seatlessly in between, so there were four levels of heads — floor sitters, sofa sitters, chair sitters, and standers, divided like the distinct layers of trees in a rainforest. Some children, including Ravi, bounced around like frogs.

"Do you have a pen?" Mira asked Baskar, eyeing the front of his maroon golf shirt, which bore no pockets. She was bored of her book — the baked baby story was a bit much given the meal she was about to eat — and thought she might invent a game to play alone with paper and pen. Solitary dots-and-squares, or a word game.

"Ahh … let's see … no miss, I do not," said Baskar, smiling at Mira and then her mother.

"But," Mira asked carefully, "didn't you just say you work at an ink factory?"

"I do, yes," said Baskar, "but it's computer ink, toner. I can't even remember the last time I used a pen myself."

Mira returned to her book and imagined Baskar typing out his grocery lists on his computer, printing them out. How did he check the items off the list?

Lala Aunty moved through the guests, offering plates of samosas and crackers and a lumpy pumpkin pâté. She brought out sparkling bottles of pomegranate and mango juice and poured them scarlet and yellow into glasses of various odd heights. "We have wine, too!" she exclaimed, and everybody looked around excitedly because none of them ever drank wine.

Uncle handed out napkins at his wife's request. When he'd finished, he went nimbly from one end of the room to the other and then to the adjacent rooms, turning lamps and light switches on and off. After each switch, he stopped and looked at Lala Aunty, as though considering which tones of light made her look best.

The thin elbowy woman rested her weight on the back of Mira's chair and began a conversation with Mira's mother.

"Do you listen to Lala's show?" the woman asked.

"Every Sunday morning," Mira's mother said. Mira thought of the Sunday mornings in the new house, when she ate a slow breakfast of toast on a napkin so she wouldn't have to dirty one of the four unpacked plates, and Ravi, having usually finished his toast in two bites, pleating it first like a paper fan, lay on his stomach in the hallway, silently drawing pictures, the crayon patterns taking up the grain of the wood floor, while their mother turned the volume way up so Lala Aunty's voice would fill the house and make it feel less new. *Ferment the batter overnight in the oven*, said the disembodied radio Aunty, *no heat needed, off only, and leave room in the pot, don't get greedy about it, or the batter will overflow and then your oven will smell*. Her mother wrote it all down, sometimes verbatim, like a handwriting exercise.

"You know, her recipes turn out pretty well when you make them yourself," said the woman.

"Have you tried the samosas?" asked Mira's mother.

"Oh yes, they are awful, aren't they? One time," she confided, "Lala made some kind of sweet. We couldn't tell what sweet it was supposed to be, and I think she used Splenda, but you know you can't use anything but sugar with Indian sweets, and anyway they were so hard we couldn't bite them, and you know what my son told me he did? He said he just tossed it up in the air — in the air! — and didn't even check to see where it landed. Somewhere in this house, there is an unidentifiable sweet, rotting under a table or inside a plant." They both giggled and then the woman fell awkwardly silent. They took large bites of their samosas when Lala Aunty came around.

"Stop eating those samosas," she said. "It's dinner time!"

Everybody who had been there before cringed. A line formed at the food table. Uncle handed them plates. The table was set with a teal tablecloth and dotted with candles that kept being nearly knocked over. The foods didn't seem to be Indian, but rather sort of fusion concoctions in swampy shades of brown and green.

"Is this a lasagna?" asked a short man with a booming voice that Mira recognized from the Hindi music radio program.

"Ahh, not quite," said Lala Aunty, serving him a gigantic amount. "It's more of a savoury pie."

"Yum, I love banana bread," said a woman with a blue hat, as Lala Aunty placed a piece on her plate.

"That's actually a lentil loaf," she said.

The doorbell rang then, but nobody answered it. The door opened and a woman stood there in a full silk sari, looking unsure of whether to enter. Lala dropped the serving spoon she was holding and hurried to the door.

"Come in, my dear," she said, "You've been a hundred hours standing on this porch." In three seconds, she had taken the woman's imaginary coat and ushered her to the front of the food line. She loaded the woman's plate without speaking.

Mira watched Ravi take a lot of everything and wondered if he would regret it. He went to sit in another room, one that had a television, with the littlest children. Book tucked under armpit, Mira reached for a serving spoon towards the safest-looking rice dish. Noting her hesitation, Lala Aunty packed Mira's plate with everything else, far more food than she would have taken herself.

"Don't be shy, come have more!" said Lala Aunty.

"I will, it all looks so good," said Mira, full of manners, because looking at the food, arranged and bedecked, she had the sudden feeling that Lala Aunty must have spent a lot of time.

She turned to sit and saw that a woman had taken her chair, and her mother's too — at the latter she felt an instant of gladness that her mother's leg wouldn't be sitting next to Baskar's anymore. She located a spot on the carpet to sit, since the cushions were all taken, and moved her fork to sort the foods into discrete mounds. The food gave her something to do, and since she didn't feel particularly drawn to eating it, she would eat it slowly; it would use up a fair amount of time.

Her mother seemed to be having more difficulty. She balanced her plate in one hand and picked up a glass of water from the clear row of glasses at the end of the table. Turning around to go back to the sofa, Mira could tell she was being careful not to tilt her plate and drop food on the heads of people who sat around her legs. Mira noticed before her mother did that the late-arriving woman had usurped her seat on the sofa. The chairs and floor cushions were all taken. People shared cushions, their backs meeting. Some squashed together on armchairs, and others suspended themselves, feet waving, on the soft red arms of the sofa. She didn't know anybody well enough to share seating, and she could have just sat on the carpet like Mira, but then, only children sat on the bare carpet, and probably Lala Aunty would make a cute worried fuss about there not being enough places, which would draw attention to her. Mira was pretty sure that's what she was thinking.

So it seemed her mother would have to stand. Mira was curious — how would she eat? Both of her hands were full, making the manoeuvre impossible unless she put something down. The only possible table on which to leave her water was the coffee table near the sofa, inconveniently low, and she couldn't stand there because there wasn't any room in between the mismatched wood dining-set chairs and the metal folding chairs and she would have to either keep silently to herself or lean over to make awkward conversation with the sitting people. They'd look up at her and ask her to repeat herself. If somebody told a joke, her laughter would float over their heads.

She couldn't keep her water on the floor next to her, due to the carpet, and even without carpeting, it was likely the glass would be knocked over by one of the small frog-jumping children, who had taken their food first and had finished eating already, some having only eaten a bit of yogurt and rice. The plates were heavy — Lala had run out of the Corelle and broken out the china. Mira lifted her own a little to feel its push of gravity, and thought that even if her mother could find a place to keep her water, she wasn't sure she could hold the plate in one hand the whole time while eating. Her wrist bones jutted like binder clips. Didn't her mother used to be fatter? She had a fork and a spoon balanced on the plate along with a napkin tucked in her palm.

What were other people doing? Mira looked at the standers. They formed a tight corner circle, and she knew her mother didn't know any of them. Mira had never before caught her mother in such an awkward moment. Was her mother as worried as Mira was, thinking about this, in this unusual rush of empathy? If she was, she didn't show it. She had a mild smile on, but wasn't smiling at anybody in particular. To join the group of standers, she would need to tap somebody on the shoulder ("Excuse me," Mira imagined her mother saying, the way she herself got the attention of a recess monitor), or stand sideways until somebody noticed her, and there wasn't even room there to stand. Even to get over there she would have to walk around several cushion-seated people, and a couple of babies lying around on blankets — she would probably crush one of the babies under her feet.

If her father were here, such a dilemma would not have existed, because first of all, he would have saved her a seat or she would have saved him a seat, or he would have told her to leave her selwar shawl where they were sitting, or to keep her purse on the chair.

Or they might have stood and shared plate and glass, minimizing the amount of food they would have to eat and coordinating into a lovely and precise rhythm, a kind of counterpoint. Mira remembered a time when they had done this before. Mira, having finished eating, had been drawing dots. Her father held the plate in two hands while her mother clutched the glass in one hand and used her other hand to eat.

"Don't touch the mysore pak, that's my favourite," he had said, and Mira thought maybe he was joking but maybe not.

"Crumbs, I will leave you crumbs," her mother responded — in a way Mira recognized as flirtatious — holding the sweet up to her mouth and threatening to eat it whole. Then she took a tiny corner bite, barely touching it with her teeth. She saved it for him on the very edge of the dish, and Mira felt satisfied that it wouldn't be tainted with the residue of other foods.

"Oh, I was joking, you can eat it," he said. When her mother picked it up again and, wide-mouthed, went to repeat her pantomime, he suddenly dipped his head forward, nearly dropping the plate, and bit the piece of mysore pak out of her hand, as though it were an offered grape.

Her father had often compared one food to another. "This is the biggest chappati I've ever seen!" he would say, and she'd also heard him exclaim, "This chappati is impossibly soft!" and, "This chappati is even more delicious than my mother's!" (He was overwhelmingly positive in his opinions, at least while expressing them at dinner parties, to aunties who simpered under his handsomeness.) They attended dinner parties so frequently because they had had an incredibly large social circle. On the drive home, Mira sat in the back with Ravi and leaned against her seatbelt to watch her parents through the gap in their seats. They always critiqued the meal together: "Did that one curry taste exactly like that other curry?" her father asked.

"All curries taste the same," said her mother.

"It's the MTR package mix, probably."

Then all four of them gazed out the dark car windows on to the highway that led them home from Mississauga to Richmond Hill. When they passed the Vishnu temple near their exit, the whole family touched their foreheads in prayer.

Often, one of her parents would bring up the time they had eaten at MTR — the Mavalli Tiffin Room — in Bangalore, only a few days after they had first met. This was their favourite story. They'd gone to Lal Bagh Road and stepped into the crowded restaurant, where patrons tucked into meals brimming out of stainless steel sectioned plates. The place wasn't beautiful, but it was the most famous restaurant in India.

"Once, the Chief Minister of Karnataka himself stood in line here to have a masala dosa," her father had told her mother outside the restaurant, at a time Mira could barely imagine, when her parents had barely known each other.

"I know that, everybody in the whole state of Karnataka knows that," her mother said, a bit meanly, Mira thought.

"You are charming," he said, very seriously, and her mother laughed aloud because — she told Mira as an aside — she had only ever heard the word "charming" in the novels of Jane Austen.

They ordered crisp paper dosas, which came to them folded into half-moons, stuffed with cumin-scented yellow potatoes cooked until they'd lost their shape. The surface of the dosa glistened with oil that highlighted the crepe's gradual gradient from white to brown, darker where it had touched the centre of the pan. The young version of her mother raised her eyebrows over the dosas and the steel plates and their messy, potato-covered hands, at the young version of her father, at the boyish, asymmetrical face Mira had seen in the wedding album. "I thought the faux-marble table was real marble," Mira's mother told her. And she said that in the middle of some forgettable sentence, his name, Ashwin, had sounded like a combination of a sneeze and a sigh.

On the way out of MTR, Ashwin had put his hand for one second on the small of Mira's mother's back and she had tensed. "She thought I was being too forward," Mira's father told her, "so I apologized." They grinned about that moment when they told it, after they'd crossed the Atlantic. In their suburban Canadian house, Mira knew her parents had no such barriers; they watched television in their bedroom, stayed up late watching the Fox Network (her father's head on her mother's stomach, folded over each other in their bed like resting cows).

They would fall asleep with the television still on, and it flashed over their sleeping bodies until morning, when Mira and Ravi would crawl in there with them. Her father would wake up and stretch and say, "Strrrrrretch!" his mouth open and his eyes closed and his arms reaching up and over her mother, purposely waking her so he could cuddle her with more results. She would blink into his cheek and ask, "Why can't you stretch without saying the word 'stretch'?" And then father and mother and Mira and Ravi would all together say, "Streeeetch!" and get the day's stretching out of the way.

Her father would eventually get up to shower, turning the TV off as he passed it, and after five to ten minutes (the three of them pretending to catch some extra zees or watching cartoons with the volume down), they would all listen to hear him get out of the shower and say aloud to himself, "Cleaaann as a whistle!" Mira and her mother and sometimes Ravi, too, in imitation, would smother their laughing reaction in the Ashwin-flattened pillow, or they'd roll around the middle of the bed, where the sheets were warm as a fresh roti; they would wait there in the space he had left.

NOW THEY WERE back in the cycle of more dinner parties, where the food wasn't very good, and her mother seemed still in the limbo of holding her plate and glass. They hadn't seemed to have problems like these before. Mira's father had always had a plan. They had glided through without Mira's mother ever needing to worry about where to sit, where to set down her glass, where to find parking ("Does this look like a spot?" she asked Mira every time), where to find a reliable moving company ("Yellow Pages," Mira said helpfully and her mother rolled her eyes), where to mail the completed tax forms, where to enroll Ravi in school, where to hold a funeral, where to keep the Great Dad mug (in the cupboard, and all take turns drinking from it, or in some kind of father shrine). In the end she had packed his things — the mug, an envelope fat with small notebooks where it turned out he'd recorded stoichio-metric calculations side by side with funny things Ravi had said, shiny pens that didn't write anymore, the graph paper shirt with the fuzzy blue coloured-in square that would remain like a notch on a timeline — all in a storage container in their new basement. It was the only one of many containers they might really never unpack, or maybe they would in ten years; they'd open it like a gift — here, here is your father in this box.

MIRA'S MOTHER RETREATED to the kitchen. The water in her glass rippled as she set it down on the countertop. Lala Aunty was in there, washing silverware, her body split in half by the pillar in the way of Mira's view.

"You still haven't eaten, what is this?" Aunty asked, pointing at Mira's mother's plate with a handful of forks.

"He's not exactly my type," said Mira's mother.

Aunty pulled off her yellow gloves. "He's not a bad type, though, you know."

Mira remembered how her father had added yogurt to everything he ate.

And then Lala Aunty was patting Mira's mother's back with her palm. "Don't worry, *beta*," she said, her North Indianness emerging through the endearment, and Mira's mother was crying while Aunty held her whole body tightly in the bend of her elbow.

Mira saw Uncle enter the kitchen. His white hair frizzed from the humidity of the cooking and all the bodies. She saw him pause, look to the wall at his left, and quietly turn off the first switch in the row of three kitchen lights.

MIRA, BORED, HAVING waited until her mother and Aunty left the kitchen then scraped her food into the trash, observed the woman who had taken the seat on the sofa, beautiful, dark-eyebrowed, sinking into the old leather. Seemingly unconcerned with the social situation going on around her, she ate silently, listening only superficially to Baskar rattle on, probably about manufacturing toner. Instead she, like half the people at the party, was more intent on the task of balancing her plate on her lap, making sure the liquids didn't drip off the side. She was about forty — though Mira had trouble estimating the ages of anyone older than herself — very carefully put together. Her sari kept immaculate pleats, fanned outward at the bottom over bronze painted toenails and three silver toe rings. Her face had a perfect shape, more like a sketch of a face than an actual face, or more like the oval you drew before drawing in the details and contours.

She was eating rice, plain white rice. Once, right after her father had died, Mira had tried to eat a plate of rice with saru and then, unable to reach the bathroom, vomited it on the tile floor of their old house. They ate rice every day, so she'd begun to eat without thinking until, with only a quarter of the meal left, she'd removed spoon from mouth and seen one white grain sticking to the steel — the last thing she had seen her father eat was at his funeral, except that he wasn't really eating. The Hindu priest had given her mother a dish of uncooked, translucent grains, and she had taken a few and placed them into his parted, dead mouth.

"Food for the journey," the priest had whispered, for the benefit of the children. Then he had given her mother a silver dropper of water, scented with holy tulsi leaves, and she had carefully let three drops fall over his lips. "To ensure the soul goes straight to God," the priest said, before closing the coffin lid, before men carried the coffin away to the ovens, where the grains of rice burned with him.

The reason Hindus weren't buried, the priest told them afterward, was that they believed cremation destroyed the material link of the body to the soul.

The woman took a bite of wheat noodles, her wrist giving a double-jointed bend. She bit into a piece of the heavy, dry, cake of lentils, and pieces crumbled down the sides of her face.

At a wedding, the priest wouldn't say anything about death parting a pair — not in the strings of monotonous Sanskrit prayer — but Mira knew, from her mother telling her, that the Hindu marriage ceremony joined one soul to another. It all sounded like such crap to her sometimes. But her parents' wedding program sheet, now preserved under cellophane in the red-and-cream photo album, explained the steps of the ceremony in neat serif type. Her mother and her sisters had hand-folded and placed those program sheets parallel on a hundred white-and-gold chairs. The notes said the bride's forehead would be marked with the red circular sign of luck, a sign that her husband would always be with her, only instead of the word "husband" they had typed the word "soul," italicized, one letter leaning into the next like a shoulder to a shoulder.

Lala Aunty was saying something. "He died last week." No, that wasn't right, thought Mira; he died five years ago. But she listened again, and found that Lala Aunty wasn't talking about her father, but about the round-faced woman's husband.

"Baskar is recently divorced, and is living out of a suitcase at the Days Inn," said Aunty. To whom was she speaking? Not to her mother — to an unidentified woman, who had asked about the other guests. "The man wearing the blazer just moved here but his wife was refused a visa and is stuck in

India." She went down the guest list like a roll call. "Shilpa's husband died some time back. Also, that woman's son went missing two years ago," said Aunty, gesturing at the thin elbowy woman. "He was abducted at the Square One Mall."

So that was why they were here, Mira supposed. She'd bitten her cheek as she tried a square orange sweet, startled at this revelation, that her family was only one of this strange group of fractured families to which Lala Aunty had somehow become the nucleus. She spit the sweet, which was grainy and cardamom-scented, back into her napkin.

She wondered whom Lala Aunty had lost, and why she was listing all these details, and why she had invited all these people here at once. Perhaps she intended to diminish their pain, but Mira felt instead that its importance had been diminished, in a too-truthful, everybody-has-their-problems way, and Mira did not want her grief divided and shared. All she craved then was to be pitied as though hers were the only suffering in the room. She imagined the room crowded with the souls of everyone's missing family members. They paused next to loved ones, held invisible conversations, ate the inedible chutney, and wandered, taking up the few remaining spots of empty carpet space.

"OH HOY," SAID Uncle to Mira, when he noticed her on the carpet. "I would have vacuumed you by mistake," he said. He lifted his eyebrows twice — liftlift! Balanced atop his palms, which he held flat and raised above his head like a bhangra dancer, was a stainless steel plate. The plate's diameter was wider than the diameter of Uncle's body, and he spun it a little from palm to palm as he paused to talk to Mira. She watched it — a spinning disc, a wheel. Did the turning of the wheel match the patterns of his thoughts? "Will you come and help me then?" asked Uncle. "I have too many paan to fold, maybe a hundred or more or so, you know how these people eat them one and then another and another, and my hands are old guy hands so it will go very slowly otherwise unless with your help." So on top of the plate must be materials for making paan; even as he said the bit about his hands being old, his hands tiptoed in the air, across the bottom of the plate, with magic agility. His words tumbled over and over as Mira nodded and stood and saw the ingredients poised above the plate — betel leaves and crushed betel nuts, a heavy can of sugar-preserved rose petals, a jam jar filled with candied fennel seed, a tiny green container of white lime.

They spread the materials out over newspaper on the kitchen table, out of the way of the guests. "If they see this then immediately they will come and eat them faster than we can fold," said Uncle.

He folded two as examples and Mira caught on, though her paan were clumsy and fat at first — "Not to worry, those will be for the clumsy and fat guests only," said Uncle. She washed the waxy heart-shaped surface of each leaf, then dried it on a paper towel and flipped it upside-down, then rubbed a thumbful of the chalky lime over it and topped it with a hunk of sweet gulkund. Then Uncle added the fennel seed and betel nut and a bit of coconut dyed pink and yellow. The leaves were laid out on the wide plate until nine or ten had accumulated, and then Mira and Uncle tackled the folding together.

"Folding paan is similar to origami," said Uncle. "You know, they use this kind of folding for all different things —

car airbags, folded, then upon crashing they boom open in your face. Telescope lenses, too, surprisingly. They fold it up so it fits on the spaceship. Also, too, you know I had a heart attack a few years ago and they put a stent in my artery — you know stent? It's like a mesh to keep your artery open. No clogs-bogs. They showed me before surgery and I asked them, how do you plan to fit such a thing in my small small artery? We will fold it, the doctor said. Origami inside my own body!" he said.

"If you eat paan, you won't get worms," said Uncle. "I mean inside your body. But on the other hand, you chew too much, you get mouth cancer."

Mira nodded. She imagined what mouth cancer might be like — sores that looked like tiny pizzas. She imagined a lens unfolding in space.

She wondered if Uncle had had anything to do with the selection of guests. No, she thought, watching Uncle gesturing in the air, his hands moving like spokes; no wonder it took him so long to fold the paan on his own. She smiled and he beamed. Ravi came up to Mira, held his still-filled plate right up to her neck. "Everyone finished a while ago, Ravi," she said. She took the plate from him and put it next to her on the table. Ravi went and sat on a cushion in her sight, wiped his hands on the carpet. Filthy, she thought, remembering all of Ravi's dirty handprints in their old house, on the wall next to the stairs. She creased the two sides of a leaf, then brought in the bottom and top. The paan's final shape was a plump pentagon. They did look like origami, thought Mira, like green origami frogs. Still, she was tempted to bite into one, but she'd had them before, knew she didn't like the taste, too sweet, and with a cold rush like peppermint. Maybe, she thought, it is possible to be reincarnated as something inanimate, and I will come back renewed, as a coat rack or a folded leaf, a handprint, a grain of rice.

There and Back Again

THERE WAS A difference between actively observing and just passively looking, or that least that's what Mira's drawing teacher had told her before she had dropped the lessons. The teacher had shown her a picture of a pigeon's foot and said that Picasso's father, an artist himself, had forced the boy to observe and sketch pigeon feet over and over until he could draw with photo precision every knot in their arthritic grasp. As a result, Picasso's skills of observation became so developed he could look at anything and, instantly perceiving details and nuances, produce his own exact copy. Mira imagined him looking at her and drawing a picture so identical to her that it was indistinguishable from the original.

She remembered this when she saw Ravi looking at his own hand. He had this habit of, when sitting in front of the TV, holding his hand out in front of him and staring at the palm, his eyes getting bigger and bigger, or whiter and whiter it seemed, then flipping the hand over to look at the back in this same way. He kept his fingers splayed so they much resembled the shape of a pigeon's foot. What could he be looking for that he hadn't already seen, there on the front and back of his own hand? Didn't he know it well enough by now? He concentrated on it the way Mira herself had started concentrating on her own face in mirrors, stretching her skin out with her fingers to examine any anomalies.

HE WAS DOING just this, staring at his hand, right before he first asked his question. He quickly put the hand away, down on the arm of the sofa, where his fingers moved like kicking legs. A piano prodigy in another life, thought Mira. It was a Friday after school, their mother had just arrived home, and all three sat watching sitcom reruns and eating unshelled peanuts.

"Check for worms before you eat them," said Mira's mother. They all checked for worms.

"Mom, why can't I be in the normal class?" His fingers kept dancing, tapping against the sofa's corduroy fabric.

For a second, Mira thought he meant the normal class of society. At school she was learning about feudalism. She and Cynthia had constructed a miniature hut with a straw roof to illustrate where the serfs would have lived. "Good work but historically inaccurate," the teacher wrote on their comment sheet. But no, he meant the normal class as in any class other than the one in room 314, where they housed all the special ed kids, or, as Mira's mother put it, the kids who didn't know up from down (which led to many instances of Mira lying on her back around the house, imagining the ceiling was the floor).

"Different people go in different classes, that's all," said Mira's mother.

Another pair in Mira's class had built a castle out of papier-mâché. LORD'S CASTLE, it said on the base; they'd written the letters in white glue and shaken glitter over them. "When they take it home, their My Little Ponies can live in it," said Mira, and Cynthia cackled *hahaha*.

"Like Mira is in her class and I am in my class," said Ravi, with a tone of finality.

BUT THAT TURNED out not to be the end of it. Ravi began asking, with abnormal frequency, variations on the same theme: "Mom, Why am I not in the normal class?" "When will I be in the normal class?" "Can I change into the normal class?" Normal-class-normal-class took on the qualities of a fugue, the phrase repeated and re-emerged with musical regularity. It took on the rhythms the Sanskrit mantras they chanted nightly. She heard her brother say it in his own primitive prayers, said quietly to himself as he lay supine in bed, "God please help me get into the normal class like Mira." He brought up the subject when Lala Aunty was over — "Next year I might be in the normal class." Lala Aunty said, "Is that right?" and patted his hand and gave him an extra handful of char-mur snacks to crunch on.

Once he called it out to Mira in the school hallway, as he walked with his abnormal-class peers and teacher. They all held hands, a wobbly string of kids of varied heights, reminding her of her plastic bracelet with the multicoloured snap-together pieces. Some grinned and others stared flat-expressioned at lockers or at Mira. The kids in wheelchairs trailed in back — like Santa Claus at the parade, thought Mira, watching the grotesque procession. The teacher was curly haired, matronly, patient. Probably she had an autistic brother.

"Next year I won't be in this class!" Ravi exclaimed from his place in the line, waving at Mira as he did whenever he passed her in the halls. The whole motley crew turned to him for this bit of fanfare. He might start a revolution.

"Indoor voice, Mr. Acharya," said the teacher, as though calling him mister would give him the dignity he wanted.

It wasn't the frequency of the question that bothered them all — Mira, her mother, Lala Aunty and even the imperturbable Uncle — as it wasn't as though Ravi hadn't ever been a broken record before. After any small reprimand, Ravi would bring up the criticism again and again. For example, when Uncle and Aunty were over for dinner, the phone rang and Ravi answered it and said "She's busy. Okay bye," and hung up in response to someone's asking to speak with his mother, and Lala Aunty suggested next time he answered he should demonstrate the same friendliness he displayed in person. "Say hello and how are you and oh sorry Mom can't come to the phone right now. Don't just say 'she's busy.'" For the rest of the evening, he asked again and again, "So I should say how-are-you next time?" and for the rest of the week, after every phone message he took, he'd ask whoever was around — "Did I do good? I did it right, right?"

"He has an obsessive personality," Mira told Uncle. They were buddies now. He loaned her books that were just beyond her. Her mother brought her along when she went to visit Lala Aunty, and Uncle would emerge from his library with a book in his hand. They would chat at the dining table while her mother and Aunty made tea and fried snacks. His current book selection was *The Wonder that Was India*, which he gave to her with a printout of a book review from when it had first come out. She could barely understand even the review, except the part that said, "His understanding of philosophy, religion, language and culture (art and prose) is just a pleasure. I am amazed to see this breadth in one person." That line made her want to know everything about the world. She carried the book around with her and beamed when people asked her why she was carrying such a big book. "Well, this is only volume 1," she would say, and point to the lines she'd underlined in pencil (Uncle had encouraged her to take notes). When he'd given her the book, Uncle had said, "It is incredible how he has captured the whole of our country, in only words!" Mira's mother had been there too, and had nodded, though Mira had a feeling she hadn't read it.

When she told Uncle that Ravi had an obsessive personality, she felt sure he would agree, and she continued, "It's like, why does he need to be in the normal class? He won't be able to keep up. He can't even understand when we watch a TV show. So I don't know how we can convince him to just stop asking." She waited for Uncle to give some suggestion, some formulation of words to end Ravi's incessant questions. Uncle twisted his hands around his mug of tea, looked straight at her, and said, mildly, "But don't you think he would like to read a book like you, Mira?"

At home that afternoon she got out *The Wonder that Was India* and vowed that she would understand every word. There would be no gaps in her understanding. She flipped to her favourite page, where she had underlined, "thirst for knowledge," "ancient wisdom," "cosmic mystery." She put the book away again and went to watch television. *Jeopardy* was on, and she got none of the questions right, though she kept on guessing. "Malaria," she said, but the answer was "leprosy." "Salmon," she said, but the answer was "herring." Ravi flopped into an armchair and said, "*Wheel of Fortune* is better because it's much easier for us to get the answers."

She turned to him and said, "No, you never get the answers. You've never gotten a single one. You just say what Pat Sajak says after he says it."

"No," he said, and smiled, then frowned when he saw that she was frowning. "But I'll be in the normal class soon, right." He said it as a statement, and he looked away and something in Mira's stomach emptied and then rushed back again, because it wasn't the frequency of his query that bothered her, but its plaintiveness, its abject tone, its lack of hope despite its persistence.

THEIR MOTHER CALLED his teacher first, and then the guidance counsellor, and then the principal. "I'm in your corner," the principal told her, "but it's not my decision."

"He's in my *corner*," she said to Lala Aunty. "As though a child's education should be a boxing match."

Next she called the school board to see if she could get him transferred to a different school where they would allow him in the regular class, but was informed he had to attend the school he'd already been assigned. She looked into private schools, calling two or three and jotting down numbers on the pad of paper by the phone — phone numbers and tuition fees. "Even the uniform would be a stretch of our finances," she said, which Mira assumed was an exaggeration, but when her mother wasn't nearby, she studied the numbers her mother had written down and tried to guess what figures they represented.

Her mother spent her afternoons pacing the foyer with the cordless phone — "He doesn't test well," she said, "But that doesn't mean anything, you know him, you know he tries so hard," she said, "I'll show you these drawings he did," she said. Her mother's voice had a certain controlled anger that grew with each conversation. Her syntax, usually a bit creative, settled into polite regular patterns, as though she'd rehearsed. Even holding back frustration, her voice fluctuated elegantly with expression, persuading and asking, "Can't you do something? ... How do you expect him to learn anything? What is he supposed to do when he finishes school? He's better off than those other kids in that class. They don't even look you in the face. They don't even walk ... no I'm sorry I said that ...," she held the phone away from her for a moment, breathed, put it back to her ear and began again.

She took an evening off from work to attend a meeting she'd managed to arrange with the principal, the guidance counsellor, and Ravi's teacher. Mira didn't know what happened in that meeting, but when her mother came home, she brought a pizza with her, and Mira and Ravi sat together at the table, in front of the covered pizza, not eating it yet, breathing sauce, waiting to hear what she would say.

"You're in," she said. "We got it."

"The normal class?" asked Ravi.

"We got it we got it," their mother kept saying, crying and opening the pizza box.

IT WAS THE autumn of Ravi's eighth-grade year when he transferred from 314 to 112, rumoured to be the easiest of the normal classes, a room that housed a group of just-turned-teenagers whose mothers didn't drop them off at the bus stop, who dated each other and smoked their cigarettes next to the No Smoking sign on school property, who applied to high school and straightened their hair and wore expensive sneakers and kissed and smoked and chewed gum and cracked wise, whom Mira avoided if she could, being only a sixth grader and inclined to carrying large books around with her. At home, not much changed. Her mother still put chicken nuggets in flasks for each of their lunches, accompanied by a pear, which she would slice and then put back together, wrapped in a napkin, zipped and locked in a Ziploc bag. The eighth graders did not carry such lunches, but it didn't matter because Ravi ate his alone on the edge of the playground, sitting on a wooden balance beam, kicking his feet in red, fallen leaves.

The only thing that changed was that now when Ravi came home each day he put his worksheets and textbooks on the dining table next to Mira's. Their mother eyed the papers with bare desperation. The deal with the school board was only a trial, and to avoid being placed back in the special education class, he had to stay above passing in all subjects. When he brought home his own book, *The Hobbit*, carried under his arm though there was room in his backpack, she counted the pages.

"There's a test when we're done reading it," Ravi said.

"*The Hobbit*," she said, pronouncing it "hoe-bit." "We'll read it out loud," she said. "It's not impossible." She had a half-finished English degree from a school in Karnataka. She'd read *Othello* once.

That night Mira lay in her bed listening to her mother and brother across the hall, opening the pages for the first time.

"An Unexpected Party," her mother began in her sing-song accent. "Well I'm glad it starts with a party," she reflected to Ravi. "You know how we go to parties, well, now we can imagine these hoe-bits having similar parties. And so many of our parties too are unexpected, like when Shailaja Aunty came the other day without even phoning."

"How is Shailaja Aunty doing?" Ravi asked.

"Oh, you know, you know," and she went on reading. "*If I say he is a Burglar, a Burglar he is ... There is a lot more in him than you guess, and a deal more than he has any idea of himself ... You know what a burglar is, Ravi?"

"Like the Hamburglar."

"Correct!"

And a few nights later, "Roast mutton? Why are these Hobbitton guys so fond of mutton?"

"Because it's delicious!" Mira yelled from her room.

"No, it's because they are not Hindus," said her mother and began to giggle. Mira couldn't remember if she'd ever heard her mother giggle. Mira got up from her bed and went over to Ravi's room. Ravi was sitting on his bed and grinning, his subject notebook sitting next to him on the bedspread, his hands together as though he had just finishing clapping. Her mother had fitted herself roundly into Ravi's desk chair. She held the book open with one hand, her chin tilted upward like a dramatic performer of Shakespeare. "Sorry Mira, no pictures," she said, and giggled again. Mira rolled her eyes, lay flat on the floor, looked at the ceiling, thought about dwarves, tried to tell up from down.

J.R.R. Tolkien became another member of the family. They left the book open at the fourth and empty dinner table place, occasionally spilled curry on it by accident. All the new family jokes involved elves and dwarves and wizards and the occasional dragon.

"Smog warning — that's what Bilbo needed, a Smaug warning!" her mother said, reading the newspaper one day.

They started referring to their array of houseplants as Mirkwood Forest. The cupboard where they kept Ziploc bags was called Bag End. When Mira slouched, her mother said she looked like Gollum.

"So I'd be Gollum due to my poor posture," said Mira, "Then which are you guys?"

"I want to be Gandalf," said her mother, "that expert in wizardry. No no, I change my mind, I'll be Thorin, no I don't like him so much, I think Gandalf. Ravi?"

"I don't know," he said, and thought importantly.

"Bilbo? How come nobody picked Bilbo?" asked Mira.

"It's the name, it's a detestable name," said her mother. "His name should have been Shobit, Shobit the hoe-bit."

"Classic Indian name," agreed Mira.

"How is Shobit doing?" Ravi asked. Shobit was actually the name of one of their cousins in India. Mira and her mother collapsed into cackling laughter.

Chapter 6 was "Out of the Frying Pan into the Fire."

"I am getting out of the frying pan and into the shower," said Mira's mother as she walked out of the kitchen and headed upstairs.

"My precioussss, give me my precioussss," they would say to each other when they wanted anything at all handed to them: car keys, chappatis, encyclopedias.

For a school assignment, Mira invented a fake world

inspired by *The Hobbit*. She called it Hichmond Rill and wrote an elaborate twenty page story about it. Her mother helped her build a giant 3D papier-mâché map. They painted it with acrylics (which her mother pronounced "a-kir-a-lix") and took Plasticine and formed little homes, pasted a legend at the bottom. In her room, she practised reading her story aloud, stealing her mother's tricks, pausing on the semi-colons and letting her voice jump suddenly into volume, wondering if she should add impromptu casual commentary in between the written words, which, when her mother did it, made the story so much easier to follow.

Mira went as Gollum for Halloween. It wasn't the first costume she'd had to explain.

Watching a recorded episode of *All My Children*, Mira's mother remarked, "This is exactly like when the army of Wargs tried to steal the treasure and it resulted in the Battle of the Five Armies."

They finished the book in late November.

"Great fellow, J.R.R.," said Mira's mother.

"I wish he was my dad," said Mira, and her mother actually laughed. She seemed to have mellowed, hadn't yelled in weeks, hadn't chased anybody down with her car in while.

THEY'D PRACTICALLY FORGOTTEN that Ravi had to pass a test on *The Hobbit*, his first real comprehension test. He had just barely managed fifties and sixties on the math and science tests, skipping the tougher word problems like his mother had advised him and spending all the allotted time on the basic calculations, his numbers round and plodding. They celebrated with dinner at East Side Mario's, where he ordered ravioli and a Diet Coke and ate most of the table's garlic bread. "Napkin on your lap," his mother reminded him. "The next one will be tougher," she said. "You can't skip any. Just do all of them. Think about the story and answer."

"I'll do all of them," he said, as he ducked his head into the plate and kept eating, nodding and mm-hmming.

When they went home, they gathered in the prayer room — more like god photos tucked into a pantry in the finished basement, much smaller than the prayer room in their old house — and performed a puja to Saraswati, the goddess of knowledge. They placed a painting of her on a centre shelf. The goddess rested in the cushion of an enormous white lotus flower and held a veena in her lap with her front pair of arms. She wore a white sari; the artist had painted its folds pale pink and trimmed the hem with gold, and Mira thought about what combinations of paint colours had been used to make the gold look so real and about how respectful you must have to be while working on a religious portrait, to avoid wearing shoes or accidentally swearing if you made a mistake. Ravi rang the tiny prayer bell while Mira placed carnation petals, one at a time, at Saraswati's feet, and Mira's mother lit the brass lamp and held it up to the goddess as though to better see her face.

It was customary during a Saraswati puja to keep a few books in front of Goddess Saraswati. Mira's mother set *The Hobbit* on the shelf with its green landscaped cover facing up. The worn white folds of its binding lay parallel to the goddess's feet. This time, it was the only book they kept there.

RAVI CAME HOME with his graded test, having gotten all but one question wrong. The question he answered correctly was,

"What is the name of the place where Smaug lives?" and Ravi wrote "On a mountain." The teacher had given him full credit, out of misplaced sympathy.

"The Lonely Mountain," Mira's mother said. She said it in a too-calm voice, one that Mira hadn't heard in a while but remembered and knew its volume and unsteadiness would escalate. Ravi had come down the stairs and handed the test to her in the kitchen while she cooked dinner. The microwave finished its time but nobody opened it. Mira's mother held the test in her hand and asked, "Did you not understand not one word? Not one word? And didn't say anything did you?," suddenly speaking so loudly it hid the sound of the test paper crumpling in her hand as she shook it. "How can you say you want to be in the normal class then? How? You remember how you came home and yelled here, normal class normal class?" Ravi pulled in his shoulders like a gull, as though his shoulders would cover his ears, and then he covered his ears with his hands. He kept entirely still, with the exception of the big toe on his left foot, which he shook and shook as though it contained all the energy of his whole body; it reminded Mira of something Uncle had said — that Buddhists believed the mind was like a fluttering butterfly, always trying to land.

While her mother yelled, Mira got up from the kitchen table and went out the side dining room door and up the stairs to her brother's room. He'd left his backpack on the bed, and she went over and opened it, took out his English subject notebook wondering if he'd written down anything at all. Ravi had written things, phrases spread out in blue ink pressed hard into the page, copied verbatim, *If I say he is a Burglar, a Burglar he is* ... the phrases growing into sentences and then entire passages, poems of the dwarves also copied neatly but with enjambment discarded … *Chip the glasses and crack the plates! … That's what Bilbo hates.*

In between the words, Ravi had drawn pictures in different colours of ballpoint pen: A tall figure who must have been Gandalf, thinner than the space between the lines of paper, his beard floating lightly sideways, a hobbit squatting squatly to eat from a whimsically patterned plate, voluptuous goblets and mean-looking elves and a shrivelled-up Gollum wearing a ring so big it took up half a notebook page, with scattered curvy lines blossoming from around him like rays from the sun, presumably to indicate invisibility. She left the book open on the bed, open to Smaug the dragon lounging in red pen, the perspective garbled so parts of his body seemed to belong to different dragons, or seemed to bulge as if eaten creatures lay whole inside.

That evening Mira saw the shadow of her mother walk through the night-lit hallway to Ravi's room.

"I finally got to talk with that teacher of yours," she said. "She'll let you take another make-up type test in one week or two weeks, she said." Mira heard her mother sit in Ravi's chair and open the book. "So then, now we will go through the important parts only." She coughed once, and said quietly, "An Unexpected Party."

BY JANUARY, RAVI was back in room 314. Two years went by, and Mira couldn't remember if he'd passed that second test at all. She only remembered taking the copy of the book when Ravi was done with it, putting it under her bed, where it remained, surviving many vacuumings.

When her mother pointed out in the newspaper a play version of *The Hobbit*, playing in a small theatre downtown, Mira talked Cynthia into going to see it.

"Smoke rings! Blow smoke rings, Gandalf!" Cynthia said to a bearded but otherwise ordinary gentleman taking a cigarette break outside the theatre, as she and Mira slipped past him into the theatre doors.

They bought their tickets and admired the programme, decorated in typography that looked like withered tree branches. "God, I'm hungry, why didn't we eat before this? There has to be an intermission, right?" Cynthia asked, rifling through the booklet. "LOOK, those men are deformed," she said, pointing.

"No, they're hobbits," said Mira. Some of the actors were walking through the lobby. Their outfits looked pieced together from Goodwill and army surplus finds. One kept removing his fake teeth to talk.

Mira and Cynthia went inside, and when the play began, they snickered through the scenes of stumpy creatures dancing foolishly with hats and fists in the air. Hobbits had their pants pulled high to make their figures seem shorter; Bilbo's cheeks had an unnatural rouge. But she hadn't expected the scenery to be so convincing. The whole theatre kept changing colour, the light would shudder from stone blues to reds so red they made the transparent air appear opaque, rich with colloidal dust, and the next second the room would shine orange as a pill bottle. Mira felt gentle surprise at this reminder that light could be controlled, pointed and aimed thin as a ruler, or filtered in lace patterns over the plaster floor. When men in rags stood on stilts, she let herself believe their height, though she knew she would mock them later ("Why can't all men be that tall?" Cynthia would ask, and they would fake sighs). Mira thought that forests had never looked so lovely in real life, littered with white paper instead of dry leaves or dirt. The fake version was infinitely more beautiful than any forest she'd seen; she wanted to go home and fill her apartment with rented birches.

Cynthia turned to her and whispered, "Bo-ring." Mira saw Cynthia waiting expectantly for her to laugh. She didn't want to, and the theatre was so silent and so resonant that any laugh would have been inappropriate. And then, embarrassed by how the play had affected her with its beauty and its compelling darkness, she laughed so loudly that Cynthia shushed her, then muffled giggles into her playbill. A creature stood centred on the stage, arched his back to expose his costume ribcage. The two girls wisecracked through the rest of it, Middle Earth not being anything that mattered much anymore.

It wasn't of any importance, a world from a book they'd all paid a lot of attention to once. There was that old argument about how half the things in school never applied to real life anyway. She thought of all the places she would never need to locate on a map. She would never need to solve a factorial or know anything about Medieval Europe or build an indestructible toothpick bridge, would never be required to read a story amazingly, captivatingly aloud. And Ravi would certainly never need to know why the hobbit had sought the Lonely Mountain, not in his job pushing grocery carts in the same Richmond Hill plaza where Mira went shopping for used CDs. Lala Aunty found him the weekend work when he turned sixteen, advising that the experience might look good on his resumé later on. He'd held the job for six months now, and Mira sometimes wondered if he'd ever do anything better than this. At the music store, she hovered by the front window, the CDs on the rack making a clicking sound as she absently flipped from one to the next and watched her brother move the carts from all over the parking lot. He would do this through the worst days of winter, and in the summer, despite his mother's sunscreen applications, his skin would turn dark. He pushed the carts, clattering and broken-wheeled to the front of the supermarket, and after the customers had borrowed and discarded them, he pushed them back again.

Le colosse

THEY WERE ATTENDING a wedding in Pittsburgh, though they hadn't been invited, and didn't even know the bride. "Go as my representatives," Lala Aunty had said, reminding Mira of her school's model UN conference, for which, as one of only two brown people in the school, she was assigned to be a delegate for India.

"Blast," she'd said to Cynthia. "I wanted to be the Czech Republic." And the other brown girl overheard her and took offence and gave her a lecture — face serious, hair shaking with the persistent nodding of her head — about having pride for where you came from, and people walking by them in the school hallway heard and so it quickly turned very embarrassing, but embarrassing in a different way from the embarrassment of attending a wedding uninvited. Lala Aunty was unable to attend herself because she was already a guest at two other weddings in town that weekend, but she had assured them the guest list was massive and nobody would care. If nobody would care, why go? It didn't make sense, except she knew Aunty pitied them and probably thought for them this would be a vacation, an occasion for them to get out of Ontario, for Mira to use her passport somewhere other than the school gymnasium.

Their motel room smelled like smoke despite the non-smoking designation, and was an hour from the Pittsburgh temple. At five o'clock in the morning, they had two hours to get dressed and drive to the temple. There were no towels in the room, but the office was closed so they would have to go unshowered, which distressed Mira's mother and gave Mira a sense of illicitness, of blasphemy. She could feel the dirt thickening on her like a new skin.

Ravi lay on the bedspread holding a blue marker, which he used to draw swooping lines on a pad of stationery. The lines swooped until there was no white space left on the paper. Already on the bed next to him was a pile of similar papers, torn from the pad. "I want to go for a walk," he said. He tossed the marker and stood up in a stretch. He unhooked the door chain and unlocked the deadbolt.

"Not too long, okay," his mother said. "You still have to change clothes."

He tugged open the heavy door and paused in the doorway before slapping a hand to his large thigh and lumbering out into the parking lot. His outline against the still-dark outside looked a bit like Alfred Hitchcock.

THESE DAYS, MIRA felt that the primary emotion of her life was embarrassment. Just hours earlier, she'd fallen down the front steps of a rest stop. Her knees banged against the concrete but she stood up quickly anyway, trying to recover prettily but failing; her windbreaker flapped around her like the wings of a pterodactyl. She saw a woman look at her and look away.

She was always falling (down stairs, on ice) or falling behind (some school adviser had let her sign up for too many classes, "You're smart, you can handle it," she'd said, incorrectly) or falling in love (with unattainable men — teachers mostly, or magazine pictures), and worse than all physical and metaphorical falling was the constant falling feeling she had, as though the organs inside her body were sinking, dropping away — to where?

Because her last name was Acharya, teachers with seating plans kept her near the front of the room, and one kept asking her to erase the chalkboard. Such an elementary school task would have once given her pride, but now as she stood she couldn't bear the thought of all those others staring at her back; she had never seen her back but believed it consisted of bony shoulders in a broad frame. The chalk brush went over the board and in her lack of efficiency she left wobbly streaks of dust. She pictured her back muscles moving inelegantly, a naked body shifting under a thin sheet, a crab scuttling just below the sand. Standing only 5'3", she needed a chair to reach the top corners, and what if she fell off the chair? Or what if, in her anxiety, she erased important information that the teacher didn't want erased, such as the exam date, or the quadratic formula — she doubted that would make the teacher reciprocate her love.

Her anxiety carried into piano recitals, held each quarter. Now that she was fourteen, she desperately wanted to quit. At the last one, she'd frozen at the keys. Her mother took a photo at the moment before it came clear there would be no performance; in the picture she looked like someone pretending to play the piano. The problem was that she'd memorized the piece as a whole and if she missed one note she had to start over, but you can only start over so many times before the audience starts yawning — "I think I need the book," she whispered to her piano teacher, who, standing too far away and blinded by the stage lights, couldn't tell what Mira was saying and just shook her head, so Mira stood up and bowed as though she'd played the whole thing, and the audience — who were just parents after all — half clapped and half waited as though expecting her to sing.

There was the time a boy asked her what she weighed and she lied. She said 102 pounds and he said that couldn't be right because he himself was 121 pounds and she most definitely weighed more than him, and he went and told the nearest group of people — "Mira lies about her weight!" The truth was that while she probably did weigh more than 121 pounds, she hadn't weighed herself in a while and didn't know. Once, she vomited, outside, on school property. The flu had come upon her as unpredictably as a mugging, and one minute she was talking to another girl and the next she had her hands up to her mouth as if to hold it back and then there was vomit in her hands, around her mouth, on the ground, and the other girl had stepped back, stepped away. One time in biology she said "orgasm" when she meant to say "organism."

YEARS LATER, IN college and afterwards, when Mira moved to a city away from her family, she would remember, in her moments of loneliness, being fourteen, and this ritual of getting dressed in a room with her mother — how it embarrassed her

— the quiet intimacy of pinning a sari, of gold against skin and skin against fabric.

Ravi was still out on his walk, and in the meanwhile, Mira's mother draped the length of her sari over the red cotton underskirt that concealed her unshaven legs (she had planned to shave them in the shower that morning), and Mira faced the wall as she put on her bra as fast as possible, cringing at the unfamiliar coolness of air against breasts. When that was over with, she put on her selwar kameez. She'd chosen a dark-coloured one specifically so it couldn't show sweat, but now she worried it was too tight at the armpits and across her chest. She lived in fear that one day it wouldn't zip. The whole effect was that she looked square and gilded, and no matter how much she blended, she couldn't get her makeup to look like her real face.

"Don't obsess, Mira," said her mother without looking, removing her jewellery from its case once piece at a time — the mango-shaped earrings, a stiff diamond necklace about a half inch wide, a bracelet constructed with twists of embossed gold. It was a lot of expensive jewellery for someone who never went anywhere. Her father had bought her mother the diamonds, on a trip to India before Mira's birth. Now the diamonds spent most of their time at a safe deposit box at the bank.

Mira heated the straightening iron by the poorly lit sink, and while she waited, she turned her head in different angles at the mirror, hoping to capture herself at her best, and knew that if she ever found that angle, she would hold her breath to let the image blossom and take root, in the same way that upon waking, she sometimes held her head completely still, to keep from forgetting a dream.

ON THE OTHER side of the room door, there were loud voices. Mira's mother sprinted to the door barefoot and soundless, the end of her sari trailing after her. Mira followed her and saw Ravi standing in the parking lot. His eyes were tightly closed and he pressed his hands to cover his ears, his fingers twitching and branching upwards. He still wore his pyjamas, the pants too short to reach the tops of his sneakers, exposing a few inches of untanned hair-covered ankle.

A man in an old grey T-shirt stood a foot in front of him. His face leaned into Ravi's as he yelled, his words echoing and magnified, "What were you trying to seeee? What were you trying to seeee?"

"Sorry! Sorry!" said Ravi, turning sideways to face away from the man, and emitting a high-pitched hum.

"What happened?" asked Mira's mother, pulling Ravi's elbow. "*Stop it*," she said to him.

"Who are you?" The man looked at her up and down. Mira felt a clutching in her esophagus. What freaks they were, he must be thinking, these Indians in fancy clothing at five in the morning.

"I'm his mom. What happened?"

"I caught this guy looking in our window. What's he doing wandering around my room in the middle of the night? Huh? Tell me, what is he, some pervert? He scared my wife to death! She's scared to death in there! I should call somebody. I'm going to call somebody."

Mira attempted to perceive her brother objectively, that enigmatic blood relation of hers who, though barely sixteen, was massive, bigger than she and her mother combined. Even this angry, yelling man appeared miniaturized next to him. Ravi's head shook like the head of a sunflower. Since puberty he had bulged outward from all sides, fat and skin spilling out over the edges of his clothing; it had become an issue of contention in their household. His chest, too, had a feminine plumpness, and Lala Aunty had adopted the awful habit of slapping him there, "Good going, Rav," she would say when he helped clear the table, then the slap and the jiggle. His skin had turned, too, into an uneven surface, bumps and flakes, in another unfair development that touched his body but not his mind. His brain was very much the same as always.

Mira imagined the man's wife seeing Ravi's eyes — dark-circled because he almost never slept — peering at her through the half-open window curtain. Sometimes when Mira lay in bed at night, she would look through her cracked open door and see him pacing aimlessly in the hallway, talking quietly to himself in stilted phrases, his eyes unnaturally large, his body a hulking rectangle, and under the trick of darkness, even she had sometimes felt a little afraid.

"It was all an accident. I'm so sorry. He'll stay inside now," Mira's mother said.

"I'm heading down to tell the management," the man insisted.

"They're closed," Mira's mother said, and the man glared at her.

"In the morning," he said.

"Please, don't."

"Just keep him inside." He glanced at Mira as he went back to his room.

"WHY DOES HE *do* that," Mira said quietly, retreating into the bathroom with the chemistry workbook she'd brought.

She solved one stoichiometry problem as she sat on the closed toilet lid, feet cold on the subway tile, erasing and pencilling numbers into an elegant, distracting solution. She was too old to be sharing a room with her family. In books, the parents always got the kids an adjoining room in a fancy suite with lots of brocade fabrics, but in real life you stayed in motels where the bathrooms had no towels and were painted yellow with yellow lighting and yellow tile, the wrong colour for a bathroom, urine-coloured — you might as well paint them brown — and you shared a bed with your mother, hoping no authorities would notice you had three people in the room instead of two.

She could hear them talking from the bathroom. Ravi had gone for a walk and forgotten their room number. He wandered past the adjacent doors, reviewing the numbers, probably reading them softly aloud. She didn't know the shape of her brother's thoughts, but sometimes she imagined they might resemble ticker tape, a two-dimensional sheet, a single line of words. He would have bent his shoulders to look in the woman's window, ducked his head to see through the glare, and covered the glass with his large, sweaty hand, thinking *which is the room is this the room*? In his frustration, he started knocking on the window, his fist determined and steady against the glass, the woman cowering inside. Had she answered, Ravi's words would have emerged identical to his thoughts, a panicked, "Which is the room? Is this the room?"

It might be laughed off if he were a four-year-old. But he was sixteen, and it was five in the morning, and the man had probably called the front desk to leave a complaint.

She heard her mother say, "Just stay in the room and don't go *anywhere* from now on."

"I didn't mean to," Ravi said, and Mira imagined his eyes closed again and his hands swooping up and then down.

Her mother's voice pleaded, "Didn't you realize it's very early in the morning? People are sleeping. Why did you wake them up? Why didn't you remember the room number, Ravi? You're good at remembering numbers."

"I'm SORRY," Ravi screamed. He began breathing a series of heavy sighs and hums. After a while, they faded, and the room became silent.

What were you trying to seeee? Mira kept hearing, as though the walls of the building had captured the phrase. Please God, she prayed, don't let us run into that man on the way out.

IF MIRA HAD been a loud girl, a confident girl, a girl over whom embarrassment rolled like water on a waterproof jacket, she would have defended her brother. She would have gone right out of the room and joked through it, diffusing the situation with a *Rainman* reference. Buddying up to the angry man, she'd say, "Sorry man, my brother's a little slow. I mean, he's no *Rainman* or anything, but you know. He didn't mean it." The man would smile, disarmed, a hand in his hair, and say that no harm had been done. Probably he'd introduce her to his son. They would date and eventually marry. Other people would stay in motel rooms to attend their wedding. Back in the room, she'd hug Ravi, her arms reaching only halfway around him. She'd say things like, "Don't worry about it," and then she'd joke-punch Ravi lightly on his flabby chest — because touching him would no longer embarrass her

— and Ravi would giggle and curl his body inwards.

Mira's mother had never even seen *Rainman*. She didn't allow those kinds of movies in the house. For Ravi's last birthday, Mira had bought him *Forrest Gump*, intended not as a deep comment on his situation, but because she knew Tom Hanks was one of only two actors Ravi would recognize, the other being Jennifer Aniston. Ravi would love the scenes of Forrest running. "Run, Forrest," he might say. They might say it together. After Ravi had opened the wrapping paper, crumpling it and saying an absent Thank You, their mother saw the video box and grabbed it roughly from his hands.

"Ravi, go get the cake from the basement fridge," she told him.

"Is it an ice cream cake?" he asked, as his mother grabbed the sides of Mira's arms and shook her, pushing her backwards and pulling her forwards as she spoke, so Mira's whole body undulated involuntarily, practically lifted off the ground because of her mother's strength, and it felt like Mira's only anchors were the fingernails cutting lightly into the flesh of her upper arms.

"Hey Mom," said Ravi. "What are you doing?"

"What do you want him to think?" Her mother whispered, scariest at her quietest. "You want him to think he's like this foolish man, on this videotape?" She dropped Mira's arms and picked up the box, striking at it. Mira said she was sorry and later exchanged the video for *Shrek*, though it occurred to her that her mother was defending Ravi from the wrong people, that the effects of Hollywood were the least of Ravi's concerns.

There had been a time when her mother had been a champion. It was two years since she'd fought with the school board to get him out of special ed, eight since she'd given the bully a little scare by chasing him down the street with her car, seven years since she'd gotten Ravi's third-grade teacher suspended after finding out that for weeks the teacher had forced him to wait in the school hallway while she taught her class — palms braced against the gritty linoleum floor because she wouldn't give him a chair — letting day after day pass with nobody even noticing him there, stepping over him like a used juice box, because it was easier to leave him in the hallway than to teach him a single damned thing.

"IT'S TIME TO leave," Mira's mother called from outside the bathroom door. They packed silently into the car, with Ravi in the front passenger seat and Mira in the back. They left the radio off and Mira dozed against the window, her head periodically hitting the glass. Ravi began to whimper.

"I didn't mean to," he said.

"Don't worry about it, Rav," said their mother.

"It's okay, right?" Ravi asked, and nobody answered. "I just forgot," he said.

"Mom, I DIDN'T MEAN TO," he shouted. "I didn't mean to," he whined.

In this way, they passed the hour to the Pittsburgh temple.

"DO YOU EVEN know the bride or groom at all?" Mira asked her mother as they drove up the hill to the temple and tried to find parking in the crowded, sloping lot.

"When will I be getting married?" Ravi interrupted. Mira's mother turned the car engine off. She and Mira exchanged glances in the car mirror.

"Well, you have time," his mother said lightly, and lifted her right hand from the steering wheel to touch the picture of Lord Ganesha they kept taped to the middle of the dashboard.

"Ganeshana madhuve" was Mira's mother's favourite expression to use when she caught Mira opting for elaborate methods of procrastination — rearranging the family room furniture into a new, better-functioning order, building a waste-paper basket out of cut-up, coiled magazine pages — rather than working on a tedious school assignment. "Do those teachers never give you any work?" she would ask, and eye-rolling, teenage-behaviour-embracing Mira would say, "I'm going to do it tomorrow." Their mother-daughter exchange was classic, with a Hindu touch, "Ganeshana madhuve," being an allusion to Ganesha, the only unmarried Hindu god.

When Ganesha's mother, Parvathi, asked him when he was getting married, he always said, "Tomorrow, my wedding is tomorrow," to remain a bachelor over a literal eternity.

But after Mira's mother had explained the expression, she had become confused and backtracked. Perhaps, she said, she had it reversed, since in those days, Ganesha wouldn't have searched for his own wife. His family would have found the girl and arranged the marriage. Maybe Ganesha had pleaded, "When is my wedding? When will you find me a bride?" and Parvathi, that clever buyer of time, had responded, "Tomorrow, your wedding is tomorrow." But, Mira had asked, why couldn't Lord Ganesha (whose title, after all, was Remover of Obstacles) find somebody to marry him? And her mother had answered, wryly, "Would you marry a boy with an elephant head?"

Parvathi had created baby Ganesha out of clay to keep her company while her husband, Lord Shiva, journeyed away from home for countless years. (In Hindu mythology, years passed like the sights out a car window; in real life you would have forgotten your husband by then.) With her powers, Parvathi granted the baby life, and he grew into a boy. When Shiva arrived home from his travels and found the child standing in front of his house, he questioned him. The boy pulled out his sword to defend his mother from the stranger, and Shiva, epic in his rage, pulled out his own sword and sliced off the boy's head. Parvathi ran out from the house screaming, and cradled the boy's headless body in her arms, crying, "What have you done to our son? What have you done to our son?" How bewildered Shiva must have been, but he wasn't the type to show it. He promised to go into the forest and bring back the head of the first animal he came across. "Why didn't they just re-attach the original head?" Mira asked. Her mother said it must have been too damaged. A mile from his home, Shiva crossed the path of an elephant, as grey as the monsoon sky, and he decapitated it effortlessly, carrying back the precious skull. Parvathi placed the elephant head above the lifeless neck of her son and pressed magic into the body — the most ancient sort of transplant. When the elephant head blinked and spoke, its surrogate parents showed no surprise.

Ravi, Mira thought, was like the crude baby-shaped clay that Parvathi had dug from the gardens behind the house, before she had given it whatever it was that made it breathe and grow and cry, or maybe he was the bleeding headless boy that Shiva left behind him when he ran into the forest, before his father had brought back a replacement for that irretrievable part. Except that there wasn't any magic to press into Ravi, and to think like that was awful, shameful, and he was still her brother, whom she was supposed to love — she did love him, in a yearning, horrible way that she couldn't stand.

Mira's belief in Hinduism was paradoxically both whole-hearted and fragmented. She prayed compulsively, but tried hard not to think about the logistics of her prayers workings; to test it too thoroughly would be for it all to fall apart. She made bargains with God. She told him — Ganesha or which-ever one was listening — she would stop wasting her money on movie rentals if only he would put Cynthia in a different French class than her this fall, so she could stop coming up with new reasons not to let her copy her homework. She would stop making craft wastepaper baskets out of magazines if her mother would let her discontinue the piano lessons. She didn't pray for important things, for long shots, such as finding out that her father hadn't actually died in any car accident, but had been found in some hospital with amnesia, and would regain his memory prompted by some small clue — finding a reminder in the way a curtain moved, or the way Jell-O tasted — and come home, weeping at the twelve lost years, the weeping evidence that he was *alive*. She fantasized about things like that, but didn't pray for them, because though she watched the occasional soap opera, she had a firm grasp on realism.

And she didn't pray that Ravi would wake up from the blur of his mind, snapping awake as though it were a nap he had been taking. But she did imagine it, her brother suddenly speaking in swiftly modulating tones instead of his blank monotone. She spent so many car rides and so many hours before falling asleep and so many commercial breaks thinking of her brother as he could have been, a Ravi who was two years older than she was instead of eight years younger. She liked to picture the two of them renting a movie and bantering hilariously through it, or shopping with him for their mother's birthday present, arguing over whether she'd prefer the sweater or the food processor. They would both have part-time jobs that involved deep thinking and would afford food processors easily. But she prayed for little things, thinking maybe they'd accumulate. Her brother had been the exact same boy for ten years, and in her experience, that was too established a pattern to expect an aberration.

Quotes from another religion told Mira there was nothing new under the sun, that nothing would ever be new again. How many more emotions were left for her to experience — true love, the dazzling emotions of childbirth. What else? In a recent French class, she'd been slapped with déjà vu as they discussed Georges Simenon's novel, *Le Chien Jaune*. It had a glossy paperback cover with the picture of a hotel café on the front, indicating an elegant murder mystery. One of the prime suspects was a large simple-minded man. They referred to him as *le colosse*. Criminals tricked him into transporting a large shipment of cocaine, and later turned him in for a reward. Cynthia raised her hand in class because she had trouble understanding the character. "I don't get it … sorry, *je ne comprends pas*," she said.

After several attempts in French, their teacher, finally relenting and using her less than polished English, had explained, "He is, you know, *un peu* retarded."

"Ohhhhhhh," the rest of the class said in unison, in understanding. No, you don't understand, is what Mira wanted to say, but — and she hated this about herself — she was a girl who thought things and didn't say them, and the class discussion continued around her. She wanted to say, you don't understand until you've lived with it. And even then you don't understand.

THERE WEREN'T MANY guests at the wedding — fewer than a hundred, which, for an Indian wedding, was the same as inviting twelve. These eighty-five or so gathered in a downstairs room of a temple. The women tucked their saris under them, cross-legged on the low-pile red carpet, pulling children into their laps. Mira played with the tasselled edge of her selwar kameez shawl until it began to fray. A Hindu priest performed the ceremony with his eyes literally closed — it seemed almost dubbed, Mira thought, the strings of Sanskrit words. Afterwards, everyone stood in an S-shaped line and waited to congratulate the couple. When they got close, Mira saw that the bride had too much foundation on her dry skin — it flaked under the temple lights. Her mother slipped an envelope of money into the bride's hand and the bride said, "Thank you so much for coming, Aunty," smiling as though she recognized them. Being strangers hadn't mattered at all.

Five hundred people attended the reception at a local banquet hall. In the lobby, Mira spotted a table with rows of crisp white place cards, and found her name written in curlicued uppercase on one side, a table number on the back. Her mother and brother had been placed at table four, but she was at table sixteen.

"We'll ask someone to switch with you," her mother said. In the hall, white tableclothed tables formed two concentric circles around a parquet dance floor. The centrepieces — low cubic glass bowls packed tightly with yellow roses — pulled and refracted all possible glow from the dim lighting. Mira scanned the tables for number sixteen and realized that some brilliant aunty had seated her at the table with all the other teenagers. Ravi and her mother were at a table more than halfway across the room.

"It's fine, Mom, I'm fine," she said.

AT TABLE SIXTEEN, she touched the eyebrow of the boy sitting next to her. He had a scar there and she had decided already that she would be fearless; these were people she would never see again.

"What is that from?" Mira asked. She heard herself speaking and liked how her voice sounded — as though it belonged to somebody bold.

"I gave it to him," said the girl on the other side of him, who turned out to be his sister. Mira tried not to stare at the girl's undeniable physical perfection. The boy was beautiful, too, even though in rooms of formal Indians, under the splendour of females, males tended to form the background canvas, content in shirts and ties. The girl looked about Mira's age, but she wore a sari, two-toned teal and royal blue, embellished at the borders with silver embroidery to mimic the looping feather patterns of peacocks. From her tight, sleeveless blouse emerged arms that were sculpted and brown, darker than Mira's. Her eyeliner looked liquid, dark and wet inside the rim of her eye. She had a deep-pitched laugh that she covered with her palm.

Brother and sister snickered through the speeches and presentations. They mocked everything. Why did the DJ wear a baseball cap? Couldn't the groom have memorized his three-line speech and delivered it with some sincerity rather than printing it out on a now thrice-folded sheet of printer paper? The girl declared there would be no speeches at her wedding, only acrobatic performances. She catcalled as the DJ introduced the couple's parents, who danced up from the entryway to the head table and thanked nearly all five hundred guests by name. Thankfully, by that time the appetizers had appeared on tables in an inconvenient corner of the room. Guests raced to the snacks, tripping over microphone cords. There were breaded pakoras with tamarind and mint chutneys, pieces of spicy grilled chicken that had to be clearly labelled "chicken" so the vegetarian aunties wouldn't accidentally pop them into their lipsticked mouths. Girl and boy nearly spilled their food laughing at how each of the uncles would accept a few lonely leaves from the salad tray and then grunt as they placed their oily samosas over them.

They returned to their tables and suffered through the thirty-minute slideshow. Bollywood tunes played on repeat as the flirtatious aunties cooed at their bald-headed husbands. Endless photos of the bride and groom were magnified onto the wobbling screen. First they were naked babies. Here they were as mischievous toddlers, subsequently precocious children. And of course, hideous braces-and-glasses-wearing-early-nineties teenagers. Finally, with each other, suddenly outfitted with shapely hair and contact lenses and perfect teeth, as if the finding of love had been a process of exfoliation, a revelation of their secret physical appeal.

Caterers served the dinner close to eleven, arranging gas burners under stainless steel trays of curries, and leaving bowls of warm naan on each table. The beautiful girl sorted her food, scrunching her face as she pressed her coconut burfi onto her brother's plate, saying "Lakshmi Aunty's are soooo much better," a family reference, thrown so effortlessly into conversation. They spoke in code, this brother-sister pair. If Mira married the handsome boy, their family would absorb her. Sometimes, when a boy at school spoke to her, instead of gosh, *he's cute* or *I wonder if he's single* or whatever it was she should be thinking, she thought *he would make a good brother*, and then felt ridiculous. She forced herself never to be curious about her friends' brothers, because she might start asking questions that were none of her business, and then she'd wish she'd just stayed quiet. But she wanted to know, did they use the same slang? Did they regard their parents in the same way? Did they talk about sex? If one of them walked in on their parents having sex, would he or she tell the other? Did they lie to each other? When they played Monopoly, did they argue over who got to be banker? Did they converse over breakfast or eat their cereal without comment? If something funny happened in a silent room, did they share knowing glances? She would never know, and so her alternate universe would remain undefined, the universe where her brother was not an almost-brother, an unfilled-silhouette, a container that didn't quite hold what it was supposed to, a cake mix in which someone had forgotten the eggs so that though it waited in the heated oven for the designated length of time, it never rose properly. She must never say this out loud to anybody.

THEY SIPPED THEIR non-alcoholic champagne as the toasts ended and the dancing started. First, the bride danced with her father. In her heels, she stood an inch taller than him, and her hair made her taller, coiled and shining in a high sphere. The bride's father appeared solemn in his dark suit, and he held his daughter's elbow with a firm grip, but at the chorus, he smiled a little and gave his hips an ironic swing. Then husband and wife danced with their heads close together, speaking quietly in words that Mira imagined were inside jokes, inside joke after inside joke, moments of eye contact, words only they understood, a language as textured as Braille.

Soon the slow song would switch to another slow song. The bride and groom would loosen their arms to wave in the other couples, and a few aunties and uncles would rise in pairs from their seats, holding their spouses and swaying sweetly and awkwardly with the quiet melody. Mira hoped the handsome boy would ask her to dance, or maybe, because she'd already decided to be brave, she would ask him. Before any of this, Mira saw Ravi move from the dessert table to the centre of the room. She scanned the hall for her mother, and couldn't spot her. She must have gone to the bathroom.

Ravi loved to dance. He found the dance floor and shifted his weight from foot to foot over the maple parquet.

"Yeah!" he said, grinning and clapping his hands with gusto. The room was silent as a field, except for the recorded music. Only bride and groom were on the dance floor, and it was apparent they didn't know what to do. They moved to a corner, crowded out by Ravi. They were like honeymooners touring a safari, and one of the animals had gotten out of hand. Some guests chuckled hesitantly but the bride frowned. Ravi, encouraged by the laughter, expanded his movements. He twisted his hips so his shirt came untucked, lifted his arms and swung them to his own beat, raised his arms high above his head, his shirt lifting and exposing the thick hairs that covered his pale, folded belly. His huge teeth glistened between his wide, open lips. His movements were large; he bent and he shook with a terrible energy, and when the song ended, he kept going.

"Ha, look at that guy!" said the handsome boy, sitting next to her all this time, seeing what she was seeing, "At least he's having a good time." He and his sister laughed together, laughed and laughed, though not unkindly.

"He's a giant," said the beautiful girl, with poetry in her tone. "The Wedding Giant."

"Who is that guy?" the boy asked, turning to Mira, perhaps by some instinct.

"YOU SHOULDN'T HAVE danced, Ravi. It wasn't your wedding," their mother would say to Ravi on the car ride back to the motel.

And years later, at her own wedding, when Mira would put her hands on Ravi's large arms in lieu of the father-daughter dance, she would remember the handsome boy's question and flinch in regret, at how she had hesitated, at how her answer had been only the cowardly one, when she'd pretended that she wasn't sure.

Around the Corner from Fantasia

MIRA AND NATHANIEL were discussing "the war effort," because Mira was learning about World War II in her grade eleven history class. She had phoned him to tell him how much she loved the nicknames, that "Allies" sounded just like the one you *should* root for, and then there were "The Big Three," "the trusteeship of the powerful," "the Four Policemen," like a football league or a comic book — "Not to trivialize," she said, because she didn't want him to think her flippant about war, "The names just get me riled up, you know? They're good names."

"What would you do if I had to go to war?" Nathaniel asked.

They loved hypotheticals. What if they were pioneers, what if they were farmers in Maine in the 1850s, what if they lived in India in times of British colonialism, what if they were in a Dostoevsky novel, what if they lived in 1939 and he had to go to war?

"I'd miss you," she said, winding the phone cord romantically. "I would send you epistles and never know if they had reached you. I would support the war effort by knitting socks for soldiers and rationing sugar and fighting for the vote and working at a munitions factory and by being generally frugal. Perhaps at the start of the war, I would make a declaration, swearing not to buy a new hat until the war was over, not knowing the war was to last another six years ... a girl did that in a book I read once."

Because she was on the telephone and he couldn't see her, she could eat while they talked. On a small plate, she had poured a bunch of chocolate-covered Digestive biscuits and was eating them continuously through the conversation, nibbling through the thin layer of chocolate and the crumbling, yielding cookie. In future months, every time she ate one of these, she would have a Proustian moment of involuntary memory, associating each bite with the low and ironic tones of his voice, and eventually she would stop eating the biscuits entirely. Having to ration sugar would be such a discouragement to a nation, she thought now. She wasn't sure what she would really do if he went to war, other than miss these conversations.

IRA'S MOTHER HAD recently begun hiding food around the house. Mira returned from school hungry one day, having only half eaten her dismal packed lunch. Checking the fridge and cupboards, she found only ingredients — cornstarch, cake mix, sour cream — which was unusual for their house, so full of people who liked to eat. The kitchen that day looked like a Home Hardware display, smelling of plaster instead of food.

Her mother had hidden the food because Ravi had become officially fat, but the subterfuge made no difference because Ravi was more determined to find the food than he was to lose weight. He searched for food like a trained pig snouting out truffles, Mira thought, but only meant it kindly — when she thought of pigs, she thought of clean infant pigs, and when she thought of truffles, she thought of chocolate truffles. Had she seen a real pig after a real truffle, it would have been incongruous with the picture in her head. And she herself had become a bit of a truffle pig, following her brother's lead until it became their daily habit to scour the house for its edible contents. In between frying pans inside the unused oven, Ravi found boxes of soft Indian sweets cut into harlequin shapes, topped in silver leaf. The siblings disregarded this elegance to take giant careless bites. In the recesses of the hallway closet, behind a rainbow of refolded gift wrap and squashed gift bags, they discovered the metallic packaging of potato chips, blending in perfectly. Their mother had tucked chocolate kisses inside the rarely touched coffee mugs on the highest shelves. They peeled them handfuls at a time, crumpling together the wrappers to form a fist-sized foil ball that rolled glittering across the glass dining table.

They were bound in their compulsion. Neither could remember the actual feeling of hunger ("I'm hungry," Ravi would say when his mother got home, though he had already eaten everything; it only meant he wanted more). They synchronized their chewing. Mira thought of eating as a hobby they had in common.

"Do you want half?" Ravi asked her in the midst of one of their searches, breaking apart a butter tart and shyly handing it to her. She took it from him and stuffed it in her mouth. Ravi copied her and giggled, crumbs flying from his baby face. It occurred to her that if he choked, she could save him, wrap her arms around him, fist below the breastbone, push the air up and clear the bolus of food clogging his windpipe, but if she choked, she would probably die. Ravi would flail his arms and yelp as her eyes rolled back into her head.

"Ravi, do you know how to call 911?" she asked him.

"Yes, you just dial 9-1-1," he said.

"If I ever look sick, or like something's just really wrong, and Mom's not home, you call 911, okay?"

"Okay," he answered. His eyebrows creased, then loosened as he resumed eating.

Mostly they conducted their feasts in the hour between when Mira came home from her high school and their mother came home from work. They ate under the pressure of this sixty-minute deadline, just barely enough time for the searching, eating, and then cleaning up (burying the wrappers in the trash, washing the dishes and putting them away). They left the television on and used the schedule of programs to mark the time. During the two sitcom reruns — usually *Family Matters* and *Growing Pains* — they uprooted fruit roll-ups under the puffy sofa cushions. When Ravi sat, he could feel them under him through the layers of cushion fabric and spongy matting, through the flesh of his bottom, like the princess and the pea. Mira chewed and chewed the fruit roll-ups until her teeth hurt and the condensed tang cut her tongue. The skin of their hands grew soft from handling the oily pakoras they found in the box of empty cassette tapes, and Ravi left a grease hand-print on the cream-coloured wall. Powdered donuts, packed in plastic, revealed themselves between pillow cases kept neatly under beds, and spilled their white dust over Ravi's shirt. Mira opened a jangling storage container of serving spoons and found crystalline coconut candy concealed underneath. The candy felt abrasive against the insides of her cheeks and sometimes left trickles of blood.

Sometimes they even ate the results of Lala's test recipes (packed into unlabelled Tupperware), though mostly their mother threw them away. The food supply was near limitless, because their mother had the habit of buying snacks in bulk at Costco. On Saturday shopping trips, Mira went with her and lunched on all the samples, while her mother added box after box to their cart.

THEY OFTEN LEFT one or two of the food items still in the package, as though their mother wouldn't notice the sharp decrease in quantity. Every couple of weeks, the food would shift to new hiding places; it was a wonder how many secret spots existed in their small house. Initially, their mother didn't comment about the food, and Mira didn't think she ever would. But one evening, as they all sat in front of the TV, their mother abruptly reached for the remote and turned it off. A singing girl on the screen stretched her arms mid-crescendo.

"Who ate all the cookies?" she asked. The question seemed trivial and kind of funny, juxtaposed with her grave expression. She looked at Ravi first. "How many did you have?"

"Only two," he lied. It was obvious he was lying, because of his delighted face.

"Then how many did you have?" she asked Mira.

"Mom, I'm fifteen. You don't need to monitor my food intake." She knew that would cut off the questioning, because lately they had been clashing, and Mira was sure her mother had been trying harder to get along. She was buying magazines with articles that said not to harass your teenage daughters about their eating habits. And there was no reason to harass her, because somehow Mira had avoided gaining weight — perhaps because she took frequent walks. She meandered with Nathaniel into the corners of Richmond Hill. She was fairly sure she had seen all of it now — she could locate all the bike paths, and knew which neighbourhoods were chummy enough to hold joint garage sales.

"Why do you need to eat like that? What's wrong with you?" Her mother said to Ravi. "Can't you see we can't even find clothes for you? Do you want to get sick? You're going to have a heart attack. You know what a heart attack is? That's what Suraj Uncle had. And now he takes seven pills every day."

Nothing terrified Ravi more than the idea of taking medications. He pressed his lips together and began to hum.

"Stop that. *Stop. That.*" Mira's mother said. Mira went and made some tea and phoned Nathaniel to tell him about this latest debacle.

MIRA AND NATHANIEL had been in the same elementary school class for a couple of years, and had met again in Tolbar Park, fifty metres from Mira's house. Mira balanced herself on the park swing, swinging, palms over the cold metal chains, sandals flung into the sand. She thought she looked pretty good. These days she liked to imagine herself from a third-person perspective, how a person walking by might see her, and this helped her to always look her best. By some luck, Nathaniel did walk by, and saw her, and came down the park path and right up to her. In order to avoid kicking him, she had to stop swinging. She didn't want to kick him, because he was fairly handsome. His hair looked exactly like a pile of golden raisins. When he opened his mouth, she prepared to give him directions. If he had only asked for directions, she still would have been pleased. Mira saw a kind of achievement in knowing a place well enough to conjure a mental map.

"You know a house here got broken into last week," he said.

"Okay."

"I mean it isn't safe, to be just swinging around alone at night."

It wasn't really night, she thought, more like twilight, and the sky was bright blue. Mira thought he might attack her. How long would it take to start swinging again, to knock him over with her bare feet, leap over him, and run the fifty metres home? She could see the roof of her house in the V made by the tops of evergreens.

"Why don't I walk you home?" he asked.

"Okay," she said, as though she hadn't just suspected him of being an attacker. In the three minutes it took for Nathaniel to meet her and then accompany her home, Mira's entire dialogue consisted of: "okay" (twice) and "goodnight" (as he handed her his phone number). Later, she analyzed this scene and decided that her silence had been the principal source of her charm.

THEIR FIRST DATE was at the Richmond Hill Heritage Village Day Festival, and she didn't know it was a date until she was walking up a set of stairs and he put his arm around her as they leaned together to read the descriptions of items for a silent auction. His forwardness surprised her because she so rarely touched other people — it was alarming, but she figured she would eventually become desensitized, the way third world children seemed unable to feel the flies that landed on them. Nathaniel had six siblings and played soccer. She thought large families and sportsmanship contributed to these inclinations towards touch; he put a hand on her shoulder when he wanted to get her attention to point at the man in the town crier costume, who rang a bell and said hear-ye hear-ye and wore pantaloons in the town's colours; he rested his palm on her thigh as they sat to watch a group of teenage trumpeters feebly play "Amazing Grace."

"My tenth-grade band played out here for the Remembrance Day parade," she said. "And the Santa Claus parade, actually. And during last year's Earth Day, they set up a stage for the choir to sing."

"This town has a lot of festivals," he said.

"Also, my Girl Guide troop met here," she told him. "My mother and Ravi used to pick me up here ..."

"Who's Ravi?" He pronounced Ravi "Raaavi," even though he said it right after her and so should have said it the same way.

"My brother." That was the very beginning of telling him things.

"I didn't know you had a brother," he said.

"Yup, so the two of them would come to pick me up. I waited outside. And across the street, where all that construction is, there used to be a strip club painted pink, called Fantasia, like the Disney movie. For a while, we gave directions by it. Where's the library? Just south of Fantasia. The high school? Around the corner from Fantasia. The townspeople despised it. I used to sit here and watch the women standing there half-naked, smoking."

He kissed her then, suddenly. She wondered if the mention of half-naked women had prompted him, and she imagined that the trumpeters were watching them, evaluating her response. Because he was kissing her, right out there in public and everything, she didn't get to tell him about the time she'd gone inside, or about the fate of Fantasia, that somebody had mysteriously set it on fire and she had witnessed it, the red flames clashing with the pink walls, smelling like burning grease. Or about how afterwards, she had snuck past the yellow police tape to collect a piece of the remaining brick as a keepsake. She had a habit of wanting to remember things, pictorial details, like the building's exact shade.

AS A RESULT of having six brothers and sisters, Nathaniel always spoke as though yelling over a crowd. In his house, they hollered. Mira didn't think she had ever heard anybody holler in real life, besides the Richmond Hill town crier.

In contrast, Mira's family could pass entire evenings wordlessly, with an occasional hmmmm from Ravi, which they ignored like noise from the refrigerator. Mira had vague recollections of a time when her mother had been called chatty. Now the carpet absorbed even their footsteps. If the phone rang, everybody jumped.

The differences in their homes delighted her. The differences in anybody's homes delighted her. Lucy Chin's house had made her claustrophobic. Cynthia's house was open-concept, expansive and expensive. It had barely any belongings in it, as though she and her family might at any moment pack up and move. At Nathaniel's house, the sofas had slipcovers. His parents avoided decorating, with the exception of potted plants, whose soil spilled and made the beige carpet brown. Their cupboards held unbreakable plastic dishes in primary colours. A dog ran wildly up the stairs.

Mira's mother had recently developed a penchant for fragile furniture. The legs of chairs curled like italicized script. The arms cradled cushions with embroidered portraits of elephants. On the walls, every room had a painting shipped from India, back from when Mira's father was alive and they could afford it. The paintings all had the same character, an hourglass woman with dark eyebrows and gold nose-rings appearing in every frame; it was as though she had wandered from room to room, stopping and posing, then moving on. The only pet they had ever owned was a Siamese fighting fish with a purple-red tail, who had no companions and so swam in an endless ellipse until he died. She had been in the room when Ravi knocked the bowl over with a misplaced elbow. "Sorry sorry sorry!" he had exclaimed, throwing up his hands as the bowl crashed against the porcelain tile; as she scooped the naked fish into her hands, it stared at her with a wobbling eye.

Mira's mother painstakingly examined the Queen Street antique shops for marked-down items, considering the house an ongoing project. At a Winners store, while buying Ravi clothes, Mira had seen her mother exhibit a rare joy at spotting a pewter carving of the Goddess Durga, whose numerous lean arms opened as gracefully as the petals of a magnolia.

The goddess was even more beautiful and more terrible than the tiger whose back she used as a throne. Each arm held a different weapon, a black shield, a bolt of thunder, a blade shaped like a slender moon. Years ago, when their mother had ventured to redesign the basement prayer room in their old house, she had told her children the story of the Goddess Durga, whose name in Sanskrit meant "invincible," a word that shook the little Mira, once its meaning had been explained to her. "Indestructible," her mother had said, wielding an angled brush to paint an enormous gold Om symbol on the blue prayer room wall. "Impossible, inhuman strength." The other great Hindu gods had combined their forces to create Durga, each forming a different part of her body. Mira's mother held Mira's chin, "the face from Shiva," pointed to her eyes, "made by Agni, the god of fire," patted her on the rear, "created by the Earth," and so on. They created her to defeat the evil Mahishasur, a demon who had received a boon that protected him from being killed by any man or god. ("A badguy?" Ravi had asked from his seat on the basement stairs.) Durga, a woman, killed the demon Mahishasur on the tenth day of the waxing moon, brandishing a trident borrowed from Rudra, the god of storms and winds and death. At this point of the story, their mother whipped her paintbrush around in an imaginary duel and the children pretended to be vanquished, falling and rolling all over the carpet, kicking their feet in the air.

Mira had been so infatuated with the story that she had insisted on dressing as Durga for Halloween. It was only a few years before she went as Gollum. Out of an old blue sari and stick-on velcro, she and her mother fashioned a gown. They stuffed Mira's mother's old beige pantyhose with crumpled tissue paper to make the six additional arms, which held cardboard and construction paper weapons. Mira wore a foil-covered Burger King crown and instead of "trick or treat" would say, more boldly than she ever said anything, "I am Durga, defeater of Mahishasur!" her extra limbs bobbing up and down. "She's a Hindu goddess," her mother explained to their bewildered Korean neighbours.

But in that ordinary department store, Durga, the Hindu symbol of strength, waited amongst ordinary objects, as though she were of the same ilk as clay garden gnomes or ceramic toads. Mira's mother saved her from the shelves and gave her a prominent position on the mantelpiece, adorning her with a fresh flower when the garden provided one.

"I like the simplicity of your house," Mira told Nathaniel.

"You can come over whenever," he said. He seemed to view this as a magnanimous offer. It was true, Mira thought, that Nathaniel's house had a comforting quality. But secretly, she preferred her own home, with its dark beauty. Even the rugs depicted ancient battles, and as a child she had imagined sinking into them and travelling backwards in history. It took effort not to pity Nathaniel for living in a place where it didn't even matter whether or not you took off your shoes.

BACK WHEN MIRA still dressed up for Halloween, she had accompanied her mother and brother on countless shopping trips. Ravi would stick his head halfway out the window and point out impressive-looking cars, of which Mira and her mother knew nothing. At the shopping centre, her mother had made a game out of having the children search through the clearance bins for Ravi's size. But then Ravi's size began to increase, not in the expected increments, but almost exponentially, his torso expanding like bread dough rising. The numbers on the clothing tag went up and up commensurately until Mira and her mother had to struggle to find his size in their usual stores. They switched from jeans to elastic-waists. They became regular customers at the city's Big & Tall Men shops, where sleek-haired gentlemen would ignore their protests and try to sell them two designer Italian suits for the price of one.

And there were further complications. Ravi wouldn't wear shirts with buttons. He wouldn't wear shirts with collars. He wouldn't wear shirts that didn't feel like cotton, or pants that couldn't be rolled up into shorts. He wouldn't wear socks of colours other than white. Clothing lay in his dresser unfolded and unsorted — because his folding abilities were such that even pillowcases came out diaper-shaped — so undershirts shared space with hats, brims mingling with sleeves, and Mira wondered whether her brother might someday emerge from his bedroom with his leg in the neck of a sweater, a human clothing rack.

Shortly before Ravi's eighteenth birthday, Mira entered her mother's bedroom and saw her leaning forward at her desk, squinting at the computer screen, clicking through websites for discount large clothing, scanning through page after page. "I can't handle it anymore," she said, and continued clicking.

"Let me take care of it, Mom," said Mira, inspired and sad, as she watched the hand twitch over the computer mouse, tendons pronounced, veins startlingly blue. Her mother pulled a credit card out from her purse and handed it over wordlessly.

"SO NOW I'M in charge of buying his clothes," she complained to Nathaniel the next time he came over. As soon as she had walked away with the credit card, she wished she hadn't volunteered. She knew it would be a chore.

"You need to regress," he said, tracing his finger across her eyebrow as though he were locating a foreign country on a globe. She didn't know what he meant exactly, and how regressing would be any different from what they usually did — renting movies (he talked through them; she didn't), playing cards (he always wanted to play poker; she argued for Spit), or going on walks (he preferred walking near shops; she liked parks). Everything but the walks they did while sitting on her bed. This had embarrassed her initially. When he first came into her room, he hopped on to it even though there was an office chair right there, which she'd wheeled out invitingly before he'd arrived. So she sat on the chair herself, until he patted the spot next to him, and then she hated the way the mattress sunk under them, and the sound of bending hinges. But it had been five months now and now she was the one to jump first on the bed and whatever activity they started with always dissolved into them kissing each other and they'd miss half the movie or lose half the deck of cards and half their clothing. They hadn't talked about sex yet, but she thought about it with a shy disbelief that it was now a possibility.

For now they used juvenile expressions to dart around topics of physical contact. "Fooling around" was ruled out because Mira had once heard a biology teacher say it. Nathaniel suggested "sucking face" and Mira countered with "necking." They decided on "making out," which Nathaniel shortened to MO. He liked secret codes; he read books about spies. During the walks, they'd stop if they saw a park, sit romantically on a park bench, MO when there weren't people to see them, and discuss all the possible places they could kiss each other ("Chem lab," he said; "Your ear," she said).

The thing she disliked about kissing was the smell of breath, both familiar and unfamiliar, and how she was never sure if it was hers or his. Alone, she would cup her hand to her mouth and breathe and smell and think — was it him or was it me? She started gargling regularly with baking soda. His body was scented most often of soap, but sometimes, if he had biked over, there was a spiced human odour that filled the room like humidity, stayed when he left. She didn't like how it seemed to overpower the room's natural smell, which smelled like nothing but which must be her own smell after all.

Another thing she didn't like was when he waxed political. One minute they would be kissing and then he would be discussing the House of Commons. He was the only person she knew who watched CPAC, but she was pretty sure he had no idea what he was talking about.

She and Nathaniel and Cynthia had milkshakes together, because Mira had wanted Cynthia's opinion, but then spent the whole time wondering if he wasn't looking a little too long at Cynthia's face, or if it was more than politeness when he offered her the extras from his milkshake. She was not imagining it, when he watched Cynthia's neck as she tilted the tall stainless steel cup to pour the icy dregs into her red mouth and then slammed it down on the table. Cynthia used Nathaniel's napkin to wipe the condensation from her hand. The conversation was mild. Mira and Cynthia compared their school to Nathaniel's, discussed the pros and cons of wearing uniforms, the unfairness of how exams came right after winter break.

"So what did you think of him?" Mira asked quietly as she and Cynthia walked home together, Nathaniel having biked in the opposite direction.

"He's attractive," said Cynthia, "but I don't think he has a very rich inner life."

APPARENTLY REGRESSING MEANT building a fort by placing a bed sheet over her desk chair and the end of her bed. Mira viewed this behaviour as a symptom of his having so many younger siblings, but she played along. A flashlight, balanced on the chair, provided the ambiance as they told ghost stories, lowering their voices, butchering the endings. From one of the secret hiding places, she brought a bag of banana chips and a box of Parle G glucose biscuits. Ravi eyed her as she passed through the hallway carrying them.

"We should draw pictures." she said to Nathaniel.

In her desk drawer, she could only find blue pens and lined paper.

"Don't you have drawing paper? And markers? Or crayons?" he asked.

"Ravi probably does. He used to draw," she said.

They went to his room, where Ravi lay on the floor, pretending to read a magazine. Nathaniel politely stepped around him. She had noticed that Nathaniel never said anything to her brother unless her brother said something first. *Say something*, she wanted to tell him. *You are usually always talking*.

"Rav, you have crayons we could borrow?" Mira asked.

Ravi considered this. "Will you give them back after?"

"Obviously. That's what borrow means."

He pointed to the closet. Then he abruptly stood up and left the room, hands placed at the sides of his head like fake ears.

They checked the various boxes but didn't find any crayons. Instead, they found several of Ravi's drawings.

"He doesn't do these anymore?" asked Nathaniel, flipping through a notepad filled with round-eyed square-headed birds.

Mira kept looking in the closet, coughing as she disturbed dust on the shelf up above her head. "He did them for a long time, took classes all the way up through high school. And then, he stopped. I don't really know why. We tried to get him to start again. Suggested all kinds of pictures he could draw. My mom would physically put the paper in front of him and the marker in his hand," she said, turning to look at him. Nathaniel kept looking down at the birds. Mira tested some markers and discovered they had all run out. One by one they left faded lines on the paper, and this seemed to her the most pathetic thing of all. Her hands found a box of art supplies on the high closet shelf, and accidentally knocked it over. They covered their heads as Ravi's collection of short coloured pencils fell over them as sharp as ice rain.

MIRA AND RAVI took a trip to Hillcrest Mall. Ravi drove. They squeezed through traffic in the narrow part of Yonge Street. People never believed it when they heard that Ravi could drive, but really his road skills were impeccable, surpassing those of any driver Mira had ever seen. It was shocking, given that, as a pedestrian, he hesitated before crossing even the emptiest of streets. He got his licence right away at sixteen, passing the test on the first try, and now he knew the roads so well he didn't even glance at the street signs. He had no temper, no rage, and so Ravi moved through the busy streets gracefully, making smooth turns with a flick of the signal, merging with a quick check over his mountainous shoulder, smoothly stepping his large foot on the accelerator as though it were a pedal on a glorious grand piano. He followed exactly every driving rule his mother had told him, never picking up bad habits. When it came to safety, he had an obsession with following instructions. This slowed him down with the speed limit — and for a while, other cars had lined up to pass him, but then his mother advised him to travel at ten percent above the speed limit (if the sign said sixty, he went at sixty-six, and so on) and in this way he blended in better and avoided being pulled over. Once he learned how to drive, his mother began sending him alone to the stores with a list of groceries. It took him a while to find everything, but he became practised at scanning the aisles for unfamiliar items.

On one occasion, Mira's mother had forgotten to write down the quantities of items he should buy, and he had returned home from the Indian store with a bag of besan flour so large they didn't have a cupboard tall enough to keep it. After that, whenever she sent him on errands, she called him "Hanuman," after the Hindu Monkey-God. Scooping the soft chickpea flour with a steel scoop, she told Mira and Ravi of the bloody war against Ravana's army, where Lord Rama's brother Lakshman received near-fatal injuries, pierced by a charmed arrow. With the flour she mixed a generous splash of water and measured with her fingertips the amounts of cumin and chili powder to create a rich batter, the same colour as a lion's skin. Rama sent Hanuman, his faithful helper, to find and bring a rare healing herb growing somewhere on the Dronagiri mountain. Mira's mother described the precious herb, and Mira speculated her description was a complete invention based on the pointed curry leaves she chopped on her wooden cutting board. She held up the tiny pieces for effect, and sprinkled them atop her roughly diced vegetables, the purplest of eggplants and plumpest of bell peppers. Hanuman had to find the plant before dawn, to cure Lakshman, who lay near dying in his brother's arms. Their enemies tried to lure Hanuman away, but he resisted the distractions. The vegetables went into the batter. Exploring the mountain between ground and sky, Hanuman still could not locate the plant. Knowing he had only the barest amount of time, he lifted the entire mountain in one strong arm, as easily as a bag of flour, and flew back to Rama, where the herb was found and Lakshman saved. Here, Mira's mother dropped her vegetables individually into a black pot of boiling oil, and as the batter coating quickly browned, a cluster of miniscule bubbles formed and flickered to the surface.

"He lifted the whole mountain?" Ravi asked, his face lovely with surprise.

"The whole mountain," she said. But later, she told Mira the rest of Hanuman's story. Yes, Hanuman had superhuman strength and undeniable loyalty. But in his youth, the gods had placed a curse on him that made him forget, for the rest of his life, his own powers. Unless reminded, Hanuman could not even remember his impossible skills, that he could lift mountains, and stretch his monkey tail to unbelievable lengths, that he could fly as readily as the tiny weaver birds and large grey herons that frequented the Indian skies, that he could grow larger than an elephant, larger than the State of Kerala. In the incident of the mountain, a crocodile had reminded him of his strength. But once the cure had been found and Lakshman had been rescued, Hanuman promptly forgot all again. Only those who had been there could remember that once, as a boy, Hanuman had flown into the sky, and mistaking the yellow sphere for a mango, had tried to eat the sun.

FOR THE FIRST time since he had started pushing grocery carts, Ravi had a job interview. It was a cash register position at the same store. "He just has to push some keys," said their mother, but even she didn't seem to have much hope that he would get it. Mira imagined the checkout line growing longer and longer as Ravi tried to remember the code for, say, navel oranges, then typed it in laboriously. "We can dress him up decently at least," her mother said, "Or they'll never hire him."

At first, Ravi tried to help, holding up shirts and saying "What about this one?" in his slow voice. He seemed to be just choosing the clothing at random. He picked up shirts with embarrassing slogans or cartoon characters, shirts that would fit people half his size. She couldn't understand how he had no concept of how much space his body occupied, that he could hold up a tiny piece of fabric and believe it would cover him. He gave up after the fourth or fifth shirt, instead spending the time humming and clapping along to the song playing from the store's speakers. Mira handed him the clothes and waited outside the dressing room, watching his feet under the door. He took off his shoes and revealed ankles that could almost be called slender. She didn't understand how they withstood the burden of his body. She watched his hands lift over the top of the dressing room door to pull on a shirt, his arms and hands forming a horseshoe shape in the air. He opened the door and his body bulged in between his slim limbs.

"How do I look?" he asked, beaming.

Why was he so happy? Didn't he realize that the pants had bunched at the crotch so their hems didn't even reach the floor and the shirt stretched over his belly where it should have been loose and flat? Where was his dressing room shame? "Those don't fit properly," she said, and handed him the same clothes in a larger size. She didn't smile. She wanted him to stop smiling. Nobody would ever have sex with him, she realized. His body would always be entirely his own.

Her mother phoned her as they stood in line at the register, to ask if she had found him clothes.

"Yeah, we're getting some T-shirts and a couple of pairs of pants."

"T-shirts? He can't wear T-shirts to a job interview. Find him some office shirts, and pants that need ironing."

"But Ravi doesn't wear shirts with collars."

"Mira, it's a job interview."

"The interview's at a grocery store."

"Oh god, Mira, I can't let him go in there and embarrass himself."

"You think his *clothes* are going to embarrass him?" Mira said, relishing and regretting the following silence. "Never mind, I'll buy something. Don't worry." She hung up. She left the line and picked up the first passable clothes she found in Ravi's size, and didn't bother having him try them on.

"Are those for me?" Ravi asked.

"Yes, and you're going to wear them."

"I don't like those kinds of shirts." He said it dismissively, as though he were refusing some vegetable curry at dinner. But he never refused food.

"It'll help you get a job," Mira said, though she felt she was lying.

"I WILL NOT PUT THAT SHIRT ON!" He stamped his foot. His shoe, not on quite properly, flopped at the heel. Other customers turned to look at them.

"Shut. Up," she whispered, conjuring up her mother's tone of voice, then ignored him and went to pay.

THAT NIGHT ON the phone with Nathaniel, she confided in him that she planned to never have children. Because she might give birth to somebody who wasn't quite right, and she might not be able to love him as much as she should. She had never said this out loud before.

"But didn't you say it isn't genetic, what your brother has? The odds are, like, zero."

"But there's the *fear* of it," she said. "Don't you get it? And even if my baby doesn't have what he has, it could have something else — Down's syndrome or something. I just can't do another eighteen years of this. What am I talking about, eighteen — if you have a kid like that, he stays with you forever. That's another lifetime of this, of fighting with him and fighting for him and fighting embarrassment. Forget it. At least now I can leave, I can do anything as soon as I leave this house." As she spoke, she knew she wasn't getting it right, she was painting it all too negatively, even though she meant everything she said.

"Well, my mom had seven kids and they're all normal," said Nathaniel. Questionable, thought Mira, who had seen his brother once lick the carpet.

"Lucky her," she said. "Your family is so blessed."

"You're going to jinx us," he said. She could tell he was angry and she didn't care. He hadn't lived through anything, he'd never suffered.

"Your life is all roses," she said.

"Stop it."

"Okay."

"So what will you do instead of children?" he asked her, peacekeeper Nathaniel, moving things along.

"Instead of having children, I will live as one of those rare childless women with long resumés and unspent fortunes. So remember, when we have sex, you and I have to use multiple, layered forms of protection."

"Ah," he said.

When Mira encountered these childless women, mostly her mother's friends, she always wished she knew their reasons. Her own mother, and the other women with children, appeared simultaneously pitying and envying. She had heard them gossiping about why Lala Aunty didn't have children. "Okay, maybe they couldn't have kids, sad and all. But there are billions of orphans lying around in India. We have a duty to them," her mother's friend Anusha declared accusingly, as though she had personally brought home several orphans. "These abandoned children are like our own children. All Indians are related. You know, we took a taxi in Mumbai and chatted with the driver and found out he was my brother-in-law's brother-in-law."

"Oh, they don't even want children," a woman named Kalpana answered. "This way they can still afford that other house in Tobermory. They don't have to buy all this Nintendo-Bintendo nonsense. What kind of an Indian buys a cottage in

Tobermory? Hiking and camping and all, as if the outside is new to them. As if they weren't raised in houses made of mud! It's simply ridiculous." Mira tried to read her mother's expression to see if she too would have preferred a second house in Tobermory.

Mira had told Nathaniel about the summer she worked at a summer daycare camp. Mostly she told him this story so he wouldn't think she hated children. For three months, she had taught four year olds a song that went: "Peel, peel, peelpeel bananas! Chop, chop, chopchop bananas! Eat, eat, eateat bananas! Go, go, gogo bananas!" At that last line the children and counsellors would scream and throw their arms in the air and jump madly across the rubber floor. One of the children in her group, Edison, had a fear of this song which was both cute and strong. The first time they sang it, when they reached the screaming at the end, he had mashed his face into Mira's leg and cried. After that, every time they sang the song Mira would take Edison on a walk to the water fountain, the one on the far side of the building. It was a relief to her, too, because she hated screaming and jumping and acting crazy. What did it mean exactly, to go mad, go insane, go crazy, go bananas, lose your marbles, lose your mind? They were such lonely phrases — always going or losing, and worse, *losing control*, but were used so casually that she always speculated about who had coined them and in what frame of mind. She pictured going bananas as exactly that, body heat melting brain to overripe banana mush, seeping sticky thick white and sweet-smelling, filling and spilling from her ear canals.

WHEN MIRA BEGAN to get fatter, it felt inevitable. She was only a little bit fatter; she noticed it the mirror, an extra lump of hip, a crease across her belly that wasn't there before. But she should have expected it, since, while dating Nathaniel, she had let her after-school activities dwindle, instead loitering with him in the Tim Hortons parking lot, having Timbits and iced capps. She ate and went to school and ate and saw Nathaniel. Her face was round now, and Mira began surreptitiously elongating her neck to minimize the flesh under her chin. In the shower, she found stretch marks clutching her thighs and stomach like pale fingers. "*Gona!*" she spat at herself when confronted with her fatness. *Gona* meant "buffalo" in Havyaka, and she had heard her mother call her brother that on occasion. Insults sounded more vulgar in Havyaka. In English, a buffaloe was a sweet, if somewhat foolish, buffoonish creature. In English, who could call anybody a buffalo and mean it as anything but a joke? But Havyaka exposed the buffalo's true identity as a disproportionate and hideous animal with fur the colour of filth. Forget that her Brahmin ancestors adored buffaloes and their cow brothers. She would think of this in passing, only years later, when she would take her honeymoon in India. An uncle would take her to watch a buffalo race — "Kambala," it was called, a traditional coastal Karnataka sport watched by thousands of people. She would want desperately to take one home, imagining herself concealing it ineffectively in her carry-on luggage, a splendid bovine that lumbered and hobbled against its friends, splashing through the muddy paddy field water at illogical speeds.

"Your sari blouse needs to be let out," her mother told her. They were trying on outfits to make sure they had clothes for a wedding that winter. Mira had tried closing the buttons on the blouse and it had flattened her chest grotesquely.

The Indian grocery store had a tailor in the back room. All three family members went, because Mira's mother needed a new blouse too, and Ravi needed a kurtha. While Ravi and their mother went next door to buy material, the tailor took Mira's measurements. She posed underneath a large poster of Bollywood's Salman Khan, his muscles swollen and hair depleted from steroid use. Blouses in twenty colours and an equal number of designs covered a row of styrofoam manne-quins with bodies that ended at the waist. On one of them, some joker had drawn red cheeks and pasted an unusually large bindi. The tailor licked over his cavity fillings. He used a brown paper measuring tape to circle Mira's stomach and then the flesh of her upper arms. In a pale blue notebook, he recorded the centimetres. His long-nailed fingers scratched across the buttons at the front of her blouse.

"Tell your mother you pay extra for large-size fabric lining," he said, tilting his head slyly. "The measurements have changed since last time, hanh?" Mira nodded but didn't look at him. She watched him pull pins from a tomato-shaped pincushion.

Afterwards, she explored the grocery shelves while Ravi and her mother had their fittings. A tower of mango boxes blocked half the entryway, open-topped to reveal the ripe-rotting fruit. Inside a bin of lychees, a brown roach scrambled drunkenly. The ready-made samosas wilted at room tempera-ture. Boxes of dhokla mix and bhel mix gathered dust. Behind glass, sweets dyed into unnatural pinks and greens had been stacked into pyramids. From the back room, Mira heard her mother talking about patterns and about not wanting to be cheated. Mira picked up a bottle of coconut extract and recoiled at seeing a large mosquito preserved inside.

When she came back into the shop, Mira's mother selected a box of bright orange round laddoos to take home.

"Leave it, don't buy that!" Mira said. In Hindi movies, they nicknamed the fat kids "Laddoo."

"What do you mean, you guys love laddoos," her mother said, surprised at the urgency. She bought it anyway.

ON A WEEKEND over winter break, Nathaniel's family travelled to Florida on a rare vacation. Because he was the oldest, they let him stay home by himself. So Mira invited herself over and lied to her mother, saying she would be sleeping at Cynthia's. Mira stood on Nathaniel's porch and wondered if, by the next time she stood on the porch, she would have slept with him already. His house smelled like marinara sauce; he'd made pasta. She wondered if he'd chosen the bowtie-shaped pasta because he thought it was more elegant and would set the mood.

"This is one of two shapes of pasta that Ravi won't eat," Mira told Nathaniel.

"He's not here," Nathaniel said.

"I mean at home," Mira said, pointlessly. She'd been hoping he'd ask what the other shape was.

They watched something on Showcase until Mira started to doze. Nathaniel collected the unbreakable plastic plates and put them away. Mira got up off the slipcovered sofa. They stepped over the needy, lumpy dog who slept on the bottom step. She wanted very badly to say that the dog's body reminded her of a scoop of mashed potatoes, but thought it wasn't the best time.

They took off most of their clothes. She slowly unbuttoned her flimsy floral blouse, which she'd worn specifically because it had buttons and it seemed more lovely to her to open a shirt rather than pull it over her head. She pictured how, around the corner, inside the now defunct Fantasia, women had dropped their clothes for decades with practised ease.

Then they lay under a single sheet on his twin-sized bed, so small that Mira had to lie sideways, but she found it romantic to settle her undressed body into the gaps of his. They kissed for what Mira estimated was five minutes.

Will we make love now? she asked herself, and then imagined herself asking it aloud. Will we ML now? she could say, and wait while he tried to guess what it meant.

But Nathaniel only said goodnight and removed his hands from her body then stayed entirely still. To propose an activity as dynamic as sex now would be like going from sitting to running without the intermediate step of having to stand.

TOO EARLY, SHE woke up to the square of white light from outside. Nathaniel breathed evenly with his mouth open. His arm formed for her a neck-rest, a little too warm. Today he smelled like fabric softener. Perhaps it was the room's sand-coloured paint that made her imagine the pale blue sheets covering their feet as rolling waves, and made the air conditioner roaring in the yard sound like the ocean. She didn't know if he had noticed that she was becoming larger. She wondered if she would soon be larger than he was. She tested the circumference of her arm against his arm, curling her fingers loosely around each as far as they would go. She shifted and put her ear over his stomach, hoping to hear the growls of morning. When she didn't hear any sounds, she pushed her ear down harder like a suction cup on a car window. He woke up sleepy-eyed.

"What are you doing?" he asked.

"Oh, nothing," she said quietly, as though she had a marvellous secret. And then she said, "I want you to be the first person I sleep with." She had thought a little about how she would present this question, and was happy she'd managed to avoid the phrase "first time." Then, looking at his vacant face, she wasn't clear whether he understood she meant *now*, she wanted to sleep with him now.

Because she didn't know what to say next, Mira told him of the ideas that had occurred to her in dreams. Later she'd find it childish that she had once associated dreams with intimacy. But now she told him that in the middle world between sleeping and waking, she had been frozen. Her eyes must have been open, because everything had looked the same in his room as it always did, the open closet door casting a tall black shadow on colourful spilled clothing, the Toronto Maple Leafs poster wilting and faded from too much direct light, his backpack slouched against the leg of the cluttered desk. But she had felt sure it must be a dream, because she couldn't move. Every attempt to turn or rise had been hopeless. And when she compared then to now, she realized she had been unable to sense the textures under her, the cool blankets or his skin, the weight of her head on the pillow, and now they felt incredibly rich, too much almost, how butter might taste after weeks of fasting.

"Sleep paralysis," he interrupted her. "That's what that's called. When you can't move."

While frozen, she continued, a figure had materialized in the doorway. In the past, when she'd had similar dreams, there had been other figures, hooded demons or bizarre creatures that stood above her until she managed to scrunch her eyes and squeeze her hands and will herself to move. Once, her ceiling fan had begun speaking to her, its blades whirling with each word. This time, it was her brother, standing at a distance, over on the other side of the room. He appeared paler than usual, and had a moustache and beard, a poor disguise. His mouth moved into the same shapes over and over, and finally she understood rather than heard what he was saying. Ravi said exactly the same words she heard him say to himself, when he thought he was alone, "I love my mom and dad and sister," simply, memorized, like lines from a play.

Nathaniel pulled away the sheet covering them so the bed was completely bare and she shuddered — in the daylight she was too aware of her body, of his body.

"So should we do it now," he said, cold and urgent, "or do you want to keep talking about your brother?" His hands went to the sides of her panties and tugged them down as she tried to suck in her hips but they swelled unbidden. He removed his own boxers, and though they had seen each other naked before, she felt that with their clothing had gone everything that had once been sensual and beautiful. His lips were dry and white at the edges and he kissed her close-mouthed and hard.

"Wait," she said. "I've changed my mind."

He sighed in an unbearably familiar way, and she collected that sigh in her memory to pull up later, along with the outlines of his ears and the first thoughts she'd had of him.

"Sleep paralysis," she said, slowly, as she stood up, moving even as she said the unmoving phrase, covering herself with the wrinkled, water-blue sheet. *Paralysis*. Later, she idly looked up the etymology and learned that *para* meant beside, *lysis* meant loosen, release. She took her time, she lingered, because though she knew it was over, she wanted to be sure.

BUT SHE WASN'T sure, and after she spent the day at the library, slowly making her way through a book she wouldn't remember later, so her mother wouldn't inquire about why she had left Cynthia's so early, she went home in the dark and her mother wasn't even there. Mira entered the house and lay down in her own bed. It had been too easy, she thought, to tell him everything. She had overshared, unloaded too much of her *baggage*. She was like an old woman with hundreds of failed relationships — she hadn't had any failed relationships, until now. The word made her think of bags under eyes, of loose skin and sagging breasts, of her clothes piled up on his floor like every single thing she'd ever told him. She felt like an approximation of herself, like the Picasso series Cynthia had on a poster on her wall, depicting drawings of bulls each more abstract than the one before, so that while the first bull possessed a full, fleshed body, the last was only a few suggestive lines. Never again would she allow herself to be so open. Who would she talk to anyway? She began to cry, noisily, hiccupping wetly into the pillowcase. Who would she tell now, about her father's picture's recent disappearance from the mantelpiece, next to the Durga carving, and her mother bringing home some man and serving him tea like an arranged bride? And about what she remembered, the information she had been waiting to bestow on Nathaniel, about how her mother had chased Ravi's bully down in her rust-spotted Ford Taurus, but when Mira had been bullied, mercilessly, torturously, her mother hadn't helped, because she hadn't even known, because Mira never complained to her, just waited every day of first grade at the school bus stop praying that Lucy Chin's face wouldn't be there, flattened against the second seat bus window, her hair shiny as gunmetal, swinging over her neck as she turned and watched Mira walk the bus aisle. The girl was always there, waiting to whisper at Mira, *don't tell a soul*, as though souls were something you could tell things to.

She would tell them to the wall, she decided through her tears, share her emotions with the wall next to her bed. She began to speak out loud, hysterically, in almost-gibberish, thinking in a rush of thoughts, *going bananas, you are going bananas, and the only one left to hear you is the wall.*

Ravi waited for a moment in the open doorway. She managed to catch only a glimpse of his too-short pants as he hurried away, the ill-fitting clothes a reminder that not much had changed. She went back to crying, softer now, stopping finally when she heard sirens like babies crying, approaching their house. Then she heard a doorbell. And an insistent knocking. Wiping her face with her palm, Mira went hesitantly to answer it, a little afraid.

On the front step, a policeman greeted her. Ravi came nearby, his face lit up because he was especially fond of policemen, who had once rescued him when he'd wandered lost around a shopping mall.

"My mom?" Mira said. A car crash, she thought. It must be.

"We're just checking on a call," he said it as a question.

It took Mira four seconds to understand what had happened. She clutched her brother's shirtsleeve now with fierce affection, knowing that Ravi had seen her, had run to the telephone, and had dialed, just as she had instructed him to do if anything ever seemed beyond their own abilities to fix what was wrong: 9-1-1.

"It's fine, we're fine," she tried to explain to the police officer, wiping her face, gasping as she resumed crying. Out on the driveway, the siren sound had been shut off, but the red lights remained, flashing through the soundless neighbourhood.

The Family Took Shape

GAMES WITH RAVI tended to crescendo to his turn. On occasional weekday nights, Mira and Ravi and their mother played Scrabble. They unfolded the board and each reached blindly into the bag of shaken letters. Mira and her mother would hold their breaths and mute the television when Ravi formed words. "C-A-R," he had spelled the last time, fumbling the letters over their squares. "Car? Is that the best word you can make, Ravi?" their mother asked. Mira glanced at his letters and then took back "car" and replaced it with "charting," building off a letter "g" that was already on the board, and managing to locate it over the triple-word-score square.

On long drives, they played twenty questions. Mira's mother would choose something easy — the steering wheel, the green clock numbers — which Mira would guess in three questions. Mira tried hard on hers. The last time she'd had to provide them with a hint after fifteen fruitless inquiries: "It's intangible." Still nobody could guess, so she had to tell them, "frustration," and her mother said, "Ohh, frustraaaation, how do you expect us to get that? Come on Mira. Now I am really frustrated."

When Ravi went, Mira and her mother asked more than twenty questions. Finally, "Is it outside the window?" Mira asked, and they looked out at the empty sidewalks, the emerald-coloured highway signs and the short glass office buildings. He answered yes, but they couldn't figure it out even after he tried explaining. Whatever Ravi had chosen, it was something he'd spotted before they'd even begun playing, before the slow lurches of the traffic jam — something outside the window from which they'd long since driven away.

LALA AUNTY HAD signed Ravi up for a bowling league, even though he should have been past games by now, even though what he needed was not bowling, which would have no effect on either his economic situation or his weight problem. He needed a proper job. She had come into their kitchen, pulled a pamphlet out from her triangle-shaped purse and placed it on the counter. Mira's mother was dicing tomatoes, lamenting that the knife wasn't sharp enough — "You need a serrated knife," advised Lala Aunty — so Mira, sitting on a stool next to the counter, snacking on stolen, dripping tomato pieces, grabbed the pamphlet with her free hand. She read the slogan on the front — "Let me win, but if I cannot win, let me be brave in the attempt." Underneath was a picture of a man with Down's syndrome, about to fling a bowling ball towards the camera. The pamphlet's earnestness embarrassed her.

"Ravi is very special, and so he is perfectly suited to the Special Olympics. It will be good for his self-image. And bowling! I know he would be good at it," said Lala Aunty, who had begun searching through the freezer for who knows what.

"I'll take a look at it when I get a chance," said Mira's mother.

Special Olympics, thought Mira, as though the real Olympics weren't already special.

Lala Aunty was pulling everything out from their freezer and putting it back in again. "You need a vacuum sealer," she said. "I will get you one. Then the vegetables, they stay fresh." The problem with letting Lala Aunty in your kitchen, thought Mira, was that afterwards, everything possessed a new order. She rearranged the spice jars, switching the places of the cumin and fennel seeds, and at least twice now, Mira's mother had tossed a handful of the wrong one into her frying pan. Lala Aunty shelled the pistachios, encroaching on Mira's single great food-related pleasure, of using her nails to snap open the smooth, dusty shells. She left the crack-prone glassware in the lower rack of the dishwasher, the kettle in the cupboard instead of on the counter, the broom upside-down against the wrong wall, and, walking past, hand on wall, Ravi had once received an unexpected handful of dust.

Mira knew Ravi would end up joining the bowling league. Her mother had started using a Brita pitcher when Lala Aunty had made disparaging remarks about Toronto tap water; she'd purchased Clairol when Aunty found grey in her ponytail; she'd had an unnecessary talk with Mira after Aunty said that nowadays kids really did start having sex at fourteen. Mira was seventeen now, and though it had been a year and a half since she and Nathaniel had ended, there was no chance of her having sex any time soon.

Lala Aunty's influence spilled from mere kitchen arrangement into actual mealtimes. She would stay and make them dinner, some gross concoction of broccoli and breadcrumbs, for example, or a mess of carrots and cream of wheat. "You're eating with Aunty, today!" she would exclaim, *Eating with Aunty* being the name of the radio show she still hosted, which she aimed to work into conversations. Even on those nights when Lala Aunty didn't stay for dinner (she had many social events to attend), Mira's mother would cook her recipes. Mira would come home from Cynthia's and see her mother sitting on the window seat under the half-circle window, listening to *Eating with Aunty*, writing down a recipe. Out the window, the vegetable garden remained unplanted even though the season approached late spring.

"We should plant vegetables," Mira said.

"Uncle said he would pick up some seeds for us," said her mother, pencil in mouth, getting up to check the fridge for ingredients.

"We should do it ourselves," Mira said.

"This recipe actually sounds okay," said her mother. "No, not okay, it sounds delicious, and isn't it funny how Lala sounds exactly the same in her radio show as she does when she's at our house? I mean, I suppose that isn't strange, because why should she sound different?"

"You don't even cook," said Mira.

"I cook you dinner almost every day," her mother said, taking the pencil out of her mouth, turning to look at her. Mira glanced down at the slanting words of the recipe — *turmeric powder, colocasia leaves.*

Six years earlier, in a whim of generosity, Mira had baked

her brother a flat birthday cake. She'd hidden it in her closet, covering it with a clean dishtowel. It was the first time she had used the oven on her own. She worried someone would detect the smell of warm chocolate and find its source. The next afternoon, on his birthday, she was up in her room and heard them all come home, and, heart palpitating, anticipating the glorious surprise — "Mira, you *made* this? That's so *nice* of you. Ravi, isn't this a beautiful cake?" — she removed the dishtowel (only a little frosting had stuck to it) and carried it down the stairs, turning the corner to the kitchen, only to see them all — Ravi, her mother, Lala Aunty — lighting the candles on an ice cream cake, which it was clear Lala Aunty had purchased ("Wasn't this *nice* of Lala Aunty, Ravi? Ice cream cake, your favourite," said her mother), and Mira ran back up the stairs, her amateur cake attempt nearly falling to pieces in her hands. She stashed it in her closet and went and sang happy birthday with the rest of them, and grinned and stood for photos and helped rinse the plates for the dishwasher. That night, she went back up to her room and hid the evidence of her cake by eating it, high frosting and all, and since she couldn't risk sneaking a fork, she ate it with her hands (like a barbarian, she thought), though she couldn't finish the whole thing, so she wrapped what was left in the dishtowel and buried it in the garbage can, making sure to drop an old banana peel on top to minimize chances of the cake's discovery.

RAVI HAD BEEN searching for work for six months now, since he had turned nineteen and left high school. The grocery store where he'd pushed carts had switched owners and let him go.

In the kitchen again, Lala Aunty, Mira, and her mother had examined a printed draft of Ravi's resumé.

"Can we cut the Objective to get it down to two pages?" said Mira.

"Yes, does he need an Objective? Isn't that the old style?" said Mira's mother.

"Objective — who cares? It is the *personality* that is most important," said Lala Aunty. "His personality must shine from this piece of paper. It must literally shine."

"Literally?" asked Mira, but Lala Aunty ignored her.

"Reading this, they should see his *warmth*, his *helpfulness*, his *good nature*."

They had been editing and proofreading and cutting and building the resumé, which described Ravi's one job experience. The rest of the space was filled with a list of times he had helped out at Lala Aunty's dinner parties by making runs to the Indian store, and with adjectives describing him ("warm," "helpful," "good-natured").

He had been trying to find a job, trying with an obsessive zeal. His resumé came in three different renditions. He left the house at eight each morning and drove around Richmond Hill and the surrounding area, dropping copies at the customer service desk of every grocery store and Shoppers Drug Mart and every coffee shop and anywhere he saw a help wanted sign. The problem was that no matter how they dressed up his resumé, he couldn't make it through an interview. Though Lala Aunty coached him before each interview and grilled him afterwards about the questions, he simply couldn't articulate his "greatest strength" and "greatest weakness," and he did even worse at the questions about specific work situations —

"What would you do if a customer didn't have enough money and harassed you for a discount?" "What would you do if you caught someone stealing?" Employers doubted he could work a register. They said as much when Lala Aunty, angry at each failed interview, phoned up the company and demanded to know the reasons behind his rejection. "You are making a big mistake, let me tell you," she said, huffing and puffing, wagging her finger as though they could see her.

They realized now that despite its trials, school had been a cushion for Ravi. In his former nightly four-hour homework period, he now watched two hours of game shows and sitcom reruns and then went outside and repeatedly circled the block on his bicycle.

DESPITE HER FIXATION with Mira's household, Lala Aunty did have her own family, which consisted only of her husband. And despite Mira's irritation with Lala Aunty, she was fascinated by Uncle, and visited him every other week. Whenever she went over to their house, he would offer her an apple or an orange and then invite her to sit on their sofa and eat it in front of him. While she ate, biting or sectioning, he would speak to her in English spotted with Hindi. Occasionally he recited Sanskrit verse, gesturing so spectacularly that his hands would catch in his long, white hair. He had been an adjunct Sanskrit lecturer in some distant past life. He often offered her a glass of fruit punch — his preferred beverage — never failing to mention that the word "punch" came from the Sanskrit "panch," meaning "five." "Five fruits!" he would tell her, and she would nod. She had only just discovered from her mother that his name was Rajgopal. But nobody ever called him that. Everybody called him Uncle, including his own wife.

"Uncle wants to know if he can help with the gardening this spring," "Uncle would like to find out if Ravi has an email address," "Uncle asks what type of apple, Mira, you prefer," were all past inquiries Lala Aunty had related from her husband. That was how their garden bloomed with perennial tulips, how Ravi learned to send birthday ecards, and how Mira grew weary of Honeycrisp apples (though she kept eating them, to be polite).

When Aunty brought Uncle with her to social outings, he tended to amble around behind her without saying much. Sometimes he would find a chair, place himself in it, and just watch his wife as she took over other people's kitchens. She would toss her body around the room, zipping over the tile floor like a cartoon, the end of her stylish selwar kameez lingering for a second in the air before following her.

UNCLE FOLLOWED AUNTY when the family went bowling together the first time. Before entering, they all stood uncertainly under the sign that said Superbowling, unsure if it was open. Inside, the place was empty, except for one attendant, and the lights were all off except above their lane. The twenty-five-cent candy machines were covered with a skin of grime.

"I will not be playing," Uncle assured them. "I will merely be in this plastic area, reading my book." He pointed at the orange plastic chairs and cozied himself into one, opening up a pocket-sized volume of the Bhagavad Gita to a yellow page.

"Excuse me, no street shoes allowed," called the attendant from up near the shoe rentals.

"Oh, I'm sorry, sir!" Uncle hastily removed his shoes. One of his socks showed a large hole, and he placed one foot over the other to cover it.

Ravi put his rented shoes on, and sat next to Uncle.

"These shoes don't go together!" said Ravi.

"No, dear, it's just the laces that don't match," Aunty told him. She began to help him tie his laces, even though, at nineteen years old, thought Mira, he certainly knew how to do up his own shoes.

Mira's mother took her turn first, then Mira, then Aunty, and finally Ravi. When Mira went up, she picked the first ball on the shelf and it proved much too heavy for her. With two hands, she propelled it across the lane and then hurried away without waiting to see how many pins she'd knocked over. She didn't like the feeling of all of the others behind her and watching, felt suddenly sure that everyone was looking at her rear end.

"Since when do Indian people go bowling?" Mira asked.

"Being Indian has nothing to do with it!" Lala said.

It did have a little to do with it, thought Mira. For example, Lala Aunty probably shouldn't have worn a selwar. She was having trouble figuring out how to wrap her silk shawl behind her so it didn't disrupt her bowling technique. Lala Aunty prepared for her turn by lifting each available bowling ball and testing its weight, passing it between her hands and making exaggerated eyebrow movements. She checked if it fit her fingers, removing her two garish rings and setting them next to Uncle. She chose a ball that glinted neon pink as it travelled slowly and without aim down the striped wood. When she hit a single pin, she jumped up and down and gave Ravi a high five. Her second ball headed straight for the gutter. *HA!* thought Mira, meanly, in her head.

"Oh, darn!" said Lala Aunty. She collected her rings and playfully stole Uncle's book. "Why did you come with us if you are not going to watch?"

"I came to see the young Ravi," he said. He held his hand out for the book.

"You're up, Ravi," Aunty patted his back. Ravi lumbered forward and picked up the heaviest bowling ball with no effort at all. Aunty shouted useless directions at him. "Keep your eye on those little arrows. Just like Arjuna's arrows in the *Mahabharat.*"

"Well, not really," said Uncle.

Ravi pulled the ball back with one hand and dropped it in front of him. Its path was perfect from the second he let go.

THAT EXACT MOMENT, the moment when the bowling ball left his hand, was the beginning of Ravi's winning streak. Mira and her mother tried to accompany Ravi to his first practice with the local Special Olympics bowling league, but a man wearing an aquamarine-and-black bowling shirt met Ravi right at the door and shooed the two of them away. When he came home from a practice two weeks later with a ribbon, Mira's mother took it from his hand and looked at it, holding the ribbon up from one satin corner, then asked uncertainly, "Should we put it on the fridge? No, we should buy a frame, right?" and Ravi clapped his hands together at this bright idea. So they framed the ribbon and nailed it to the wall of Ravi's bedroom, next to a poster of a yellow Lexus. His luck in bowling transferred into other things — his skin seemed slightly clearer, he lost ten pounds. His laughter seemed easy, natural, uncompulsive. When anybody asked him how he was, he'd say, "I'm doing pretty good!" After one match, he came home and told Mira and her mother, "My friends all were cheering for me!" and Mira realized it was quite possible nobody had ever cheered for him before, and more than that, he'd never had friends before. Afterwards, she and her mother and Lala Aunty would ask him often, "How are your friends?" and every time he'd say, "They're cool guys and girls. They're good friends of mine."

Lala Aunty took the credit for this new, lighter, popular Ravi, and seemed to think she could affect similar change in Mira's life by taking her shopping. Mira preferred to do her shopping alone, so she could scour for secret, beautiful, often second-hand finds, but Lala Aunty went on about how before Mira went off to university she needed to start wearing the right brands in the right sizes — "None of your clothes fit you properly," she said, and hinted that if Mira herself took up a sport, maybe she would lose some weight and it wouldn't be so hard to find a husband. "You're young still of course, but every year girls will be snatching them up and then when you are twenty-six-twenty-seven you'll see only the baldies and fatties are left."

So they shopped together at Hillcrest Mall one Saturday after dropping Ravi at bowling and her mother at the dentist. Mira wondered if Lala Aunty planned to pay for everything or if she was meant to pay herself. She stopped in the food court for a cup of coffee and Lala Aunty expressed surprise that at seventeen Mira was already drinking coffee — "A bit early for coffee, isn't it? Must mean you don't have enough of your own natural energy." She expounded on caffeine and how she couldn't possibly sleep at night if she had coffee in the afternoon. Mira interrupted her — "Chai, then? They have chai everywhere now" — but Lala Aunty complained about sugar and about how Westerners were exploiting Indian culture to an inexcusable degree.

"Just look at our influences on fashion," Lala Aunty said. She directed her remark at the mall's biggest department store, indignantly, as though the mannequins were her oppressed ancestors. "You know Indians invented sequins?"

"This might look okay, right?" Mira asked, holding up a black Indian-inspired tunic.

"You could get that for a hundred rupees in India," said Lala. "The price of a cup of coffee here."

"But I would have to buy a plane ticket to India first," replied Mira, draping the shirt over her arm in subtle rebellion.

"And when is the last time you went to India? It has been a long time, isn't it? A million years roughly. Since before your father passed?" Lala Aunty asked.

"We haven't gone since then," Mira said.

"Go then! Why not? You kids don't even know how big the family is."

"It's *my* family," said Mira, checking the sleeves of the shirt for stray threads.

"Yes, of course, I know that. Actually, you can buy even more clothes there. You wear only black T-shirts or what? Ravi can stay with me and Uncle. You and Mom go and when you come back he will be fluent in Hindi." Lala Aunty took the shirt from Mira's hand and kept it firmly back on the rack.

"I guess we can go now, since I'll be buying all those cheaper clothes in India," Mira said, asserting to herself that Indians certainly had not invented the sequin.

THEY PICKED UP Mira's mother at the dentist — "Which kind of floss did they give you? The cheap kind, oh this is the good kind. Good," said Lala Aunty, checking the toothbrush, too, to make sure it was soft-bristled. Then they drove to the bowling alley to pick up Ravi, and when they got there all shifted seats so that he could drive.

"Well, then, how was it?" Lala Aunty asked. "You struck 'em dead, I think, right? Striked 'em dead."

"Put your seatbelt on," said Ravi. "It's the law."

Aunty fastened her seatbelt. "Hit lots of those pins, eh?"

"I did pretty good," said Ravi, beaming out the windshield.

"Can we stop at my radio station for *just* one moment?" Aunty asked. "I have forgotten to bring home my recipes for Monday, and I *must* test them out once more before delivering them to the public."

Ravi hummed and frowned. He took the extended route and they parked in the near-empty lot next to the building where Aunty worked.

"Come in with me, I absolutely must show you my office," she said.

The four of them ascended a narrow set of stairs to the offices of Indo-Toronto Radio. Her cooking show was the most popular on the station, and had been running for an abnormally long time. When she'd started, it had been merely a Sunday morning show, but now they put her on right before dinner time every weekday. Toronto Indian women listened to her from their kitchens, followed her advice over even the smallest measurements of garam masala, which was odd given that Aunty herself was unable to stick to a recipe as written (the reason her cooking was often subpar).

For Lala Aunty's radio career, Mira held a private respect. She liked to imagine those women, under the influence of Aunty's voice, running for the appropriate cupboard as soon as she named an ingredient. When the show ended, her instructions continued to guide them, as they fermented their white idli batter in their turned-off ovens, admired the air bubbles that formed overnight, inhaled the light sour smell, and consulted the notes they'd taken from Lala's show. Lala Aunty's instructions filled recipe books across the city, were pencilled into margins of newspapers, copied on Post-it notes. New Indian wives, who had never before so much as purchased rice flour, would present their husbands with dishes of curried goat and diamond-shaped almond sweets. The husbands — setting their expectations low — would open the foil in their lunches and find thick onion uthapams, dark orange mango pickles, and crisp happalas the colour of tropical sand. Their colleagues would ask them what they were eating, and the husbands wouldn't know the names of the foods at all. "But this isn't just a show for us ladies," Lala Aunty announced now and again on the radio, firm in her feminism, and each time, another husband would learn to make a rich tomato saru.

In fact, there was a framed poster on the hallway wall of a shining pot of tomato saru with Aunty stirring it and smiling. Chopped coriander lay scattered over the surface, and Mira thought, that coriander is no longer fresh. The poster was over a decade old, though with all of Aunty's primping and dyeing, her hair was roughly the same genre of black. The age change showed only in the absence of lines around the photograph eyes and in the flamingo lipstick she had long since stopped wearing. The name of the show, *Eating with Aunty*, was printed across the bottom in chubby letters, somewhat surreally, since Mira had heard Aunty say those words so many times.

The picture portrayed Aunty as Mira's family had first met her. For months after Mira's father died, Lala Aunty had arrived at their door with pots not dissimilar to the one in the picture. Mira's mother, stoic in mourning, had listened to Lala's descriptions of whatever food she had brought with her, and Mira had wondered if the descriptions could penetrate her mother's deadened thoughts. The descriptions of food would turn to details of what she had cooked for other families, families in worse situations than theirs. "So we're not the most pathetic, then?" Mira had heard her mother ask once, and Lala Aunty had responded, "Oh no no no no," repeating the word "no" another dozen times in a soothing rhythm that Mira had repeated to herself later when she tried to sleep. Back then, she would awake in the mornings and hear her mother on the phone with Lala Aunty. She phoned her at dawn, knowing she would be awake. It became a goal for Mira to wake up before her mother made the phone calls, so that she could pick up the extension in her room and listen. They were her phone calls, *too*, she needed soothing, *too*. "Aunty?" her mother would say into the phone and Lala Aunty would say, "Good morning, Shilpa! I am cooking porridge for Uncle. He is still dozing as usual …," slipping into a narrative without waiting for a question or reason for the phone call. It had been such a relief, Mira recalled, to hear another voice that early in the morning. Their house was always so silent, not even cars made sounds out the window, since they didn't live on a main road. "Why not come over?" Lala Aunty would ask — exactly the right question. Mira's mother would gather up the children and say, "We're going to Lala Aunty's!" and Mira would pretend she didn't know this already and would sing, "Lalalala! Lalalala!" in lovely ascension, like a vocal exercise. Lala Aunty had been just what they needed. But that was over a decade ago, and now her role had changed, the way words can change, when formed in different mouths.

NEXT TO THE stirring, smiling photo of Lala Aunty was her office door, which they entered. She went to her desk and rifled through file folders, pulling out recipes.

"I'm doing an eggplant curry on Monday's show. One of Uncle's favourite recipes. You know he can't cook at all," she chattered as the other three looked around. The recording equipment was in an attached room; the place seemed to be set up as many rooms attached to each other in a long row. This was the space where she prepared and answered her fan letters. The room was clean, with corkboards all around where Aunty pinned pictures of foods she'd made and pictures of herself with special guests who had visited and cooked with her — Bollywood actors, local members of parliament, Indo-Canadian authors — and a calendar with all her appointments colour-coded in pen. She'd brought in a small refrigerator and kept it unobtrusively under the desk. Next to an aging, beige computer she kept a kettle, an assortment of teas, and a bear-shaped jar of honey.

"Come, I'll show you around," Aunty started to say, but then they heard some shuffling and footsteps in the next room. "Oh, somebody is here, who could it be?"

A man in a blue golf shirt emerged and said, "Oh, hello." Aunty introduced him as a producer for a Tamil music show. He shook hands with Mira's mother and then with Ravi — clearly he'd mistaken Ravi for an adult. Mira stood awkwardly behind her mother and brother because the room was cramped. "Now, how do you folks all know Lala?" the man asked, and then inquired as to whether they were from the Toronto area and whether they listened to his show. He smiled at Mira's mother and smiled even bigger when she said she loved the intros in his music show. Imagine he asked her out right now, on a date. He seemed the type to be smooth enough to hit on a woman even when her children were standing right there. He didn't look at Mira at all — but, of course, she was standing behind everyone else. And then the man turned to Ravi, still smiling, looking *intelligent*, Mira thought; the man's eyes had *intelligence*, which you heard people say a lot about eyes, and people took it for granted, but Mira never did, because she had looked so often into her brother's eyes, and had found only the undeveloped expression you might see in the eyes of a squirrel, a bird, a creature who didn't know you from anybody. Ravi looked like everybody else, until you looked into his eyes. Mira saw the man look into Ravi's eyes and ask him a question. She didn't hear the question, but she heard Ravi's response, "I'm not sure," a standard confused answer of his. He said it in his slow tenor and it came out like he was humming a tune. Mira watched the man's face change as he realized the sort of person he was speaking to.

"Well, then," the man said.

"Ravi suffers from some retardation," Lala Aunty said, putting an arm over Ravi's shoulders.

No he doesn't, Mira thought. She balked at the lack of specificity. The word retardation sounded so much worse than what he was. In the half-second pause, Mira wondered how her father, in the same situation as this man, would have reacted. *Kindness*, she thought, *infinite compassion*, and then was unsure of how much she'd glorified him, and if instead he'd say, as this man did, "Ah, okay, I see," satisfied at having the problem addressed so squarely.

DESPITE THAT SNAFU, it seemed Ravi's luck had continued. Lala Aunty called them up the next week and said she had mentioned to the man at the radio station that Ravi had been looking for work for some time now and she showed the man his resumé, and the man had found him a job. "Nothing to do with radio, but his brother-in-law is looking for a driver. He does deliveries — food manufacturing or somesuch," she said. "It's a good start, you know. Why didn't we think of these driving jobs, he is such a good driver. Then maybe he can go on to TTC driving, post office work, airport limousines ..."

For Ravi, the best part was wearing a uniform, a royal blue T-shirt with the company's logo. He came home with smudges of grease on his pants from warehouse work. He lived in high anticipation of his paycheque, which would come in a lump sum after his two-month trial period, and though his arms ached from all the heavy lifting, he said, "My arms are hurting," with enormous pride. Because it was summer, and on the hot and dry side for Toronto, his left arm, propped against the window frame in the sun, turned a deep mahogany colour, much darker than the rest of him. At night his mother applied Myoflex ointment to his arms, and in the morning she layered on the sunscreen.

"We should fashion you a sleeve," said Mira, "just to cover that one arm."

"You must be joking!" said Ravi. He had learned a new expression.

RAVI'S LIFE HAD a rhythm now, regular as a sine wave, as full as anyone else's, with work and his new extracurricular. Midway through the bowling season, Ravi came home with a trophy — it had a figurine of a man bowling, in plastic the colour of brass, seam lines running down the sides of the man's body.

"Look at this trophy!" Ravi said and held it high up over his head. "They said I might get a big trophy," he continued, after all the congratulations, and gave his mother a sheet of paper from his coach. It announced that their team had qualified for the regional semi-finals, taking place over three days the following week.

"It's a good thing they sent this paper, or we wouldn't know what was happening, Rav," his mother said.

"Good thing!" he said.

"Should I put the trophy on your shelf?" Mira asked him, and he nodded and gave it to her and went to the living room to watch *Wheel of Fortune*. As she travelled up the stairs and into his bedroom, she heard him repeat the letters after the contestants. Earlier that year, Uncle had installed a glass shelf that cut across one wall of his room. It was held up by smooth metal brackets painted dark blue. Glass might not have been the best choice, because the grey dust covered the surface and made it noticeably opaque. She dusted off a corner and placed the trophy there, noting the other items displayed: his grade eleven photo in a cardboard frame, a sandalwood statue of Lord Ganesha, a model car with lacquered, lifted, butterfly doors.

While she was there, she made his bed, picking up the sheet and tossing it upwards to shake off the short sharpened pencils that often collected in parts of Ravi's room. There lay maybe twelve pencils on the floor, so she gathered them and opened a desk drawer to put them inside. They fit in the space between the curled drawings and unused watercolour sets and red-penned assignments from the normal classes. She found a familiar copy of *The Hobbit*, pages smashed and bent up against one side of the drawer. She remembered when they'd read the book aloud and seen all sorts of hidden significances — *There is a lot more in him than you guess, and a deal more than he has any idea of himself*. It seemed so cheesy now, like a quote they'd put on a Special Olympics pamphlet; every quote everywhere seemed to be a melodramatic metaphor for Ravi's hidden abilities. But as it turned out, he did have hidden abilities, and Mira wanted, if she could, to not become what she might be becoming: the sort of hardened person who dismissed things just because they felt sentimental or impossible.

Later, in the evening, when she came downstairs from her shower and found Lala Aunty in the kitchen with Ravi, when she hadn't even heard her knocking or opening the front door, and didn't even know where her mother had gone, she let it go. She herself was not the person who rightfully should be sitting there with her brother — next to the kitchen walls painted in two clashing colours with white wainscoting in the middle like some kind of mediator — going over bowling rules, under the half-circle window that framed the half-circle moon.

LALA AUNTY WOULDN'T let them buy fries at the bowling alley, even though all the other tables of spectators had them.

"Vegan brownies," she said and pulled out Tupperware from her purse. The brownies tasted like bowling shoe insoles, but Mira figured they hadn't come here to eat anyway. She and Aunty and Uncle and her mother were all present, and Mira had brought her friend Cynthia. Ravi, in a new violet bowling shirt, stood with his teammates. He stood on his toes to wave at his family.

"Focus on the game!" yelled Mira. She was making an effort because Cynthia was there.

"What a great shirt," said Cynthia, untying and retying her hair. "We should get bowling shirts but wear them, like, as dresses."

"Over tights?" Mira suggested.

"Or without them!" Cynthia winked.

"Hey, don't make these implications when I am here," said Uncle, looking up from the book he was reading on the history of bowling.

They'd been there forever, watching other teams bowl, and now Ravi's team was finally up and halfway through a game.

"They're winning, right? Are they winning?" asked Lala Aunty.

"They seem to be winning," Uncle said, and everybody agreed.

It was hard to tell from the team's demeanour. There were five people on Ravi's team. Three of them (including Ravi) waited quite emotionlessly, another seemed excited about the fries he was eating, and another maintained a miserable pose with his chin in his hands.

Ravi went up. Unusually, there was no build-up to his turn.

He flattened his lip and his face squeezed as though converging at a central point. All of this was only visible to the rest of them in profile, as he did a surprising sprint, swung his arm, and let the ball go.

"Ohhh, look at that, that's good right?" Lala Aunty asked.

"Better than I could do," said Mira's mother.

"I've never been bowling," said Cynthia.

"We'll take you," said Lala Aunty.

"No, I don't really want to," Cynthia said, and went to get fries.

"Ahhh, the old Dime Store," Uncle said. Everybody looked at him. "That's what they call the 5-10 split."

The game continued. Aunty ate several brownies, Uncle wowed them with bowling facts. The bowlers moved in staggered patterns. Mira thought it was like watching an array of lines and circles. A person was just a set of lines with a circle on top. The bowling ball was a second, odd-placed head, startling when it took its hollow spin. The lines-and-circle person paused there, waited for the crash, and retreated slowly backwards part of the way before turning. The next figure lifted a ball and played out the same actions. Except it wasn't just that one team; all the players in the whole spacious space moved those movements. Each team had four-to-six people, and occasionally two players from different games would act in synchronicity, parallel as they released and returned. They were like some kind of media player music visualization, matching a tune that might have been audible under the sounds of people talking, occasional claps, a vague announcer's voice, and heavy urethane rolling over wood.

The bowling alley lights shone white and unforgiving on the strange features: smiles that didn't form correctly, over-large placid foreheads, unfocused gazes, round moon faces, fleshy hands, legs that didn't stand, wheelchairs wheeling bulky and metallic, distended bellies, underdeveloped chins, thick glasses, hairless skulls, and coarse-haired, shuddering, disproportionate limbs. The bowlers kept their almost-unison, exclaimed in warbling voices, blundered beautifully with terrible motor skills.

"Have you seen that movie, *Freaks*?" Cynthia asked Mira in a whisper, but they all heard. "It's this really old Tod Browning movie about a bunch of sideshow freaks, like a midget and a bearded woman and people with crazy shrunken heads. But what was cool about that was that they didn't use costumes or CGI or whatever, so they used real, actual freaks, people who looked like that for real. And at the end there's this part where they're all just sort of running together and yelling 'gobble, gobble, gobble'…"

Cynthia kept going and Mira thought, I have to make her stop talking, oh god how do I make her stop talking? I have to defend him, because I have never defended him, and I can't let this idiot friend of mine say these idiot things, and I have to do something before Aunty does, because there is only so much control you have over the shape your family takes.

"Stop it," Mira said.

Mira's mother looked at her in surprise. Aunty and Uncle stayed silent.

"Pardon?" Cynthia said.

"Just stop, okay?" she said, and hesitated here. What did one say in such confrontational situations? Her chest was pounding, and she wished she hadn't started this. "This is a tournament for the Special Olympics," she said slowly, "… and these people here are special … and Ravi is special, too, and he might not be like you with your perfect brain, but don't you ever use the word *freak* near us again," and then Mira laughed inappropriately because she saw Cynthia's disbelieving expression, and after all, this was her one good friend in a school of people and she couldn't lose her. "Forget it," Mira said. "Nevermind."

And as she was thinking of how to recover the situation, she saw that Ravi had finished his game and come to stand with them. There he was, standing just behind Uncle's shoulder, listening with the alertness of a feral animal. Lala Aunty excused herself for the bathroom and Mira's mother and Uncle cleared throats and scratched arms and retied shoes while Cynthia said, "Crap, I'm sorry." Ravi was looking across the room at his teammates, and Mira knew that he had heard her repeating the word "special" like a bargain store announcer, and was now noticing their irregularities for the first time.

THE NEXT DAY, though the tournament was supposed to continue, Ravi declared, simply, that he wasn't going. It was breakfast time and they were in the kitchen, always in the kitchen it seemed. The radio was off and just the three of them in their pyjamas and morning hair.

"I'm not going to play bowling anymore," said Ravi, hunched over his cereal spoon.

"No?" asked his mother, and shook her head at Mira.

When Ravi left the room, Mira stood up from the table to put her orange juice glass in the sink. Then, she leaned over the island until her face nearly reached the other side, where her mother was standing, adding skim milk to coffee.

"You never should have taken him out of the normal high school class," Mira said. "After all that work to get him in there in the first place."

"Mira, that was ages ago," said her mother. She set down the milk. "You remember those exams. He wasn't sleeping."

"You think he liked it in there in 314? He hated it. He knew they weren't normal. He *knew* it. After twelve years of school, his diploma has a fucking retard stamp on it. They didn't even let those 314 kids leave the classroom at the lunch hour. His whole life practically he ate lunch with *freaks*. He *hated* it."

Mira was startled when she saw her own face in the window of the microwave, glaring and monstrous.

"I don't know what you want me to do about it now, Mira," said her mother, and left the kitchen. There was only the sound of her bare feet sticking to the tile.

Out the kitchen's semicircle window, on the side street, Ravi rode his bicycle, the frame engulfed by his huge soft body. He wobbled around at a slow pace. It took effort to ride a bicycle that slowly and keep balance; Mira imagined an invisible force holding him up against gravity, which was, of course, invisible too.

They didn't know it now, but at the end of the summer, Ravi would receive no payment for his driving job. His employer was taking advantage of him, would claim he had failed the trial period, and wouldn't reimburse him for gas, so his compensation for those hours of work was only one dark arm and thousands of kilometres of mileage on the family car. After Mira left for university, Ravi would rejoin a bowling league to fill the open time, a bowling league populated by ordinary people, and though he didn't win as often, he still brought home an occasional ribbon or certificate and pinned them all up on his bedroom wall, and if you walked by his room and saw that wall, you might really think it was the room of a champion.

The Girl Who Couldn't Be Hypnotized

THEY MOURNED RAVI'S luck thoroughly, without hope for resurrection. Months and then a year passed without paid work; he volunteered at their mother's office. When Mira graduated from high school, it was without excessive ceremony, and when she left for university, the transition was in some ways seamless, because she kept coming back. She came home every weekend, spent the weekdays craving home. She could have predicted that she'd miss her mother's chappatis, discussions with Uncle, silence, and watching TV in a room unpopulated by girls in tank tops. But then there were the atypical longings, for the shadow of her brother's head moving around the hallway at night, for her mother's face, twisting as she scoffed at typos in the newspaper.

She desperately missed Cynthia, who she phoned once a week and who had adapted swiftly to university life. In the background of the phone calls, she always heard a heavy bass line from a subwoofer, and other voices to whom Cynthia kept turning — "Mira, you won't believe what's happening," she'd say, and then what was happening would turn out to be some girl putting a lot of marshmallows in her mouth or that the girls in their dorm kept finding pubic hair on the toilet and couldn't figure out whose it was. Cynthia never said she wished they'd gone to the same university — why would she? But Mira thought if Cynthia asked her just once, she would transfer right out of this supposedly elite place.

Her own boringness felt amplified by her surroundings; her sense of humour was fading from a lack of conversations. In the few exchanges she did have, she'd think of a joke and then hesitate to use it. The few times she said something funny, everyone looked surprised. Through the door of her room, she heard girls bantering, propping their bodies up against the walls of the corridor. She'd try to wait for them to leave before she went to the bathroom, but would generally run into a couple of them group studying in the lounge with their notes spread on the hard carpet, or evaluating each other's outfits before jetting off to parts of Toronto she'd never seen.

As a result, she became the best student she had ever been. Her particular passion had always been chemistry, and this was elevated here by the scale and quality of the lab equipment — the gleaming test tubes and pipette tips they threw away instead of bothering to clean, the unrusted metal scoops she used to measure compounds so precisely on the digital scale. She titrated and distilled and centrifuged and autoclaved; her lab partner mostly just wrote stuff down.

As an elective, she took adolescent psychology, and became obsessive over it, even though they spent most of class time watching coming-of-age movies. Mira wondered if she had come of age yet. *These are adults*, she thought, looking at the preening people around her in class. If she dated a classmate, she would be dating a man, and she'd have to refer to him as handsome rather than cute, though she compromised in her head by using the word "guy" and describing him as "dashing" or "attractive." The course's textbook became her bedtime reading. She scanned the textbook index for words that were relevant to her life.

She didn't bother fully unpacking her belongings in her dorm. In November, her cardboard boxes still contained rolled-up sweaters and unopened packages of pens. On the Friday of the first November weekend, she stuffed her textbooks in her backpack along with underwear and a toothbrush — everything else she had extras of at home — and caught the subway in her usual routine. Even the walk to the subway stop made her uneasy, disoriented her. When walking downtown, to see which way was south, she had to stop and look for the CN Tower, and when she stopped, she disturbed the flow of the crowd around her, who parted and kept walking, brief-cases swinging. She once saw a car halted in the middle of an intersection, trapped by the unfortunate timing of traffic lights. The cars around it honked in violent cacophony, and the crossing multitude of pedestrians — gloveless, shivering, stylish — swore and jeered; one pounded the car's hood with his fist as he passed.

She took the train to Finch and then caught the GO bus to Bernard Terminal, where Ravi picked her up and drove her to the house. It took forty-five minutes total.

On the bus, she looked out the window at Yonge Street and half-napped, head knocking against the Plexiglas, falling in and out of dreaming of a time-shifting Richmond Hill. A decade and a half earlier, the town had produced a book chronicling its history, *Early Days in Richmond Hill*, and her dream started there, with the old pictures of churches and women in hats and carts rocking along behind horses. The dream progressed through the decades like a time-lapsed film of plant growth. She knew the city's age by the buildings, everything eerie yellow and grey, except the pink of Fantasia, constructed and disappeared, and then the buildings turned steel and blue and new. The churches stayed where they were and that's how she knew it was always Richmond Hill and never some other town, and also by Yonge Street, which remained constant — as streets should — though the dirt and gravel turned to pavement.

After putting her bag in her bedroom, she went to give her mother a lottery ticket, a small gift she'd purchased at Bernard Terminal. Her mother was in the kitchen, reviewing a dinner menu Lala Aunty had written out on several Post-it notes and stuck all over the refrigerator door. Mira had planned to spend the weekend doing problem sets and maybe renting a movie; she had forgotten that her mother was throwing a dinner party Saturday evening, or sort of a dinner party-baby shower, where both husbands and wives attended and played silly baby games and ate the same South Indian food they always ate but had cake at the end (pink or blue or yellow, depending). These parties were really thrown by Lala Aunty, who spearheaded the food preparation and guest list (inviting her usual hodge-podge of families), and oversaw the cleaning.

This time, when Lala Aunty showed up, she bustled around their house, inspecting the stove for splatters and making sure the bathrooms had toilet paper, and abruptly gasped to Mira and her mother, who were peeling fruit over the sink, "Oh my GOD, I haven't planned any games! I brought so many prizes — " she gestured at bulging canvas bags she had left near the front door, "— and forgot the games themselves!"

"That's okay, we'll just let people talk to each other …," Mira's mother began to say.

Lala slapped at her waist. "Are you kidding me? A baby shower without games, no way. Mira, go on the internet and plan some games, will you? Quickly quickly, just two-three games."

Mira grumbled once or twice about being ordered around, then went to her mother's computer and searched through baby shower websites for games that wouldn't scandalize this group (she eliminated the one where all the guests tried to estimate the circumference of the pregnant woman's stomach using long ribbons of toilet paper and the one requiring her to melt chocolate into a diaper) and collected together all the required materials in a big cardboard box, which she tucked under the dining table for later.

The guests started arriving around seven, though the e-vites had said six. They came with gift bags, CorningWare full of food, and boxes of chocolates that they'd picked up at Shoppers Drug Mart. Because it was a baby shower, most of the guests were closer to Mira's age than Lala Aunty's or her mother's. Lala Aunty's friends were getting younger and younger; she seemed determined to be young by association. Mostly these young people were new immigrants from India, with ages difficult for Mira to pinpoint. Some she addressed as "Uncle" and "Aunty" even though they were only twenty-five, because they *seemed* older. The men wore shirts tucked

in and congregated immediately in the living room to discuss
— what, she wasn't sure. The women arrived, some frizzy-
haired and some sleeker, in fitted selwar kameezes with long
transparent sleeves, and directly sought the kitchen to start
the search for serving spoons in sizes best suited to the foods
they had brought. It was impossible to guess which wife
went with which husband unless you saw them enter in a pair,
which normally didn't happen because the husband would
drop the wife at the door and then go search for a parking
spot. Husbands were often thinner than their wives or much
taller or nearly shorter. Some young couples had great gaps
in their levels of attractiveness; that was Mira's favourite
kind of couple, the muscular with the dowdy, the frowning
with the vivacious, odd couples, the products of semi-arranged
marriages and internet romances, standing together like vari-
ables to be multiplied, and they did multiply, cobbling little
families who over the years would grow to look more and
more like one another as the frumps picked up fashion advice
from their daughters, the dour cheered up from the accom-
plishments of their sons, the bubbly personalities flattened and
the brawny-bodied softened from allegiance to their nine-to-
five jobs.

Ravi showed people where to leave their shoes, and Mira
collected their jackets (which they wore despite the warm
weather). The house grew heated with the crowd of bodies.
The pregnant woman whose name Mira couldn't remember
— Sheila? Shyla? — lowered her papaya-shaped body into a
comfortable armchair which Lala Aunty had pulled into the
kitchen. All the women congregated around her, feeling at her
stomach and offering up their nieces as babysitters.

"Are we all here, shall we start the games?" asked Lala Aunty. She called the men in from the living room and they stood around the perimeter of the kitchen, crossing their arms and leaning against the counter or the refrigerator. Mira's mother made sure the stove was off and ushered children in to sit on the tile floor, and had just managed to quiet the rowdiest one when the doorbell rang and chaos exploded again.

"Come in! Come in!" the uncles shouted, though they wouldn't be heard outside the door, and the aunties started chattering about dinner and the deliveries of their own children while said children raced toy cars around their feet and Mira ran to answer the door.

A boy stood there on her front step — no, a man, an adult, a guy her age, anyway — and he held a tub of Neapolitan ice cream.

"Your hands must be freezing," said Mira, and then, "I remember you." She remembered him but couldn't place him, but of course he must be some acquaintance of her mother's or Lala Aunty's, but he was her age, and the word attractive certainly applied. He was about Ravi's height, but seemed taller because he was much thinner, and had an unusually even skin tone, the brown as uniform as Lala Aunty's pleather handbag.

"I don't know why I didn't put it in a bag," the guy said, and the word "bag" surprised Mira by matching the word she had only just used in her head. She took the ice cream from him and he wiped the condensation from his hands on the sides of his shirt, which was white with pinstripes that seemed to stretch his frame out farther. Mira moved backwards so he could enter, trying to think of what to say next, and wondering why he had been invited, and whether he had a wife who had already arrived, who was already in the kitchen, her age indistinguishable from Mira's mother's. Before she could speak, a large group of uncles and aunties wandered near, and she felt a gnarl in her chest at having missed that moment of aloneness with him, when she might have shown a personality that was impressive, or at least endearing.

"Harshvardhan, you decided to come after all!" Aunty exclaimed from the back of the group. Harshvardhan — what a name, thought Mira, whose mother had blessed her children with only four letters each. Perhaps he shortened it; it was obvious from his accent that he'd been raised in the U.S., and all the Indian people she knew here tended to nickname themselves for convenience — Ashumantha became Ash, Venkatramana became Venki — and their full names on official documents always seemed to describe different people entirely.

"And you brought such a big tub of ice cream!" said one uncle.

"It's all mine!" said another uncle, taking it from Mira.

"Ah, the three-colour kind," said an aunty. "My *absolute* favourite."

"Well, I didn't know if the baby's a boy or girl or what, and I thought chocolate is sort of a boy colour and strawberry a girl colour and the vanilla is whichever. I don't know, it made sense to me in the store," Harshvardhan answered, without any trace of shyness at being accosted by so many new people at once.

"Great rationalization! What a thinker!" said one uncle, patting him on the back.

"I don't know, I myself have a partiality for chocolate, and I am most definitely a female," said an aunty, her hands on her hips.

"I'm sure an uncle will share some of his chocolate with you," said Harshvardhan.

"We have no such divisions here — men, women, et cetera," declared an uncle.

"Complete equality," agreed another uncle.

"Any ice cream for any person," said an aunty.

"I scream you scream we all scream for ice cream," said an uncle.

"Yes, Uncle," Harshvardhan discreetly shot a smile at Mira, who thought the ice cream must be half-melted by now.

While they reassembled in the kitchen, the uncles talking about their preferred flavours of ice cream — mango, pistachio — and when they'd first tried it and how ice cream differed from kulfi and whether kulfi was better than gelato, Mira dreaded having to run the baby shower games. She would have to fake an excitement that matched the energy of this group; enthusiasm was not an emotion she wore naturally. When she'd been assigned the task of planning the games, she hadn't realized she would have to lead the group through them, and hadn't realized that one of the guests would include an appealing and unmarried person her own age. She fretted, remembering other times she'd been in such situations, the times she'd been at campus social gatherings and ducked into the bathroom to regroup, and when she'd shamed herself and family by freezing at that piano recital as her mother shook her head in the audience and Ravi asked in the car ride home, "Why didn't Mira play the piano? She plays the piano at home all the time," and the hypnotist — she would never tell anybody about the hypnotist.

It had happened only months ago, at the very start of

the school year. She'd forced herself to go because though it was only weeks into the semester, she could feel the friendships forming around her while she remained solitary as an unbonded atom. Girls in her hallway had already established their five p.m. dinner routine and ceased inviting her after her fourth shy refusal. It wasn't that she didn't want to join them, but rather that she couldn't see herself eating in front of them. The unusual nature of her eating habits became evident to her when she saw the other girls biting noncommittally into pears or leaving huge salads unfinished. Over the past few years, Mira had developed a mental block — she *could not* leave food on her plate. If she tried to combat this issue by taking smaller portions to begin with, she ended up just going back for more. If she were alone, she could sit in front of her plate using one tine of her fork to pick up the specks of food that were left (crumbs, bits of herbs), and a half hour could pass before she decided she was done. The only people she ever ate in front of were her family and Cynthia, who had been around since before the weird eating had evolved, and it had happened gradually and so lost its power to startle. At family dinner parties, Mira either slunk off to eat with the children or she wandered from room to room so that nobody noticed. She was terrified of eating an entire dinner, in a college cafeteria with limitless food, in front of the most ordinary girls she'd ever seen.

She'd reflected on her increasing fatness before, but for the first time now it struck her as really awful. Mira didn't want to be somebody who ever even thought about food, wanted to be the sort of being she'd once heard a priest describe at a temple lecture she'd attended with her mother, a person who had thoroughly liberated herself from physical desires.

The hallmates went to frat parties three nights a week, taking scissors to the hems of each other's skirts. Mira had gone to one of these during orientation week, where at the door of a house of castle looks and proportions, a boy wearing a white visor (pointless — it was nighttime) had asked her and the girls she went with, "Are you in or are you out?" and Mira wanted to laugh, though she was a little intimidated, but what was this, a cult? A secret society? Anyway, she had seen the same boy at general chemistry office hours the last Monday afternoon. One of the girls said, "We're in," shaking her hair with unconscious confidence, and so he'd passed to let them enter. Inside the castle were boys in T-shirts standing around, girls dancing boredly to overplayed songs on a carpet that squelched with beer — this is it?, Mira thought, I put on earrings for this? But then what had she expected? Princes? Jousting? And then she tried not to hate herself for her inability to dance; they stood the bunch of them in a circle (we could have done this in the dorm, she thought) and she self-consciously mimicked their movements, thinking, with each shoulder shrug or hip gyration, what limb she should move next.

And then the hypnotist, whose show she only went to see because she had called home to talk to her mother and Lala Aunty answered instead, and asked her, "How many friends have you made?" (only Lala Aunty would ask such a question so specifically) and Mira didn't have a number to give her. Later, Mira was taking a shower in the big shared bathroom, pausing in her leg-shaving to pull at the flimsy curtain to close the persistent gaps on each side of the shower, when she met the eyes of a girl who was brushing her teeth.

"You want to come see the hypnotist with us?" the girl

asked through her toothpaste, offhandedly, clearly expecting her to say no.

Mira said, "Yeah, all right," ducking carefully behind the curtain before she could catch the reaction. She walked to the hypnotist show with four girls and felt like a puppy they had brought along, dangling around them as though on a leash, since these girls had clearly solidified their relationships, and girls tended to travel in groups of four, according to all the chick flicks she'd ever watched. The four split into two rows while walking and Mira tried to gauge which pair's conversation would be easier to join — the first row compared fashion choices and the second compared leg injuries, and Mira had never kept up with trends or broken a bone. She chose the second row so she could adjust her pace to the girls in front of her. She laughed occasionally and tried to find a place to jump in. One of them monologued dazzlingly about the time she had cracked her fibia or tibula or one of those parts mostly unacknowledged except on lean, volleying girls. Mira thought the word fibia, tumbling in her head, would be better used as the name of a pretty girl who liked to stretch the truth.

They had gone early and found seats close to the stage before the rec room filled with students. The show began and the hypnotist asked for volunteers, and Mira of course did not volunteer, never would even think of doing so. But then the hypnotist, apparently wishing to engage the audience further, began pointing at people and asking them to come up on stage, even descending into the middle pathway and pulling people up from their seats. He got to Mira and eyed her, sized her up, and though she cowered, the girls she was with helped him urge her onto the stage. The hypnotist — wearing a black shirt and a bronze tie and speaking matter-of-factly — explained as he lined them all up that there were some people who just couldn't be hypnotized.

Mira had never seen a hypnotist show and felt sick at the prospect of what she might be made to do — to crawl and bleat like an animal, to shout obscenities, to act in lewd scenes of the type she knew to expect from college shows — in front of an audience that wasn't just that day's audience, but one that would witness her life over the next four years. The hypnotist began his screening process, a series of steps with evocative names like Stiff Arm and Invisible Shackles. Her peers on the stage fell into sleep, their heads falling to their chests. Their eyes closed and their arms dropped as they followed instructions. "A completely susceptible group," the hypnotist marvelled, and then he saw Mira, sweating in her spot in the lineup and waiting to fall asleep herself, wondering if she would remember any of this, wondering if she was in fact hypnotized already, and he said, "Except you my dear. You didn't concentrate did you?" He waved her dismissively and Mira slunk off the side of the stage. She had to make her way around the others and across to the stage stairs and then down the aisle and then over some people to her seat — she tripped over legs because they refused to get up. They just looked at her and some tried to hide laughs. She never could figure out if the others had just been pretending when the hypnotist made them squawk and moan, or when he made that one girl look into the crowd and see a massive naked orgy. Certainly she was glad that hadn't been her, but while in the weeks that followed nobody remembered the other participants, the four girls in the hall remembered her. One found Mira eating alone in the dining hall and slapped her on the back and said, "Concentrate!" right as she opened her mouth to take a bite of her bagel. Another girl waved her necklace in front of Mira's face, and another began to refer to her exclusively as "The Girl Who Couldn't Be Hypnotized." She announced it every time Mira went by. It wasn't an endearing nickname, as it could have been; under the veil of humour she imagined darker intentions, a knowledge of her insecurities. It occurred to her too late that they might only be joking.

NOW AT THE baby shower, she tried to foist the games duty on Lala Aunty, who responded with, "Oh, no no, I can't take credit," as though organizing them had been a massive undertaking. And the game hosting wasn't a massive undertaking either — all Mira had to do was stand up and give some instructions. She could be as involved or uninvolved as she needed to, she reassured herself.

"Okay, the first game is Pass the Parcel," she said, from the corner of the room.

"Pass the parcel! Alriiight, pass the parcel!" they shouted.

"I'll play the music and you guys pass this gift around, and when the music stops, you unwrap the top layer of wrapping paper and follow the instructions written there."

They were all confused. Harshvardhan re-explained, "She'll play the music and we just pass the parcel around until the music stops."

"Tunes! Play some tunes!" an uncle shouted.

Mira played a Bollywood mix and they began passing it around, some playfully clinging too long to the package, and others tossing it hot-potato. The music stopped the first time and they all reacted together with immense eagerness. An uncle tore the blue paper and read Mira's hastily penned instructions, which said to imitate a baby; without pause he squirmed and goo-gooed baby-like over the floor. The next time the music stopped, the aunties oohed at the new colour of wrapping paper revealed, out-of-season, Christmas-coloured, and the selected aunty wrapped a cloth diaper around a baby doll while her husband timed it, shouting, "Go!Go!Go!" while others agreed that she must be breaking some kind of record. Other victims underwent baby-food taste tests, told fairytales. Some were made to wear hilarious baby bibs throughout the rest of the game, others to drink ginger ale fruit punch from baby bottles. She kept thinking Harshvardhan was watching her, but couldn't be sure with all the aunties in the way. Regardless, the possibility gave her adrenaline. Why had she been so worried about any of this? She wished she could play now; she wanted to be in the game. When the parcel landed on Harshvardhan, he belted out a nursery rhyme in remarkable falsetto. The last layer of paper instructed the player to give the parcel to the mother-to-be. She unwrapped the parcel and cooed over the stuffed elephant, squeezed his plush tusks.

They replenished chips and drinks and played the second game (baby charades), then evacuated the kitchen in one big horde while the aunties set up the dinner buffet table. Mira saw Harshvardhan looking at the family pictures hung across the living room walls. Most were regular 3" x 4" pictures framed in wood of varying shapes, sizes, and shades. Mira's mother had arranged them according to a template from a decorating book; their edges collectively form a precise rectangle. She was glad most of them featured the thinnest versions of herself, in the nicest clothing she owned. At the bottom left corner of the rectangle, he stopped, squinting and eyeing the blurred photo.

He turned to her. "That's your brother, right?"

"Yeah, Ravi. He'll be around; I think my mom sent him out to buy ice."

"And your name is Mira, right?"

She nodded. "Do you ever shorten your name?" she asked him.

"It's just H," he said, almost absently, then added, "Not because I don't like my name, but because it saves time. Was this picture taken at a wedding?"

She looked more closely at the picture, moving tentatively near him. The pictures spread in front of her — faces aging and regressing from one to the next, her father only in the oldest ones, his clothes and hair a relic, her mother forcing a smile, Ravi failing to look directly at the camera.

"I think so. Yes. A wedding we went to in Pittsburgh. But that was a while ago."

"I was there," he said. "You sat at my table."

She looked and looked at his face. There was a small white scar on his eyebrow, the only break in his skin tone.

"Your brother started dancing, remember? And I asked if you knew him. And you pretended not to. I saw the three of you guys all leaving together afterward."

"Now I remember," Mira said.

NORMALLY, MIRA WOULD have filled a dinner plate and retreated to her room to study, but today she stayed downstairs and hovered. She mingled with uncles who advised her on RRSP contributions, and aunties who asked her how she got her hair so straight.

H seemed to be moving parallel to her, so that they were never in the same conversation. Mira finished her food quickly and returned to the buffet, serving herself with nearly the same quantities she'd taken the first time.

Lala Aunty approached her. "Mira, will you go pour water for people?"

"Yup, I'll just finish this quickly and then go around."

"Maybe go now, so your mother has a chance to eat?"

"I'll go in just a second," Mira said, irritated, since at a glance around she could see that most water cups were still full, and that plastic water jugs had been placed within reach of the guests.

"You shouldn't eat so much, Miru," Aunty said, handing her a water pitcher.

It made sense that somebody like Lala Aunty, who made her living making meals, and who herself needed to lose twenty pounds, would notice Mira's gluttony. Mira's mother had either missed it or avoided commenting, and though Cynthia talked constantly about anorexics, it was in her usual derisive, hypothetical way. Aunty picked up a pitcher herself, and they went around to the seated people, offering them water, pouring it into their plastic cups, trying not to let the ice splash.

When they were back in the kitchen refilling the pitcher, Lala Aunty said, "I think your father knew his father back home. They went to college or some-such. And you know Harsha, he goes to your college, even though he's from the States. Cheaper, I think, but still a top school. Smart family."

"He goes where?" she hoped he wouldn't overhear.

"Same as you, you didn't know?"

"No, I met him at a wedding once, apparently," Mira said, "but hadn't seen him since then."

"Oh, you will be great friends! You should ask him for a ride back to school."

"He's going back tonight, though, right? And I wasn't planning on leaving until tomorrow ..."

"Come on, Mira! It's to make some friends, that's all. What do you do here anyway? Same as at school, most probably."

When she had finished offering the guests water, Mira went to her room to pack up her clothes. She pulled off her selwar kameez and searched her closet for what to wear. Originally she'd planned to return in the same clothes she'd arrived in — old jeans, high school sweatshirt, bus ride clothing — but now she tried on everything she owned. Her breasts in the mirror seemed to form a horizontal cylinder under her shirts. Pants wouldn't zip shut and her thighs were too tight against the fabric. Adding jewellery didn't help. She tried on a necklace and the pendant looked like a tiny grain of rice next to her swollen face. A lovely hair band only isolated the accessory's own beauty, emphasizing the deficiencies underneath.

She picked up the phone, heard her mother speaking, hung up, waited five minutes, pacing around her carpet, stepping in between the discarded clothing. When the phone was free, she called Cynthia and said, "I feel fat, Cynthia, ugh, I feel fat."

"HAHAHA are you joking?" said Cynthia. There were voices in the background. Mira told her about H and her fashion dilemma, how nothing fit correctly. "Well don't take a laxative, you have to sit in the car with him."

"Cynthiaaa," she said.

"Borrow from your mom," said Cynthia. "She always wears those flowing ethnic tops." So Mira borrowed a shirt from her mother's closet and wore it over her jeans. She refreshed her eyeliner. What a genius Cynthia was. She imagined the sentimental message she would write in Cynthia's next birthday card.

When she went downstairs, she looked around for H, trying to get up the nerve to ask for a ride back, but didn't see him. The aunties and uncles had started to leave. Ravi was pulling jackets out from the closet in heaping armfuls and her mother was bringing out yogurt containers brimming with leftovers for the guests to take home. She figured he must have left already, without bothering to say goodbye — why would he say goodbye? With half-relief, she dropped her packed bag on the closet floor and went to help her mother, but Aunty intercepted her on the way.

"He's outside waiting in his car for you," Lala Aunty said.

Mira imagined what embarrassing words Aunty might have used. ("Will you drive Mira back? She has no friends. Take pity on her please. And move the seat back, because she needs extra room.") Out to the road she went, and checked for him in the cars, knowing he was watching her. A honk sounded and she went to it, squinting to see him behind the windshield.

"Thanks so much for bringing me along," she said. "I hope it's not a huge hassle."

"Not at all," he said, and immediately turned the radio on.

Mira counted the songs that played. It was an inoffensive soft rock station with occasional excerpts of banter. They drove out of the empty residential streets and on to Yonge, and she thought of the conversation they would have had if, five years ago, she hadn't pretended her brother wasn't hers. She could have demonstrated her commitment to the community by discussing the dilapidated buildings of downtown Richmond Hill and how if only they'd replace the adult video stores with coffee shops and classy bookstores, the area could be revitalized. She would have pointed out every baby in every stroller and every non-vicious dog and awwwed over them so he'd see her potential for motherhood and pet ownership. She could have identified the bands playing on the radio, so he'd see her as culturally attuned.

After counting nine songs, she reached out and turned the radio off. The highway was empty and H raised his distinctive eyebrow at her sudden move. His shirtsleeve wrinkled as he turned slightly towards her, keeping his eyes on the road. He smelled like the gum he was chewing.

"Once in high school, I came down to the kitchen and saw Ravi making one of those microwave pizzas," she said. "The personal-size kind, you know, Lean Cuisine or whatever. He picked up the box and read the instructions. I checked it afterwards, like I actually took the box out from the garbage and read it myself, and it said you're supposed to heat the pizza for two minutes, let it sit for a minute, and then enjoy! I was at the table eating crackers and Ravi read the box and put the pizza in the microwave and then he set the time on the microwave for *twenty* minutes. He waited there in front of the microwave, and it seemed like too long to me because I'd eaten a lot of crackers, and how long does it take really to melt some cheese? But I didn't say anything. I stayed there to see what he'd do. It caught fire. He opened the door and there was a little flame and he blew on it a couple times and hit it with his hand and I guess the flame was small enough that it went out. It was smoking, the crust was all burnt and the cheese had gone past melting, it was congealed and the oil had turned it orange. Really, it looked like the face of a burn victim, and Ravi didn't even look at it, he just started eating it, and clearly it was too hot and was hurting the inside of his mouth, and there was no way it tasted any good, but he just kept eating it. And I didn't stop him, I just watched him eating this disgusting pizza, disgusted, like why doesn't he know he shouldn't eat that —"

When she pressed the heels of her palms to her eyes to hold in her crying, he put his arm around her and pulled the car to the shoulder — like a gentleman (Aunty would have said).

A COUPLE DAYS later he phoned her, saying he'd found her number in the campus directory. He invited her to a silent auction with him because, he said, "You seem pretty quiet," and they went, using their scanty part-time earnings to bid on student-produced art, tickets to campus shows, dinners cooked by quirky local chefs. They won a dinner and had the meal in H's apartment with his two roommates, who said, "H talks about you constantly," and, "Wow you really are as gorgeous as H described," while a man in a tie-dyed shirt served them plates of sautéed kale. "I have this issue," Mira said, like a joke. "I can't leave food uneaten on my plate." "Um, why would you?" H asked. He seemed as pleased as though he'd cooked it himself. Mira had never eaten kale before, but the flavour was incredible! Better than candy!

Better than samosas! She thought in exclamations; she wanted to write poetry with clichés about waking up from a dream, about food regaining its taste.

After that, H and Mira began cooking weekly dinners together — Hungarian mushroom soup and beet salad and palak paneer. Mira stopped snacking in the afternoons so she'd be hungry enough to fully appreciate their efforts.

They made pumpkin ravioli from scratch after H accidentally carved his jack-o-lantern so eagerly it collapsed. For Halloween they went as gold and silver. They dressed head-to-toe in their assigned colours, painted each other's faces with makeup they weren't sure was non-toxic, and wore squares of white cardboard on their chests with the symbols from the periodic table. He blended her name into words — mira-cle, mir-coincidence, mir-pressure; over time they stopped making sense.

Before winter exams, they quizzed each other — she read him facts from her adolescent psychology book. "Can you believe we're adults?" she asked, and he responded by pointing out that they could neither rent cars nor legally consume alcohol yet, though at least they would be able to drink soon, since they were in Ontario. She read him the parts that bothered her the most — about mother-daughter relationships, about the need for father figures, about developmental disabilities. They fell asleep together on Mira's bed, textbooks over them like blankets. In the morning, Mira woke up next to H, with hot pink highlighter on her blue button-down. Nothing much romantic had happened yet; he'd kissed the side of her head a couple of times and occasionally draped his arm across the back of her chair. Mira wasn't even sure if they were dating or just good friends, but he looked sleepily at the marker stain on her shirt and said, "You should probably rinse that with stain remover," and he began to unbutton it, the pads of his fingers on her skin. He made excruciating eye contact, his eyes dark in the morning and his hair at all angles. Mid-unbuttoning, he stopped to collect the textbooks and notebooks and pens and highlighters in one single armful and placed them gently on the area rug. Then he lay back down and kissed her. He pressed one hand flat on the skin between her stomach and breasts and held her bottom lip between his teeth as he slid his hand slowly, firmly sideways. A small sound escaped from Mira's mouth and into his and then her thoughts kicked in — oh god, I just moaned into his mouth and his hand is on my stomach and I should lie on my back so that gravity flattens it — so she turned from her side to her back and H lowered himself to kiss her stomach. She let him undress her and then undressed him, dropping their clothes with their study materials.

In November, Mira happened to stand on a scale some-body had left in the dorm bathroom, and found she'd lost twelve pounds. She and H had been taking evening walks (digestive strolls, he called them) to a new Toronto destination each time — Chinatown, Kensington Market, the Distillery District — instead of what she used to do, which was watching library-borrowed movies on her computer while eating honey-roasted peanuts from the jar on her desk, dropping crumbs into the keyboard and constantly rewinding to rehear a line of striking dialogue. She'd stopped going home so often on week-ends, and thus avoided the heavy dinner party meals and her family's limitless temptation of hidden snacks. And she often spent the night in his room, eating packaged oatmeal for breakfast instead of the dining hall pancakes.

In hardly any time, she was just the size she wanted to be. One weekend, when homework wasn't too heavy, she pulled a large selection of clothes from her closet and packed them neatly into a duffel bag. She took the old route (subway, GO bus) home for the first time in weeks. She called out into the hallway, but nobody was home, so she left her shoes on the front rug and skipped upstairs to the alcove in her mother's bedroom where they stored the sewing machine. Under the cone of light from a standing lamp, she threaded the bobbin, selecting a thread from a rainbow of spools in her mother's collection. She tried the pedal and tested out her desired switch on a scrap fold of fabric. She altered her clothing to make it fit, turning shirts and pants inside out to narrow legs and nip in sleeves. Ends of fabric and short inches of thread accumulated on the carpet and she swept them together in a pile using her bare toes.

It was nighttime when her mother came home, and Mira was trying on a newly slimmed skirt and sweater in the full-length mirror behind the bedroom door. Her mother pushed the door open and jumped at the sight of her. "Miru? I didn't know you were here. And I didn't recognize you," she said, holding her daughter's shoulders, squeezing them, turning her around and watching the mirror. "I thought you were some stranger, hiding in the house."

"You were out?" Mira asked.

"Yes, just got home," she said. Her hands still clung to her daughter's shoulders, and Mira wanted badly for her to let go. The hands were veiny and dark. It seeemed like everyone was aging; months ago, on a visit to Lala Aunty's house, Mira had gone upstairs to use the bathroom because the main floor one was occupied, and on the counter she had seen an open box of hair dye, in a shade slightly blacker than natural. A pair of flimsy, transparent gloves hung over the box's lid, darkened at the fingertips. Drops of dye had stained the counter, and later, Mira had noticed the sides of Lala Aunty's scalp, similarly stained, the colour leaking over the hairline. Aunty had been in her forties when they'd all met, so she must be nearing seventy. Now, looking at her mother, Mira wondered guiltily, *How old is she?* She wasn't exactly sure, and only then remembered that her mother's birthday was only three weeks away. Aunty was organizing a party, and had sent an email, which moved further down the list in Mira's inbox. Subtracting the years in her head, she figured out the age — forty-three — which wasn't technically old at all.

"It's late," Mira said to her mother. "Were you out with Lala Aunty?"

"I was — well, I had a date."

Mira noticed now that her mother was wearing a green dress, though she never wore dresses, and gold earrings.

That her mother had a date didn't bother her. Now that Mira had found love, she had the generous feeling of wanting everyone else to find love, too. She understood finally why matchmakers wanted to make matches, and anyway it had been fourteen years since her father died and it was a bigger shock that her mother had waited so long, past the time when she was slender and long-haired and needed supporting and didn't need reading glasses.

"What took you so long?" Mira asked. She aimed for a jokey tone and held her breath for this to be the moment their mother-daughter relationship would advance into a mature friendship like the ones described in the sidebars of her adolescent psychology textbook. They would compare birth control pills and make fun of their boyfriends together.

"It's not like nobody wanted me," Mira's mother said. And then she told her about the men who had pursued her, the widows at dinner parties, the attempted set-ups by Lala Aunty, and the time twelve years ago when a man had approached her in the unlikely location of the mall parking lot, and proposed to her. "Come home with me to my mansion," he had said, and held out a ring he'd just bought at Sears after observing her in the bedding section.

"The bedding section? For God's sakes," Mira said. What a crazy, she thought, reminding her future car-owning self to lock the car doors when she went to the mall, thinking what a good, funny story who knew her mother was funny?), until her mother told her, with an expression of wonder at her old self, that she'd said yes, had looked at the three hundred thread-count sheets he held in a big plastic Sears bag in his other arm, that he had purchased already for their marriage bed, and followed him into his car — "But what about your car?" Mira asked, the safest, most inane question, and her mother just shrugged — and he'd driven her to his house, which was in fact a mansion, Tudor-style, coniferous-lined driveway, and she had stayed there in luxury for three days. "I didn't sleep with him," her mother said, "I just watched television all day while he went to work. I think he had a thing for Indians. But he was nice enough, and when I decided to leave, he let me leave."

"What about me and Ravi?" Mira asked, looking over at the clothing she had just sewn, at the still-hot iron on the ironing board, at the sewing machine light that she hadn't yet turned off.

Her mother waited, and grimaced before saying, "You were here."

"By ourselves?" she asked.

But her mother didn't answer, just looked at her as Mira stood up and brushed off her skirt, though there was nothing there — it was a comfort to feel the slim cylindrical shapes of her legs — and her mother grabbed her hand with her old dark, shrivelled one, like the forked branch of a tree, like a wish stick, but Mira shook it off and went to her old bedroom to check the bus times. She could still make it back to catch the last train. Her mother lingered behind the closed door, her feet two blunt shadows in the gap between the door and the carpet. Mira pictured two small foxes, sitting, thinking. On the bus back downtown, she tried to remember those three nights when she was six and her brother was eight. Was six not old enough to remember? She wondered what they had eaten, and whether they'd turned the house lights off before they went to sleep.

TO H, MIRA confessed everything terrible she had ever done, how she had watched a home video of herself at age four, practising the piano in her living room while her brother sat on the adjacent sofa, colouring in the margins of a magazine, and when four-year-old-Mira finished playing, she turned and scowled at Ravi — for no reason — until she got his attention and then when he turned his head mildly around, she said, "WHAT?" in a vicious voice and banged her hands against the piano keys in what struck her now as hilarious discord, and then Ravi turned away but in the video she could see he was still watching her, his pupils stealthy in their corners, catlike. She quoted to H a line from a Komunyakaa poem about that tenuous state between innocence and experience, *Where did we learn to be unkind*? Where had she acquired that animal meanness; was it instinctive, innate? Where had she picked up that quality of voice she used only on him, the sound of it like an extended claw? From where had she taken that stinginess that embarrassed her now, that let her eat more than her share of whatever gummy snacks or slice of cake their mother had left for them — was it evolutionary? And what of the emotional stinginess, how she didn't want to touch him, how she cringed from Ravi's needy, forgiving, open arms, his childlike greed for affection? "Gimme a hug!" he would say, and she still couldn't do it. When he had tried to watch TV with her, she would, without looking at him, say, "I'm watching here," an indirect command, so that if he complained to her mother, she'd be able to say she hadn't actually told him to leave. She'd sometimes sat in the back of the car when he was driving, even if it was only the two of them.

"That's all normal behaviour for siblings," said H, and he curled his hand comfortingly against the back of her head.

"Yeah, but not when your brother has a disability. I'd cheat when we played Scrabble Junior, which is ridiculous, I mean, it's not as though I needed to cheat, so I don't even know why I did it."

"That's a little awful," H admitted, "but it's not as though you still act like that now."

She had mostly grown out of that impulse to treat Ravi badly, but if her cruelty were a jar of infinite depth and she had poured and poured into it so quickly, so forcefully, could she ever, even in her delicate new contriteness, empty it again?

"You're a good sister," said H, but it wouldn't ever quite be true.

ON THE AFTERNOON of her mother's birthday, Mira was in H's room. They were studying together on the floor, his textbooks overlapping hers. H had physics on Monday, and her adolescent psychology exam was on Tuesday, but she already had her notes practically memorized. She had purchased a gift for her mother, a crystal water pitcher in the shape of an elephant. She put it in a white cardboard gift box, cushioned it with bubble wrap.

"I have this fear," she told H as she highlighted with her three-colour highlighter, "that I know is irrational."

"Mir-rational," he said, alphabetizing his flashcards.

"Imagine I go home one day and Ravi is totally normal —"

"You wouldn't be happy about that?"

"Well yeah, I'd be happy about that," she answered. She was flipping backwards through the index of her textbook. Hypnosis. "Have I told you I can't be hypnotized?"

"I've hypnotized you," he said with fake intensity. "That's what the H in my name really stands for. What do you think he'd be like?" H asked. "Ravi, I mean. Non-autistic Ravi."

Mira imagined Ravi sixty pounds thinner, a med student holding forceps to a yawning body cavity, or on the television, an expert on immigration, speaking in a speedy, low pitch, informedly, to an interviewer — "What this country needs is ...!" slamming his fist on the desk.

"He'd remember every terrible thing I have ever said or done to him."

She reached D in the index and looked for disabilities, but the textbook didn't cover it.

"He'd know you were just a kid and he would forgive you," H said.

She took her phone into H's bathroom and called home. With her free hand, she arranged the selections of soap and shaving cream by the side of the sink. Ravi answered the phone and she asked if he could pick her up from the subway station. He was shrill and lethargic, distracted, always pacing — she imagined she could hear the slow clomp of his feet on tile. Twice she confirmed that he would be there. He was reliable, though sometimes he heard things wrong. But she couldn't blame him for this, as she couldn't quite blame her mother for wanting to escape, for her temporary vacation to a home more beautiful and a life less complicated than theirs.

Her mother had taught Mira about reincarnation, and had once confessed to worrying about what she would become in those future lives, emerging from that chrysalis of death. Mira couldn't expand her thoughts to what God considered pardonable. It was enough for her now that H could overlook her former cruelty, and to convince herself that a hypothetical healed Ravi might let go of every single incident in which she had caused him pain. But in her mind, forgiveness seemed just an emotion that came and went like a hummingbird, a dragonfly, an imp, an enchantment — a flimsy, mercurial thing.

Rare Birds

MIRA WANTED FEATHERS on her wedding cake, rising outward from the middle tier.

"Every slice like the rear end of a pigeon," said H, when she showed him pictures on the internet.

She pointed out that the feathers would be violet rather than pigeon-coloured. They had chosen a theme for her wedding — wild, rare birds, an idea that had come to her as she wandered around H's neighbourhood one afternoon. Walking in front of her was a man carrying a plastic bag in each hand. His slow-moving breadth blocked her path. Mira adjusted her pace because she had nowhere to go; she was killing time while H cooked dinner. He had shooed her away because she had a habit of washing the dishes as he dirtied them. ("Mira, I still need that spoon.") She had the gardens and garage doors memorized, their colours and bare patches. She knew which yards had solar-powered lights tucked into their soil, disguised behind rocks, brightening as the night darkened, illuminating the undersides of shrubs.

Her eyes went to the man's bags. Each looked heavy, and she tried to figure out what they contained. Milk in the left, probably — she recognized the plump bulge of the milk bag — and seasonal fruit she guessed, pears, just what H was adding to their salad with crumbled gorgonzola. She was hungry as she observed the second grocery bag, and found that by squinting she could read through the plastic the words, "Wild Bird Feed." She looked at the man with new interest and pictured wild birds hovering inside his home, sitting on dowel perches, tweeting bossily as they ate their striped sunflower seeds from his rough palm, but then she realized the feed would most likely go into a feeder on his front porch.

"Wild, rare birds!" she shouted at H as she burst into his apartment.

"Nope, just chicken," he said, patting her back with his oven-mitted hand.

Mira began setting out plates and forks and explaining.

"See, I wanted a theme for the whole wedding, to sort-of unify everything. Is that not the perfect theme? And it gives us a colour scheme — peacock feathers! — we could take all the colours from peacock feathers ... am I only allowed to wear a red sari? What are the rules?"

"So a peacock blue sari?" H eyed her. "Yeah, that could look okay."

"And lots of gold jewellery — from my mom, don't worry. Should I wear a fake nose ring or is that tacky?"

"No, I adore nose rings. Get a real one. Feathers in your hair?" H asked.

Mira thought about it. They took their places at the tiny

round table. H hopped back up for the water pitcher and returned.

"And sewn on the back of the sari," H continued. "That could be your train. And we could train little birds to carry it for you. I'll be in charge of that part. Trainer for the train-carrying trainees. Except I don't know how they'd feel about carrying feathers from one of their shorn brethren."

"Haaaa," Mira fake-laughed, selected a crouton from the salad bowl and threw it at him.

THE NEXT DAY, she woke up before dawn while H still slept, and found that her head had dislodged itself from its usual position over the hollow of his neck, under his pushed-around hair. She had a pharmacotherapy class to get to, one of the last classes in her second year of the PharmD program, but she liked to set her alarm ten minutes early and lie awake, looking up at his ceiling, perpetually surprised that its slope had become so familiar. H was the only other person whose apartment she had stayed at regularly, which she thought was lucky. It would have been difficult to get to know many ceilings; she considered the possibilities, flat or popcorned or dotted in spackle, and was glad she hadn't wasted time on them. She moved her head around H's neck and shoulder, fretting that she wouldn't be able to find the right spot again, that he would wake up and she would tell him, "My head doesn't fit," and they would try together, hopelessly, for hours, until morning, until the next night, to piece together their skulls and limbs. The light would change in the room and then change again and then she would be forced to leave.

They had chosen a July wedding date, even though Mira had originally wanted it in winter. Her hair frizzed under any sign of humidity, strands rising like dry question marks. She had wanted to have her hair straightened and shiny and curled out and in at the ends in the same hourglass shape as her body in a sari that an aunty would gather and tighten neatly around her. In winter, her jewel-toned sari wouldn't appear excessive, even in the brightness of daytime, and she wouldn't have to wear patches to keep the sweat stains from her silk armpits. For the reception, she had a vision of a hall filled with white trees. She wasn't sure exactly how they would stand, since potted soil would look ridiculous and be a tripping hazard and uncles would probably discard napkins in them. But she'd have lights threaded through the branches (H said this would resemble his sister's first dorm room), glowing in the dark hall. Between the trees, a V-shaped path would lead to the mantappa where the wedding ceremony would take place. Mira wanted the mantappa's pillars painted gold — fake gold didn't seem as vulgar in winter — and the platform covered in a blanket like a snow drift. Two Hindu priests lived in the area, and she would hire the one that didn't mumble. He was youngish, and they'd hear his tenor voice in the very back row of seats (they expected a guest list of three hundred since H's family brimmed with popularity and Lala Aunty would probably have a list of her own); his voice would resonate through the trees. For the reception, she could wear a shawl over her shoulders and then when she stood up to dance she would casually drape it over the back of her chair, like an evil queen in a Disney movie, and all the aunties would marvel at how fair her shoulders were, especially for a South Indian. The menu would include every imaginable curry — "Both veg and nonveg? Are you sure?" her mother had asked — and the spiciness of the food would warm them appropriately in the cold weather. Somebody would call up the tables by number and guests would return for seconds as the caterers refilled each stainless steel buffet tray, kept hot over a blue flame.

But a summer wedding made more sense, she realized, discussing it with her future family members and tallying up the reasons — no snow to keep long distance guests from attending, no bulky winter jackets and dripping footwear, her degree would be finished so she would have ample time for planning, H's mother had the summers off and could help with arrangements, they could take outdoor pictures, and then she came up with the bird theme — so she marked the Canada Day long weekend on her wedding planning calendar, decorating the square with a glossy sticker of a bouquet.

EIGHT MONTHS BEFORE the wedding, she journeyed to Gerrard Street to buy saris, and took her mother and Lala Aunty with her.

"You know we could find all of this stuff much cheaper in India," Aunty said, referring not only to clothing but to favours, centrepieces, and printing invitations. Mira reminded her that she was already taking her honeymoon in India. They had scheduled their trip for the monsoon season, and she anticipated spending all her time wrestling broken umbrellas and taking long naps in humid rooms.

Her mother parked the car in a lot near an elementary school and they hurried through flurries to the first in a row of clothing shops. The store window had hanging strings of coloured glass beads that clicked together as the wind came through the door. Three mannequins stood behind the strings — one headless, one bald and painted a copper colour, one wearing a synthetic light brown wig. They had been dressed in Indian dresses of varying styles, dupattas tied haphazardly from shoulder to waist. Two were red, in cheap chiffon, one-size lehengas that fell loosely and revealed half a foot of plastic midriff. Boneless arms posed out from ill-fitting cap sleeves. But the third was a blue so pale it was almost silver, embroidered in silver, with patterns of stemless flowers mingling at the corners of their petals. She could wear it with a peacock-blue blouse to match her theme. It hadn't been made into a dress yet, was just a piece of fabric pinned so it skimmed the mannequin's frame.

It hid the body's hollow beige like the dresses Mira had searched for in her fattest stage of youth. And it reminded her of an incident before that, when she'd been a little girl in a different Gerrard Street shop. Her mother looked for a jubba that Ravi wouldn't refuse to wear (one with no buttons, no high neck). Mira had fallen asleep for an hour under a rack full of blue dresses, woke up to a ceiling of different-length blue hems, like a low, textured sky. She sat up and they brushed her face, smelling like the incense that burned in a dish on the store's counter.

"This one's nice," she said now to her mother, and to the shop woman who approached.

"You can't buy the first one you see," Lala Aunty interjected, and then looked closely at the fabric and said, "That's too simple for a wedding sari."

"No, not right for a wedding sari at all!" the woman agreed, leading them to a carpeted staircase. Up the stairs were the expensive proper wedding clothes which Mira scanned through quickly.

"Aishwarya wore this kind of sari only," the woman said, pulling a square cellophane package from the shelves, "How nice you would look! With a flower garland in your hair and one gold pendant like this," she gestured at the part in her own hair.

Mira humoured her. The woman showed them a series of saris, explaining which part of India each one was from and in what style they should be tied. Then Mira retreated into a makeshift dressing room while her mother and the store woman passed possible reception outfits to her over the cardboard door. Lala Aunty lowered herself into a nearby folding chair and gave her opinions, having Mira pose in every dress.

She really only wanted the blue sari she had seen first, and so after commenting diplomatically on every outfit in the upstairs of the shop, she told them firmly, "I'll get the blue one I pointed out for the reception and then we'll think about the other one."

But when they had finished returning all the tested fabric to the shelves, and once they'd finished chattering about bangles and bindis and Aunty had bought three pairs of gaudy earrings for Mira that spanned the length of her neck, they descended back to the front window and found that somebody had already purchased the blue fabric displayed so prominently in the window. An assistant was in the process of dressing the copper-skinned mannequin in some subpar material, attaching it over the hinges of elbows.

They left the shop after a fruitless search for a similar sari. At a shop two doors down, they bought a traditional red sari for the wedding and a dark green one for the evening function. "Christmas colours," exclaimed the store's owner, as though that were worth celebrating.

IT ALL FELT like a compromise. Mira had attended nine weddings in her life. Most were weddings of family friends; Indian weddings that followed the same stale but colourful structure, with an occasional tweak of having the bridegroom arrive on the back of a flamboyantly dressed horse. A few had been the weddings of high school and university friends. One was Cynthia's three years earlier — surprising, since Mira had always imagined Cynthia holding out until her thirties rather than getting married at twenty-two, right out of university. She'd held it in an old, familiar church on the side of Yonge Street in historic Richmond Hill. Two of their former high school teachers had made cameos, nodding from their seats in pews, nearly unrecognizable when not standing at the chalkboard front of a room. Each of those weddings had possessed its own charm, but Mira wanted hers to stun, to be recalled among the best of weddings, not to blend in with the others and be discussed and forgotten over the car ride home.

But she compromised on the photographer — she'd wanted artful black and white shots of the side of her face as she got her makeup done, of her petticoat on its hanger, of Ravi's hands blurring as he danced, of H laughing into a spotlit microphone — but they couldn't insult H's cousin who always took the photographs, and she had a feeling all the pictures would be posed rows of aunties holding plates of half-eaten idlis. She despised idlis, but had included them on the menu because, her mother reasoned, many of the uncles had health problems and *expected* idlis, which were easy on the stomach. For her rare bird theme, and to make up for the cancelled white trees, she'd thought up centrepieces of twisted, nest-like branches, with wood carved bird eggs sprayed gold and turquoise.

"Eggs?" asked H. Mira told him this idea in March as they flipped through bridal magazines on the sofa. "And how do you want these eggs, Bridezilla, scrambled or fried?" he asked, "Or devilled? In an omelette?"

She looked at him mournfully.

"Or wait, wild birds, right?" he continued. "How about ostrich eggs?"

She kissed his ear.

"We'll put them on the menu." He gathered her up, crushing the page of a magazine. "Except half our guests are vegans …"

"Okay, you're right, no eggs, but what about the branches?"

He agreed to it, and they ordered branches to be set in small brass pots. When the branches arrived in the mail, they stored them in her mother's basement with the other wedding supplies. The more Mira looked at them, the more they seemed to have nothing at all to do with her theme — they were bunches of twigs she could have found in the yard.

"Let's just hold the wedding outdoors," Mira said to H when the hall they wanted turned out to be booked on their desired date. She fantasized about having the ceremony at Mill Pond, until she remembered about the swans that had lived in the pond, and how a decade ago somebody had snapped their necks. She didn't think she could hold her wedding, given its theme, among the ghosts of all those murdered birds.

They scheduled the religious part of the wedding to take place in a temple basement, though the floor needed refinishing and the ceiling beams were dark and low.

When she went to see the temple's set-up, she found that the mantappa, the pillared platform on which the wedding ceremony would be held, was bright orange, though the priest on the phone had told her gold.

"It is gold-colour," the priest kept saying.

"No, it's orange!" Mira almost shouted, but did not because she was in a temple. H suggested they cover it in flowers, but the flowers Mira longed for were overly pricey dahlias and orchids. Given their graduate student salaries, they ended up ordering white carnations that would bulge cheaply down each pillar.

She didn't think the things she wanted — her wedding plans, other things — were unreasonable. In fact, they were often ordinary; once she'd read the real estate section of the paper and said to H, "Imagine we moved to a house outside the GTA," and another time they'd been in a café, and observing a woman's tall, wine-coloured shoes, she'd said, "Imagine I owned a pair of those," and H always said, "I can't imagine it!" as though it were wholly unimaginable, until, over the telephone, midway through one of his jokes, she'd said, "Imagine we got married," and half-waited for the usual answer while at the same time imagining him saying, softly, in a romance movie voice, "I *can* imagine it." He wasn't sappy enough for that; he just laughed at her, and she worried about him breaking up with her. But after he had hung up the phone he drove immediately to see her, still wearing his pyjamas, and proposed properly, or improperly, because he removed his pyjamas and hers shortly afterwards, flinging them in his ironic, dramatic way. Even as her clothes were being flung, Mira fantasized about him ending the relationship, an even more painful end now that they were engaged. It hurt her chest to think of never washing dishes in his apartment again, of having nobody to phone — who would answer her terribly timed phone calls? She called him when he was already sleeping, when he was in important meetings, during funerals, during the basketball finals, and he answered, would probably answer if, by crazy accident, he were at the circus hanging from some acrobat's legs, swinging, letting go, mid-air, he would answer and say one of his absurdities, a pun on hanging and hanging up. She thought of him breaking up with her, saying, "I don't know, Mir-kat," speaking in endearments right up until the end.

She took a strange pleasure in these break-up fantasies. But it made her think, guiltily, that maybe H was only the person she was meant to date before meeting the person whom she was actually supposed to marry. And now she would go to her honeymoon — in India of all places, staying with his grandparents in Karnataka and then hers in Kerala, under torrential rains — and return to move her belongings from her Toronto walk-up into his. She'd never live again in a space that was only hers; she had spent innumerable hours in his apartment but still hadn't grown accustomed to the way mugs were kept upside-down in the cupboard, or the way he ate cereal instead of bagels for breakfast. Soon she'd be changing the name on her driver's licence and other identification. It felt as though she were severing the link to those other Acharyas, the ones that had been with her from birth. H's family was so flawless; it was like being adopted, plucked from her home, or like singeing off fingerprints whose touch she had pressed to countless surfaces.

MIRA TOOK RAVI with her to sample wedding cakes, partly because H had only a mild sweet tooth, partly because she was exhausted of his bird-related humour. And because she didn't know anybody who enjoyed cake as much as Ravi did. He ate the Sara Lee unthawed from the freezer.

One of her classmates, who had just gotten married herself, referred her to a bakery. Mira had sketched her own design. She wanted it to be avant-garde, with mad hatter layers and faux (non-toxic) feathers.

The shop said Patricia's Cakes in a white scripty font on the window. In the window display were hundreds of cupcakes, arranged in a daunting mountain of tiers. These were the only real cake inside the store. The door opened to a small white room with display cases around the walls, filled not with cakes but with their pictures, next to colour swatches and photos of varieties of fondant bows. A thin, efficient-looking woman stood behind one of the cases, her blue-jeaned legs magnified disproportionately through the glass.

"You could have called it Patty's Cakes," said Mira.

"Well, I could have," said the woman, and handed Ravi a menu. "These are the flavours we have available. Obviously for the inside we have chocolate and white cake and we could marble those, but then we've also got lemon and red velvet and coconut and the others you see listed there, and we could always add some kind of flavouring — amaretto or orange or whatever you like — to the frosting or to the batter, and frosting-wise there's buttercream or you could do a rolled fondant, depending on the design. Shoot — I didn't even ask you about the event. Is it a wedding, birthday ...?"

"Wedding," said Ravi.

"Oh, right, you told me that over the phone."

"Actually," said Mira, "I've sort of drawn out the design I was hoping for." Suddenly her piece of notepaper seemed ridiculous, dog-eared as she pulled it out of her purse.

The woman looked at the paper for a moment. "Hmm, well, this cake would collapse under its own weight. It's structurally impossible. It wouldn't stand," the woman said. She asked about the other details of the wedding.

"Well, it's a bird theme. Wild birds. Rare birds," Mira told her without conviction, and then described the dress and favours and invitations and the other odds and ends she'd collected.

"It's like you can't decide if you want the wedding to be elegant or garish," the woman stared at her and then came out from behind the counter. "But that's a wedding, you know, it's a business. I hate to sound skeptical. Anyway, we can work with this theme of yours." She pulled out a notebook and outlined the simple shape of a three-tiered cake. "A white fondant cake, and I'll airbrush a peacock feather over each layer. So your guests won't have to floss out the fake feathers. Okay?"

"Okay," said Mira, glad Ravi was with her instead of H, who would never have stopped making fun of how rudely the woman had dismissed her sketch. Ravi wandered to a picture of a cake shaped like a race car. His fingertips left oval prints over the glass counter.

"Did you want to sample the flavours now?" the woman asked, and, without waiting for an answer, she directed them to a high round table in the corner with two tall wooden stools. She retreated into the kitchen, behind a nearly invisible door.

Seeing a groom cake topper with a striking resemblance to

H reminded Mira that she should probably phone him for his opinion. Mira checked her handbag and realized that she'd left her phone in the car. "Rav, I'll be two seconds. I'm running to the car," Mira said.

"She'll bring out the cakes for me?" Ravi asked and Mira nodded, darting out the door.

Out by the car, on the phone with H, she saw Ravi through the window, eating methodically through small cubes of cake. He wore long denim shorts, eyes wide and head bent over a dessert plate. When he was little and had birthday parties, there had been other people — boys from school that their mother invited — but after a while the guest list dwindled to just the three of them. They would eat pizza, then the cake (too sweet, bought from Loblaws) and give him his gifts (shirts, sets of coloured pencils). They took pictures if they had remembered to charge the camera batteries. Each year's photo was identical to the last — Ravi hunched over the round blue cake, knife posed over a frosting rose, Mira or her mother (whoever wasn't taking the picture) standing with hands on the back of his chair. Ravi was thirty now; the legs that came out of his shorts were covered in dark hair. Probably he would celebrate his seventieth birthday the same way, minus their mother. Even now, Mira and H occasionally cooked dinner and invited him, and he acted as though he were their child. "More milk," he would say, holding up his glass. He would be the same in forty years, but grey-haired and smaller, changes imperceptible over the leisurely movement of time. Now he dipped each cube of Patricia's cakes in one of the mini ceramic bowls that held frosting, lifted them to his mouth with a level expression of joy.

"YOU KNOW WHAT we should do, is we should save money by getting companies to sponsor our wedding," said H to Mira as he rolled uneven chappatis.

"I don't want Google stamped across the back of my sari," Mira said. She was trying to produce a chickpea curry from Aunty's telephoned recipe. She distracted him by kissing his shirt-covered back and took the rolling pin from him.

"Hey," he tried to get the rolling pin back, then gave up and sat down at the table, where all their freshly printed wedding invitations were laid out to be addressed.

"No, see, I saw it on TV where they were able to get tons of stuff they wouldn't have been able to afford. Like the cake — we could get like a crazy flamingo cake. It'd go perfectly with your theme, Mirabello-mushroom."

"I wish I had cake now," she said, giving up on the chappatis and sitting down with him. The invitations smelled pleasantly of chemicals. The neat squares were night blue on the outside, embossed with a stylized silver Ganesha. She opened it to see the blue letters on the white background, with a tiny RSVP card tucked inside. H had had them made by a friend of his who did desktop publishing, so Mira hadn't yet seen them. The letters inside cordially invited guests to the wedding of Miss Mira Acharya and Mr. Harshvardhan Narayan. Below that were the date and time information for the ceremony and reception, and the words "No boxed gifts."

"No boxed gifts," Mira said.

"Oh yeah, my mom told me to have that put there. Apparently it's a polite way of telling people to just give cash."

"It's a rude way to tell people to just give cash. It's rude to mention gifts, period!"

Mira and her mother had discussed this issue over the years. There were four possibilities with wedding gifts: creating a registry (classic), not mentioning them at all (the most elegant option), "No gifts please" (the subtle bragging of the rich), and "No boxed gifts," which they'd decided was the most hideous option, an option for people with no shame.

"But we'd rather have cash than receive eighteen rice cookers," H said, smiling and moving his chair close to hers, as if he couldn't handle being so far across the table from her.

"God, I just feel like I'm compromising on everything! You shouldn't have to compromise for your wedding. I mean, I changed the cake design and we have that godawful mantappa and have you looked at the centrepieces? They look like beaver dams. And now I have to settle for these tacky wedding invitations so all my friends and relatives think I'm asking them for money."

H got up abruptly, silently pulling back his chair. "I'm sorry you feel like you're settling," he said, before he headed up the stairs. Mira sat for a moment and then retreated to the living room, leaving the trapezoidal chappatis uncooked on the counter.

HER BRIDAL SHOWER was a crass affair. Cynthia hosted at her apartment and seemed to confuse it with a bachelorette party. Fifteen girls attended, most of whom Mira barely knew ("You remember Sophie? From my office?"). They sipped pink rum punch poured into paper cups from a large plastic pitcher and ate wheat thins with dyed-orange cheddar until the pizza arrived. Cynthia had baked cookies in inappropriate shapes. By the end of the night, the girls were weaving drunkenly over the carpet. Somebody suggested they go to a corner bar ("Popcorn! Doesn't that bar have free popcorn?"), so they did. A tiara appeared on Mira's head and she wore it sadly through the evening and until the next morning, when she woke up early, having crashed at Cynthia's. She climbed, hungover, over the other sleeping girls splayed across sofas, to her gifts, and opened them. Tissue paper, wrinkled and scotch-taped, went into an empty gift bag. The night before the bridal shower, the night she and H had argued, she had gone to bed and found him already asleep. In the morning, she frothed the coffee and he distributed the cereal, but they spoke only in nouns. "Milk?" she grunted, "Sugar," he replied. Mira opened her gifts quietly, as not to wake the other girls. Instead of bevelled glass jewellery boxes, she found she'd received erotic card games and poppy red underwear.

She drove right to H's apartment and entered to find him standing on the kitchen table, replacing a lightbulb. He held his frown and she held one of the presents up to him. It was a novelty bride voodoo doll. Hanging from her bouquet was a pouch of pins for the groom to use nefariously on what was basically a bride-shaped pillow. H examined it thoroughly and, not looking at Mira, he removed the pins and set them down on the table. Then he took the doll and kissed it squarely (for a surprisingly long time) and started laughing as Mira wrapped her arms around his knees and kissed his brown calves. "You bird," he said, bending to hold up two fistfuls of her hair, like wings, "my rare bird." Mira thought of the first time she had visited his family, taking her passport because it was across the border in Upstate New York. She had always evaluated other people's houses, how the floors creaked in tune with her movements, how the stairways angled into landings, how the sofas had acquired new contours in age. At H's family's house, in contrast, she had complimented his mother's cooking (exactly like her own mother's), talked pharmaceuticals with his father (a doctor), watched two romantic comedies with his sister (H searched for a better entertainment), and was back across the border before she remembered to notice how the pet hair swept through the air like ghosts.

ON THE MORNING of the wedding, Lala Aunty pinned Mira's sari and bent in front of her — softly groaning, joints cracking — to adjust the crisp folds. Mira's mother took the mango-shaped earrings purchased long ago by Mira's father, and, so that they would fit through the small holes in Mira's ears, she dipped the ends in Vaseline. Outside the reception hall dressing room's double doors, Mira heard Ravi pacing — "They delivered the cake!" he called out, muffled through the door. She heard him clap his hands.

She followed Ravi to the kitchen, dressed but for her hair and makeup (the stylist had yet to arrive), and found the cake placed alone in a huge chrome refrigerator. The fondant was smooth and white, the cake woman had painted peacock feathers climbing up the cake, their shapes pendulous as teardrops; their centres had an iridescence Mira hadn't realized could be achieved with frosting. At the top of the cake she had perched a peacock figurine made entirely of sugar, turning his long neck to glance behind in a way that made you wonder what magical thing he had seen.

A caterer came around to check for fridge space. "It's a magnificent cake," she said, leaning in to move it slightly, to make room, but the cake board stuck stubbornly to the metal bars of the fridge shelf. It looked like she was being quite careful, but — and Mira knew it would happen before it happened — the cake wobbled and fell forward, its painted feathers, glimmering layers collapsing, toppling like a child in a dress.

"Oh no," Ravi said. He stepped back with his hands up, as though worried someone might blame him for this disaster.

"I'm sorry, oh my god, I'm sorry," the caterer said.

"What are we going to do? We have to go to the temple!" said Mira's mother.

"I'll pay for it," said the caterer. "I'll find you another cake, I'll go right now."

"What will we do?" Mira asked. "We didn't even order a second dessert."

"I'll find you another cake," the caterer said again, and bolted away.

"We'll probably never see that foolish character again," Mira's mother said.

"Everyone will be waiting for cake and we'll have to say there isn't any," said Mira. "It's like the wedding won't even be finished! How can we dance without cutting the cake?"

"Who am I going to marry?" Ravi asked. "Is she here yet?" Mira and her mother looked at each other and at the ruined cake, which looked even more exquisite after it had sunken into itself on the floor.

"What do you mean, Rav?" their mother asked.

"I can't marry her if she's not here."

"You know this is Mira's wedding today, right?" their mother said finally.

He paused. "Oh … but I thought … because …"

"Because?" Mira asked, wondering if it were actually possible that in the preceding months, during every discussion of flowers and cake, Ravi had been making plans of his own, thinking it was all for him, anticipating a joint life without knowing how unlikely it was that he would ever have it.

"Well, because I got to pick the cake and all that," he said. "And because you said I should wear the jubba because it was a special day."

"I'm sorry, Ravi," their mother said, and paused.

It was evident he was struggling to hide a number of emotions, or perhaps struggling to finally take grasp of this inkling he had, that only the smallest, vaguest differences separated the quality of his life from anyone else's. "That's all right," he said.

"But when I get married, who am I going to get married to?" he asked.

It had been a long while since he had asked about a potential marriage. Once, Mira had heard her mother brush off the question and then later that day had seen her crying quietly in front of a picture of Lord Ganesha, whose wedding had also been delayed in perpetuity. Another time, during the malicious flash of Mira's teenage years, Ravi had approached the door of her room and asked how old she thought he should be when he got married. She had said to him only, "Who would marry you?" before getting up from her desk and closing the door. And minutes later, even after her conscience kicked in, she had thought of the horrifying trap of marrying somebody like Ravi, imagined arranging his marriage on false pretences, maybe to a destitute Indian village girl, and realized the idea's cruel impossibility.

"Well, what kind of girl do you want to marry, Rav?" Mira asked, in spite of her instincts, adjusting the collar on the jubba he'd worn for his wedding day.

"A pretty girl," he said, and smiled broadly.

"No ugly girl is marrying my son," said their mother. "She'll *certainly* be beautiful."

"Indian, do you think?" Mira asked him.

"Maybe," he said, considering.

"A girl from India would be just great really," said their mother. "We India-grown girls have some sense."

"I say marry an American and get citizenship," said Mira.

"She should be smart, too," said Ravi.

"Very important. She better have a good job. I wouldn't mind a doctor in the family," their mother added.

"Or some unique profession, like an art dealer ..."

"What is this nonsense, art dealer! Doctor or engineer or maybe business-type. And she must be responsible. Preferably knows how to cook some proper chappatis, unlike this one." Mira's mother pointed her eyebrows at her.

Ravi's bride would perform complex surgeries and make round chappatis and quote Baudelaire, thought Mira. Or she would do none of those things, she would instead twitch her fingers and pace the halls at night, chew the beautiful tangled ends of her hair, and the pair would live in convenient, mirrored ignorance that anything was wrong with the other or with themselves.

Mira took a clean plate from a stack on the counter and slid it into the cake, pulling it up with a heavily iced chunk from the side. She put it within their reach on the counter and dipped her henna-covered fingers into it. They shared the cake in the spacious chrome kitchen, spoke through the blue frosting to imagine Ravi's bride. It was seven in the morning still, and they had yet to adorn Mira's hair with its plait of white jasmine flowers whose petals would drift to her shoulders as she prepared to adjourn to her guilty, happy life, where her only problems would be all-consuming in their triviality. You should cry before your wedding, thought Mira; sentimentality and tradition should gather themselves up, folding and unfolding like the pleats in a sari. You should be teetering, reeling; you should be on the very edge of elation. What she felt instead was a clean absence, a suspension, a sensation she only ever remembered feeling once, on an airplane, where she had bitten into a soft roll the way she bit now into her wedding cake, and because the altitude and roaring engine had overwhelmed her sense of taste, she could perceive only the food's fragile crumb yielding under her teeth.

Ordinary Fears

THEY HAD DRESSED Lala Aunty in a silk sari, which, like Mira's wedding sari, had been purchased on Gerrard Street.

"They were really nice to us at that store," said Mira's mother, "gave us this and that discount — and then we ate at Udupi in Lala's honour —"

"Did you order bad-tasting food in her honour?" Baskar asked, scruffing up the back of her hair with his hand in a claw-shape.

It was too soon for that kind of comment, Mira thought, given that they had just prepared her mother's closest friend for cremation. Now her mother was telling Baskar about it as they sat on the couch and watched *The National* on CBC. She talked right over Peter Mansbridge.

Mira was in the kitchen, watching them over the half-wall between the two rooms. She was sorting Tupperware, matching each container with its dishwasher-warped lid and piling them into the tall cupboard. Ravi sat at the kitchen table, helping. He unhurriedly lifted each item and evaluated it. Mira had gone with her mother and two of Aunty's other friends to dress the body. The girl who worked at the funeral home led them to a room with a plush cherry carpet and two Victorian parlour chairs and a coffin on a stand. She opened up the coffin for them, nodded nervously and respectfully. She was about Mira's age, and later, at home, Mira looked up what series of educational choices someone required to work there. The girl gave them instructions and left them alone. Mira's mother described how Mira had taken out the sari and its blouse from a white plastic bag.

"I didn't know what to do with the bag," Mira said, jumping into their conversation.

Baskar turned to look at her. "Well, you should just have put it down somewhere. On a chair, or on the floor. What does it matter?"

"That's what I did, I put it on the floor near my feet. But then I kept accidentally stepping on it and it would make that rustling plastic bag noise, so I moved it to the floor a little farther away. Then that funeral home girl came in again and she kind of looked at it, like I had littered. I was planning to pick it up when we left."

"Eh, she didn't know which one of you it was. Probably thought it was Anusha. She looks more like a litterer." Baskar got up to bring a bowl of banana chips from the kitchen. He opened the cupboard like it was his house.

"Can I have some?" asked Ravi. Baskar dropped a fistful into one of the Tupperware lids.

"Anusha Aunty kept saying how nice Lala's face looked," said Mira's mother. "I didn't really think it looked that nice. They powdered her face with talc so she barely even looked Indian anymore."

What Mira wanted to talk about was not a plastic bag or Lala Aunty's new, dead, white face, but about what she had seen when they took off the sheet that covered the body. "When we took off the sheet ..." she began.

"Don't tell me you saw her nude," said Baskar.

"No, she was wearing a very modest undergarment," said Mira.

"*Athe*, is what the ladies in India have nicknamed that kind of bra. You know *athe* actually means 'aunty' in Havyaka," said Mira's mother.

"How appropriate," said Mira, "naming a supportive garment after a supportive family member."

"It reminds me of my favourite aunty growing up," said Mira's mother. "She wore one just like that."

They had tried to put the sari blouse on Aunty, but could only get it to fit over one arm. The arms had swollen near the armpits. They had become so enlarged that Mira had a sudden worry that Aunty would expand to completely fill the wooden box. The funeral home girl would open the coffin to inspect the body before setting it aflame, and she would see a rectangular block of flesh in the exact dimensions of the box, bloated like a bowl of pho left too long in water, with eyelids and nostrils and birthmarks embossing it like the sides of dice. One time, on Aunty's instructions, Mira had left dosa batter to ferment in the oven, but used too small a container, and the batter had bulged out and on to the oven floor. When she looked inside the oven, batter was still rising and breaking the surface tension, pouring active and bubbling, pale and alive down the sides of the bowl. Now she wasn't sure she would ever be able to look into such spaces — this included stifling

open ovens, refrigerators before the light clicked on, gas fire-
places, home air vents that seemed to exhale at her, toaster
ovens with their hot red elements, the wooden chest she kept in
the upstairs hallway with tennis balls and bicycle helmets and
badminton racquets — without imagining Aunty's flesh, solid
and liquid at the same time, taking up its hollow space.

Her mother and Anusha lifted the body and Kalpana put
the left sleeve over the hand. Then they switched sides and
Kalpana attempted to manoeuvre the right hand into the right
sleeve, but said it was unnatural. Mira tried, but almost fainted
at having to bend the heavy and inflexible limb into arrangements she'd never seen Aunty maintain while alive. So in the
end, they just tucked the blouse over top of the arm and hid
that side with the sari pleats. Aunty went into the afterlife with
one naked shoulder.

MIRA HAD THE guilty feeling that none of them were being respectful enough, mournful enough. When her father had died,
though she had only been five, there had been whole rooms
in their old house she had avoided, not in fear, but in a suffo-
cating instinct towards reverence. She had not even wanted to
look in those rooms. She did not feel this way now when she
visited Uncle's house, now inhabited solely by him. But she did
feel — looking upon the kitchen stool Lala Aunty had pulled
up to the stove and rested her ample rear on, as she held the
end of a long spoon in a saucepan of milk sweets that needed
endless stirring, her wrist moving as gracefully as Martha
Graham choreography — that all Aunty's furniture had upon
her death turned immediately antique. Belongings she had used
last week now felt like ancient relics.

The news was still on and Baskar kept eating the banana chips and wiping his hand on the sofa. It was possible he had picked that habit up from Ravi, who wiped his own hand on his pant leg a moment later.

The phone rang and Mira answered it and heard Uncle on the other end.

"I can't find the aluminum foil," he said, pronouncing "aluminum" as "al-you-min-ee-um."

"Lala Aunty kept it in that drawer next to the silverware," she told him.

"Oh okay," he said, worriedly. "Will call you back if I can't find it, then?"

"No problem, Uncle."

"Is that Uncle? You say hello for me!" Baskar called out.

"Baskar is there?" Uncle asked. Her mother and Baskar had first met at one of Lala Aunty's dinner parties, and it had taken her twenty years to agree to date him.

"Yes, we're just watching the news," said Mira.

"Good good news, no, not good news, but you know. Will let you go," Uncle finished and hung up.

Mira put the phone back in its receiver on the counter. "I am worried," she said, watching her mother take Baskar's oily hand, "that Uncle just spends all day going around the house and turning the lights on and off."

While travelling from her downtown apartment to her mother's house, she had seen a man on the subway, sitting just in front of her. She faced forward and he faced sideways, according to the perpendicular arrangement of seats. Upon hearing a noise of moving paper, she looked up from her novel to see the man holding a newspaper up so it covered his face.

He seemed to be reading it, until she saw him turn the page so violently its pages flapped and snapped in defiance of their natural creases. The side of his face was visible, and it squeezed together as though around a pivot, all features converging at his harsh purple mouth. It was obvious that in holding the newspaper he was both trying very hard to control his twitching, and also to conceal himself. His face loosened again and he muttered, and then repeated all three actions — flapping, squeezing, muttering — and continued repeating them until he finally exited at Bloor. This is what it was to try and hold yourself together, Mira thought. This is what grief would look like embodied — repetitive and beyond restraint.

BASKAR PUT HIS wet mouth over the spot where her mother's shirt left her shoulder, an unrefined kiss, and Mira thought of how his breath smelled like dog food, literally, like the smell that inhabits a house with a dog, and which the owner no longer notices.

The television showed images of filled hospital beds and packed ERs.

"Oh, there's York Central — no, it's some other place, never mind," said Mira's mother. She shooed Baskar away, and Mira wondered if she noted the smell of his saliva on her skin. York Central was the hospital where her mother worked, in the health records department.

"Crowded, eh?" said Baskar, wiping his mouth with the back of his hand.

"Uncle said when Lala went by ambulance, they got priority to go in but still had to wait to see a doctor. I'm not saying it would have saved her necessarily, but who knows?"

"Time is of the essence when you're dealing with heart trouble," said Baskar.

On the TV, they announced the changes to the Ontario Health Insurance Plan.

"OHIP doesn't even give us eye exam coverage anymore," said Mira. She'd been seeing floaters in her eyes lately, and read that it was a sign of old age. She was twenty-eight.

"Not a problem for me — 20/20!" said Baskar.

"Hmm," said Mira's mother. "You and Rav should see a movie together," she said suddenly to Baskar.

"Which movie will we watch?" said Ravi, who joined them now in the living room. He chose the dark green loveseat and leaned diagonally into it.

"We will one of these days, but got a lot of stuff to take care of at work. Toner doesn't make itself."

"All right, Baskar-the-Grouch," she said. Baskar crunched messily through his banana chips, and Mira reminded herself that he was nobody important to her.

Now somebody interviewed a doctor over the backdrop of a busy waiting room. Mira surveyed the people, mostly elderly couples. In each pair, Mira tried to guess who had the ailment. While the doctor waxed on about health care privatization, a couple stood up together as they were called inside. They held hands and shared a side-to-side gait, stocky figures and lumpy faces. She imagined Baskar and her mother like this in thirty years, shuffling together with twin hunched backs. She added Ravi alongside them in the image, a third bump in the row.

After her mother had first started dating Baskar, Mira had asked her, over the phone one night when H had to work late, what had made her contact a man who had initially so repelled her. Because it was *she* who had contacted him and not the other way around. "Oh, Lala kept mentioning him, kept pushing him on me," her mother said, which wasn't the most glowing reason, and wasn't enough for Mira, and so her mother asked her if she remembered the time they had all gone to the mall together to buy Uncle a birthday present. Mira did remember the story her mother told her, of how she had forgotten her purse inside somewhere and only realized it after they'd gone out the building doors, so she told Ravi to wait there on the street while she and Mira ran to find it. When they returned — the purse safely under her mother's arm — Ravi was standing next to a man. They were roughly equal in bulk, with identical dark hair colours and wearing similarly puffy jackets. The two of them looked the same; the man could have been Ravi in fifteen years, but the man had dirt all over his face and big, flaking hands that held a piece of cardboard with green marker words saying, "Need money for food." Instead of the word "FOUR" he'd written the number "4," slashing it across the cardboard. "Ravi, come back here, what are you doing?" her mother said, and from her tone he must have known he had done something wrong, so he made that expression of his where the whites of his eyes stretched high up, like Dracula's, and he'd said, "Making friends, Mom."

"This is what someone does when he has no proper role models," Mira's mother said to her. She told her that when they went home after that, she had prepared dinner for the two of them — Mira had gone home to her own apartment — and tried to watch some sitcom on television, but she grew tired of explaining the jokes.

So, love having come and gone in the first third of her life,

Mira's mother replaced it by phoning Lala Aunty and asking for Baskar's number.

"*ATHE*, FUNNY HOW you've reminded me of her," Mira's mother said. "She wore those funny old bras, big enough to be shirts of their own. So big it showed under the sari blouse. You know what we called that, when the bra showed? We said Sunday was longer than Monday." She rarely spoke about her childhood, and did it now with a voice of confession. "My favourite aunty, she was. Four decades ago. God, I am old now."

"Old is gold," said Baskar.

"I used to sit in her clothing cupboard, which smelled like roses." She told them how she had watched her aunty spit out the window (she had acquired from her husband a love of paan-chewing) and pull up the hem of her faded cotton slip to kick away ants.

That other aunty had washed her bras in a reservoir with hard navy soap, then left it to dry in that mirage-inducing weather, up there on the clothing line like fat white gulls.

"We used that clothesline as a badminton net," Mira's mother said. In her childhood, she had lived in a valley outside the city of Kasargod.

Every other week, Mira and her mother played badminton against H and Baskar in the community centre's open badminton hours. The first time they'd gone, her mother had scoffed at the yellow plastic birdies they provided, which she said had no weight to them. The birdies flew flimsily across the gym, embedded themselves in the wire mesh around the light fixtures, went too easily over the back boundary line. "Out!" Baskar kept saying. "Out, again!" After that she had gone to Canadian

Tire and bought two tubes of Yonex white goose-feather birdies with heads made of Portuguese cork, and she and Mira hammered them relentlessly at Baskar while H laughed good-naturedly and Baskar pretended to cower under his racquet.

Those feather birdies were the kind her badminton-obsessed relatives used to buy — of course, they'd called them shuttle-cocks then but Mira's mother had dropped that term because Baskar kept saying it suggestively.

"At home," she said now, "I spent so many afternoons watching my uncles play badminton." Mira had seen these uncles play, on a long ago visit to India. They played shirtless and with their lungis tied up to expose their active knees. After that, the aunties would play, using slightly older racquets and the birdies that were missing a feather or two. They wore their floral, cotton nightdresses, which swirled and collected the red dust around their anklet-wearing ankles. The uncles played with wordless intensity, hitting net kills and only speaking to call out the score, but the aunties used underhanded swings and took breaks, approaching the clothesline to gossip through the gaps between fragrant, billowing saris.

"My aunty had a quick, low serve that fell just over the service line every time. All the opponent aunties would say, 'Waah!'" ("Waah" did not mean anything, but was one of the preferred exclamations of aunties.) She told them her aunty had stopped playing when she became sick and began to spend her time lying on the cot in her bedroom, complaining of throat ulcers and holding scraps of old fabric up to her face to blot her nosebleeds.

When the other uncles and aunties had gone inside for tea, Mira's mother and her small cousins would race to the court

— which wasn't really a court but a space of hard dirt used for drying areca nuts in hotter months — and select the oldest racquets and barest birdies from the bucket where they were kept. They'd choose their partners and organize mini-tournaments. The racquets were so old their splintery wooden handles had to be smoothed down occasionally with a bit of sandpaper reserved for that purpose, and if an ambitious player tried to smash the birdie too viciously, it would catch in the racquet's grid, spreading the strings until they no longer held their perfect squares.

"I was playing badminton when she died," she said. "I was winning my game, partnered with one of my girl cousins, against two of my brothers." One of her brothers had just accidentally hit a birdie up on the roof, when another girl cousin proclaimed the death of the aunty. The girl stood on the marble front step of one wing of the house and all the children dashed towards her just as they'd run to the badminton court before.

Mira's mother did not run with them. She went up the side stairs to the terrace and then up another level to the highest point in the house. "I was sure it was there somewhere, that birdie." She climbed out the window, on to the roof extension, and stood up, bare feet gripping the crimson slate tiles. On the roof, she saw not only that one birdy, but dozens of lost birdies laid out over the slate like fallen snow, except at that point she'd never seen snow, so couldn't make that comparison and thought only of feathers, of birds retiring their tired wings and resting their tired limbs on the rooftop, unreachable by even the tallest cousin.

She looked down to the gull-like undergarments hanging between saris on the makeshift badminton net, and yelled,

"Athe!" "I didn't know if I was yelling about underwear or my aunty!" she laughed. Nobody had heard her anyway.

Maybe *I* could gather those birdies, she thought after a minute, and stepped forward. Her foot slipped right over the wet moss that coated the roof, and she landed hard on her side. She seized the edge of a beam to keep from falling. If she had fallen then, she would probably have died, knocking her head on roof tiles, cement corners, and then the hard ground.

Eventually, she managed to slither back to the window. She never went back up to collect her bounty of birdies, though she knew she could have bartered them for any number of store-bought apples and clementines. "That's how I got my fear of heights," she said. High places terrified her after that: roofs, ladders, tops of coconut trees, and all the famous suspension bridges she would have opportunity to visit later in life. Mira had assumed her mother had simply always been afraid of heights. "My relatives always wondered what had triggered that phobia of mine, when I had always been an adventurer." They missed learning of the reason, because they were inside her aunty's bedroom. They opened the dark, sweet-smelling cupboard to find a sheet to cover her, and said, "Throat ulcer, must be," and repeated those words for the weeks that followed. It was only now because of her job at the hospital that Mira's mother realized her aunty must have died of undiagnosed throat cancer from eating all that paan, which was stuffed with sugar-preserved rose petals and carcinogens.

The most startling to Mira was the very last part of the story — which her mother told as an offhanded coda — how, after the aunty's death, they moved her husband into a different room, already inhabited by three single uncles and an older cousin. A newly married uncle moved into aunty's old room with his wife, who acquired the old cupboard like a hermit crab.

BASKAR GROANED WHEN the phone rang the second time. Mira answered it, and it was Uncle again.

"Hope I am not disturbing you," Uncle said.

"No, Uncle, not at all. Did you find the foil?"

"Yes, I had found it in that drawer you mentioned, but see, I have used it all up. But you know, it is night and I am quite concerned at driving nowadays during nighttime, now that I'm an oldie. Otherwise, I might go to the store …"

Mira doubted that he would need foil so urgently, but said, "Actually, Uncle, I'm positive Aunty kept more foil in the basement. More everything, really. Foil, Ziploc bags, Saran Wrap, and all that."

"In the basement?"

"In the crawl space," she said. Many times, she had seen Lala Aunty emerging from the tiny door with materials for food storage.

"Oh, but my arthritis. I don't know how I will get it out from there," Uncle said.

Baskar began massaging her mother's shoulders. Mira turned away.

"Uncle, let me just drive over there and get it out for you," she said.

"I can go, Mira, if he needs help," called her mother.

Baskar groaned.

"I'll go," she said to her mother, covering the receiver.

"Are you sure? That isn't necessary, only that I wish I had more foil," Uncle said.

"I'll go too," said Ravi.

"No, Ravi, you don't have to go, stay with us," said Mira's mother.

"Fifteen minutes, I'll be there," Mira said to Uncle. From the kitchen counter, she took her keys, put her shoes on, opened the door, and waved at her mother, who was getting up to put away the banana chip bowl, and Baskar, who turned the television off and lay over the sofa like a lumpy slipcover. Ravi imitated him, stretching out over the loveseat and yawning, hanging his head over one of the armrests.

She drove down Highway 7, imagining what it would be like to be afraid of driving at night. There *was* a sense of danger in sitting inside a quiet, dark machine, rolling along the dark city streets, the lights of passing cars white and magnified, stretching into long cones. Her night vision was good, but still she was sometimes tricked by glare on glass. And her father had died in a car accident, and it occurred to her that she didn't even know what kind of car he had driven. Toyota Tercel? Pontiac 6000? Her brother, ironically, was a skilled, brave driver, untouched by those associations. Baskar had said there was a posting for a delivery driver job at his company, and that he could give them Ravi's resumé and a recommendation. She hoped he would follow through. Lala Aunty would have made sure he did.

Reaching Uncle's driveway, she could see his shadow travelling around from the yellow square of one window to the next. She watched him for a minute before getting out of the car.

The broken front door had been labelled in his block letters, "Lift door to open." She reminded herself to see about getting it fixed, took off her shoes, and rang the bell. The outline of Uncle's body moved behind the narrow block glass by the door.

"Mira, here you are. You drove safe?" Uncle took her hand and brought her inside. "Do you want an apple to eat? Or an orange? I have both. Or maybe, no, maybe used up the apple already."

"That's all right, Uncle. I'll just run downstairs and get you the foil?" then felt a little guilty, as she had nowhere to get to.

"Come have an orange with me," he said again, and so she agreed. On the kitchen table and counters and chairs and any other available surface, Uncle had placed newly cooked dishes of food. Mysore pak crumbled beautifully in cupcake wrappers, and steamed vegetables held their colour under the kitchen pot lights. Innumerable curries — made with rich beet root and translucent cabbage and soft, formless eggplant — surrounded them. She isolated and identified the aromas: fresh chopped coriander leaves, roasted mustard seeds, asafoetida warming in oil. The reason no apples remained was that they filled a fruit salad, mixed with quartered purple grapes, narrow coral-coloured slices of papaya, and white cubed pears, all fattened and flavoured with ice cream and mango pulp. She hadn't known Uncle could cook. It seemed it was his own kind of mourning, a hunger tangibly replaced.

Uncle gave Mira a tangerine and she peeled it in one long strip, adding it to a vast heap of peelings already dampening an old *Toronto Star*. She ate the sections and watched him wrap a dish in his last piece of foil.

Then down into the basement she went, down unfinished wooden stairs she felt she might fall through. The basement was predictably cavernous, but also like a split-level within a split-level. Mira had never been inside the crawl space, which spanned half the basement. She knelt in her jeans on the cold concrete and stared at the door.

In the rectangular black space, the ceiling was so low she would have to stay kneeling. She scanned the area before entering. The crawl space didn't have additional light, so she could only see its contents from the glow of the rest of the basement, which didn't reflect too well. The foil was visible in the far back corner, maybe ten metres away, in long narrow boxes with glistening metal teeth. The room smelled of camphor and cloves and of dust, dust which coated her hands as she touched the floor. She could make out old clothes in leaning piles, drooping candles, pieces of garden rope, Dasara dolls with human faces, and one large carved wooden chest. For a second, she didn't think she'd have the nerve to enter; she would have to return up to Uncle and pretend there had never been any foil at all.

What made her go in anyway was the vague thought that her fears and her family's fears, too, were only the usual ones — small spaces, heights, driving in the dark, dying alone. Mira pointed her body in the direction of the aluminum foil, partly sure that she wouldn't be able to turn backwards. And then she was crawling in the crawl space, and could hear Uncle as he paced upstairs from room to room in his rendition of grief's repeating pattern: adjusting the lighting, phoning the only people he knew, cooking perfect versions of all the mediocre foods that his wife had once made.

Sublimation

ON THE FLIGHT to India, Mira spoke to her baby as though the baby would understand.

"Tungsten is the metal with the highest melting point," she said, adjusting and tucking a blanket and then pattering the tips of her fingers lightly on her son's arm. "The only letter of the alphabet that doesn't appear on the periodic table is the letter *J*."

Maybe this wasn't how one should talk to a baby, but chatting kept him quiet, and the trip to India took fifteen hours, not even including the six-hour layover at Heathrow, where she had sleeplessly pushed the stroller through Harrod's and purchased an expensive tin of hard candy, which she had eaten piece by piece over the second leg of the trip, trying to guess each flavour by taste alone. The journey had nearly ended, and they had caught their connection to Kerala. The baby had been awake since they'd left Mumbai. Every time she heard her son begin to whimper, Mira had a dipping feeling of anxiety in her chest. He might not ever stop crying. They might escort her off the plane. She'd discovered the best way to quiet the baby was to ease into mild, one-sided conversation. Naturally, she began to run out of things to say. She had started by telling stories — *The Three Little Pigs*, *Little Red Riding Hood*, even a French play she had once memorized, *Le Cerf-Volant Magique*, though she'd learned these stories so long ago that she kept forgetting the orders of events. Since the baby had been born, she and H had been stocking up on children's books. The baby's room already had a bookshelf. Flipping through them, she was a little surprised to realize she didn't enjoy all the truth-bending in children's literature: the personification of animals and suspension of disbelief. She wanted her child to read about the real world, however simplified and beautified; she preferred to find the wonder in things that were actual and concrete, things she could see for herself.

Mira wasn't a natural mother. She was self-conscious about baby talk, hadn't yet mastered the cooing glissandos of motherese. It was H who fed the baby with spoon helicopters, whirring mashed bananas in figure eights through the air as the baby jiggled in anticipation.

While pregnant, H had suggested that she should have nude photos taken. She had thought he was joking, but he wasn't. Mira declined, but after that, every time she showered, she stopped to look at her unclothed body in the bathroom mirror. Her body looked like ovoids overlapping, burgeoning with heavy, fluid weight. It was gorgeous but foreign. Though she could take folic acid and refrain from drinking, she felt she had very little effect on what would develop inside of her. She read books full of pregnancy words — ovum, pablum, womb, embryo — that sounded like words spoken underwater, or like the suction of an emptying drain. At the pharmacy where she worked, her stomach was hidden behind the counter; the regulars must have just thought her face was getting fatter. When the baby was born, people said it looked like her, but she couldn't see it.

She had brought the baby to India for his *Namkaran*, his naming ceremony. She and H had planned to travel to India for their honeymoon, but they had postponed it after she had been hired for a job right after her graduation from pharmacy school. H had fewer holidays now, and would meet her there in two weeks for the ceremony. Secretly she hoped to grow used to the baby in this time, and that he would latch on to her during H's brief absence.

Flight attendants slowed their carts near her seat, offering beverages and extra blankets.

"His eyes are so big," one of them said, an Indian girl with a neatly cultivated British accent. "And he's so well-behaved. He's barely even cried!" She widened her own dark eyes and shook her head at the baby, then moved to the next row. Mira mumbled about melting points and precipitates, and the baby intoned a series of pitches and exposed his gums. She hoped that the baby's first word would be scientific and impressive, maybe "amnicentesis."

The plane landed, and the baby began to cry from pressure in his ears. Mira gave him his pacifier. As soon as the plane stopped, the air conditioning turned off, and the temperature inside the cabin began to rise. There was some mix-up at the gates, and it took another hour before they let them exit the aircraft. Passengers stood in the aisles and complained loudly about their connections. They pulled bags from overhead bins, and as a man opened one compartment, a backpack fell out and landed on an elderly woman's neck. She began to shout at the man about how she was going to sue him, trying to get his name. Finally the doors opened, and the crowd pulled forward.

The heat in the Mangalore airport felt nearly unbearable. It had been more than two decades since she had last been to India, and she had no memory of this humidity, how drops of perspiration could replenish themselves continuously on the surface of her skin. Her handkerchief grew damp from constantly wiping her forehead. She was still wearing clothes appropriate for the Canadian winter and ended up stripping off the layers of sweaters and balancing them on top of a cart. The baggage belt moved slowly, in stops and starts, and Mira placed herself right at its opening, worried somebody would make off with her luggage. Finally she spotted her suitcase with several others, already off the belt. A malnourished, dark-skinned employee in an olive green uniform was perched on top of it.

"*Adhu enna* suitcase," Mira said in her faltering Havyaka. Speaking this language was even more difficult than speaking to the baby. The man smirked and insisted that she let him pull her suitcase so she could handle the stroller. She agreed after hesitation, because her mother had warned her against these fellows — "coolies," she had called them. It was mere metres to the arrivals area, but Mira didn't have the energy to argue with the man. She tipped him with her only bill, twenty Canadian dollars, worth nearly a thousand rupees.

"Mira!" she heard a voice call out, and turned to see her mother's sister Jayashree skittering towards her. She looked like a narrower and tanner version of her mother, her bones bending out at awkward angles, her shawl tied behind her in a firm knot. Her feet, encased in brown rubber sandals, made loud brushing and smacking noises against the floor. Her brother Ram, tall and golden, jogged up behind her.

"Jayashree Aunty!" Mira faked energy, reaching out her arms shyly to embrace her aunt. Ram shook her hand up and down. He was one of the few men who looked appealing in a moustache. It animated his face, fluttering as he spoke.

"Flight and all was good?" he asked, waving away the employees who hovered around waiting to see if they needed help loading. He spoke in English. Her mother's family mostly spoke in Havyaka, but for her sake they would flit in and out of English, and sometimes Hindi, by accident.

Jayashree cooed at the baby, picking him from his stroller and kissing his cheeks. She tossed him up and down and handed him to her brother. Ram held him up in front of him, his laugh wonderfully resonant, but then stopped abruptly. He said something quickly and quietly to Jayashree that Mira didn't catch.

"*Chelo*. Come, come, I have a Jeep waiting," Ram said. "We'll go direct to *Ajjimane*, no stops, unless should we go to temple?"

"Ayyyo, they haven't taken bath," said Jayashree, hitting him on the arm, and he hit his own forehead with his palm.

"What am I thinking?" he thundered, and he ushered them quickly to the waiting vehicle.

They clambered into the back of the Jeep, lined with a bench on each side for them to sit. The back door was completely open, with no glass, and Mira clung tightly to the baby with one arm and with the other hand she clutched a leather loop on the ceiling. She had changed into a light cotton sari in the airplane bathroom (a feat in the confined space) but since she didn't wear them very often she struggled with trying to keep the *pallu* in place. Hurtling over the unpaved roads, the Jeep made too much noise to talk, so Mira stared out the back.

Kerala was nothing like Mumbai. She knew Mumbai from documentaries where she had seen the old streets and the filth that covered them, the humans and dogs starving openly under Bollywood billboards. Uncle had told her that the city had its moments of beauty; he described schoolchildren in navy flooding the streets after classes, flowing en masse under a radiant blue sky cleared, for a moment, of its smog. He said that on some days, the scent of vendors roasting spiced peanuts or sweet ears of corn could actually overpower the city's human stench. Palm trees surrounded the concrete buildings in lines, leaves flapping under the weight of rain in monsoon.

But in Kerala, she saw no tall buildings breaking the sky. The road on which they drove meandered atop a mountain, and on each side Mira saw brilliant green rice fields divided into squares, cushioned in knee-deep royal blue water, reflecting an angled image of their Jeep as they passed. Children ran half-naked but healthy alongside them, rolling rusty bicycle tires with sticks, as though from a different era. Cows stood stoically and emitted loud "ommbayyy" sounds, their suede sides shuddering with the vibration. Their vehicle passed the occasional house, their plaster walls painted deep blood red. The soil here contained iron, turning it rust-coloured, like powdered tempera paint; it stained the children's feet as they flapped hot against the road. Until Mira had seen Kerala, she had never thought colours existed with such brilliance. Their hues appeared richer in Kerala, saturated, as though if you touched the plants or objects or even people, the pigment would rub off on your hand. It made Mira think of the bright wetness of Bingo markers. She felt like a character in *The Wizard of Oz*, landed in this Technicolor place where every red resembled rubies, where her own tears might be blue instead of clear and where, when a woman blushed, she felt it as if in her own skin.

The Jeep turned off the road at what seemed an unmarked spot in a field. Mira couldn't see anything that might have signaled the entrance to the home where her mother had grown up; Ram and Jayashree knew by heart where to tell the driver to turn, and suddenly a road into a valley emerged. They disappeared down the road, easing bumpily down the steep incline, rocks flying out from under the wheels. At the bottom of the road was a metal gate painted orange. A skinny cousin stood balanced atop the gate and unlatched it, swinging along with it to let them through, whooping at them and waving.

"*Nilsi … nilsi*," Ram yelled back to them as he leapt from the stopped Jeep onto the dry ground. *Nilsi* meant wait, Mira remembered, and she stayed where she was, unsure. "The bitches are ferocious," Ram shouted to her, and Mira startled at the language before realizing he meant the guard dogs that were running wildly around the property, jumping and snapping their jaws. Two uncles helped Ram round up the dogs and tie them safely away. Relatives began spilling from the house like ants, crowding around and opening the door and taking her suitcase and the baby easily from her. Three small children she didn't recognize hugged her legs and took her hands and pulled her out. They chattered at her, calling her three different things — *Akka*, *Athige*, and *Chikamma* — and she struggled to remember what each one meant. *Akka* was what you called your older sister or a sister-type, *Athige* was your older female cousin, and she couldn't recall about the last one; really, none of these relationships made sense to her anyway. Luckily, since she was older than all the children, she could just call them by name and didn't need to bother with any of the titles. She worried about meeting more of her aunts and uncles and deciding how to refer to them.

The children gave her a tour, a boy of maybe thirteen named Gautham proudly translating some of it into English. Mira's mother's house consisted of three buildings forming a U shape. Her grandparents had died years ago, but fifteen people still lived in the house permanently, and Gautham told her they always had at least five visitors. Mira's grandfather had built a schoolhouse up the hill and all his children except Mira's mother had become teachers who hiked up there every day in their beaten sandals.

Two of the house's buildings were painted glossy red, and the third, newer structure had been recently whitewashed. There were slate roofs, and the windows didn't have glass, but instead had peacock blue shutters they could shut at night. The children led her from room to room so quickly that her sock feet kept sliding across the white marble floors (she had been wearing sneakers under her sari and left them at the entrance but kept her socks on, not thinking of how much dust they would collect). Stopping in front of one closed door, Gautham motioned for her to look inside, and Mira pushed it open to find a modern toilet. Even though there was a bucket of water instead of toilet paper and water had been splashed liberally all over the room, Mira was impressed. She had dreaded crouching with the last of her pregnancy belly hanging over that dark hole in the ground.

"Mira Athige, I hear you are a scientist?" Gautham asked shyly, lingering as the other children dispersed.

"You could say that," Mira smiled at him, thinking about how much younger children seemed in India than North America.

"I, too, am a scientist." Gautham looked up at Mira to judge her reaction.

"Is that right?" asked Mira. "A biologist? Chemist? Physicist?"

"All of them, Mira Athige. I am all three. And which are you?"

"A pharmacist, actually. Lots of chemistry involved, and biology, too."

"Then tomorrow you must show me an experiment!" Gautham said.

He left Mira to freshen up, giving her a thin cotton towel and a perfumed bar of Mysore sandalwood soap wrapped in lavender paper. The scent of sandalwood soap was what made it real: she was in India, the country where her parents had spent their youths, the country that had become almost entirely irrelevant once they had left for Canada. After the birth of her children, Mira's mother had called home maybe twice a year, even when the internet made the phone calls cheaper. Next to the water-damaged bathroom mirror, a fist-sized pregnant spider crawled thin-leggedly down the wall, and Mira let out a soft cackle, drying her face and heading downstairs.

The aunties invited her to sit on the marble floor, handing her a plate neatly arranged with crisp plantain chips and bright carrot halwa. Her great aunt added a dry *holige* to her plate, the regional specialty, a paper thin roti made from lentils and jaggery. She dabbed it liberally with ghee, and Mira put one hand to her stomach and the other hand up to fake protest, as was the usual routine, pantomiming her need to slim down. Another elderly aunty served her coffee, *caapi*, in a stainless steel cup. She brought it out with another cup and poured the milky liquid back and forth between the two to let it cool. Mira pushed the milk skin aside and sipped the coffee, tasted cardamom and cloves.

Two young girls had claimed the baby, undressing him down to his diaper and letting him crawl freely around the marble floor. One tried to feed him rice pudding.

Mira ate slowly, trying to identify the people in the room who chattered to and around her. She would never learn all their names; when she guessed she was often wrong. Her mother had four sisters and four brothers, but one sister lived in Mumbai and would be arriving the following week; one brother had recently moved to Dubai, and another lived in Australia. She recognized her eldest aunt, Laxmi, a silent, serious woman who wore a wrinkled sari tied in a no-nonsense knot at the back. Despite having two children, she was wiry and with muscular arms that made Mira embarrassed of her own body's descent into softness. Jayashree and another sister looked exactly the same, so when she wasn't sure she called them both *Dodamma*, the word for aunts older than your mother. She called Ram, who had met her at the airport, by the title *Dodappa*. Laxmi and her husband Krishna had two children, Gautham and a girl who looked like pictures she had seen of her mother as a child. This girl came to Mira and told her that people often asked her if she were Shilpa's daughter, and so she and Mira were somewhat like sisters. But we have never met before, Mira thought, but would not, of course, say to the child who smiled widely and wore a tiny gold nose ring. Jayashree also had two children, a stylish teenage girl who wore jeans with her short selwar top, and a younger boy who carried his cricket bat wherever he went. The other sister had only one boy, who spoke so quickly that Mira couldn't recognize a single word. The youngest brother's children were loud and numerous; there were at least four, with alliterative names that Mira could not distinguish from one another. Ram had only recently married, so he had no children. Mira could not remember which wife matched which husband, and she did not even begin to figure out her mother's cousins, eight of them, who lived in a house on the other side of the valley.

She tried to hold conversations with people. She thought of her father in this exact situation more than thirty years earlier, when he had come to meet his bride's family. The volume and rapidity of her father's words had often escalated as he spoke. Lala Aunty had once described her father's voice as thunderous, but that did not capture the way Mira remembered it, because thunder was only a consequence of lightning, but her father's voice had been a force, a prime mover; when people spoke to him they waited for the pauses of his breaths. Growing up in Mumbai he had learned to shout over street noise, to haggle violently with salespeople, to give roaring speeches as Head Boy of his school. He had spoken Hindi as a child, so here even he must have felt stifled, as Mira was, by the unfamiliar language. Even for those who spoke English, she had to slow her words and repeat them.

Krishna, Gautham's father, came to sit next to Mira and asked, "*Magana kannige enthathu?*" Mira smiled hopelessly at him, shrugging her shoulders and looking at Gautham.

Gautham translated, "His eyes, what is wrong?" pointing at the baby.

"Oh, nothing's wrong with his eyes," Mira said.

"*Mathe, awana bayi?*"

"His mouth is fine, too," answered Mira, understanding that one. She thought of how she had whispered the story of Little Red Riding Hood to her baby on the plane and suppressed an uneasy urge to laugh.

Krishna stood abruptly and went to speak with Ram.

THAT NIGHT MIRA went to sleep under a mosquito net, on blankets that smelled like incense, spread over the cool marble floor, with the baby lying quietly beside her. Frogs warbled whimsically outside the house, and she could hear singing voices from the nearby mosque. When her eyes adjusted to the darkness she saw geckos creep out from behind light fixtures, trapping insects with their tongues.

"Geckos stick to the walls by intermolecular forces between their footpads and the surfaces. London dispersion forces," she said to the baby before going to sleep. She wished H were there, so she could talk to him, so they could share the foreign feeling of being in India, or imagine what lives they would have had if their parents had never left, or make gentle fun of the relatives, smothering their laughs in the fragrant blankets.

She awoke to the clang of pots being washed at the side of the house and a bucket clattering and splashing down into the well. The sun had just risen, lighting the room in stripes of orange. She added the ten-hour time difference to the time on her watch, estimating it to be around six. She took the baby and checked the bathroom, but it was occupied, so she gathered her clothes and towel and went to use the old bathhouse in the garden.

It was more a jungle than a garden. The family grew mango and coconut and areca-nut and banana trees, spreading them across the acres and acres of their land. One of the children had told her yesterday that a monkey lived in the mango grove, as well as a family of peacocks that they often saw drinking water from the reservoir. Mira stepped barefoot across a path of stones to reach the bathhouse. She found Ram headed in the opposite direction, his hair freshly wet.

"Good morning!" said Mira.

"Ahh, *meevale hovuthe*? You are taking bath?"

"*Appu, appu.*" Mira nodded vigorously and then felt silly.

Ram's face became serious, and he clutched Mira's arm. "Your boy, something is wrong."

"No, he's fine. He slept nearly straight through the night."

"Something is wrong. Krishna has informed me. I will do healing for him, don't worry," Ram assured her, and continued back to the house.

Mira wished again that H were there. The family was boisterous, and caring despite having only seen her twice in her life. Her mother had told her that her brother and brother-in-law practised homeopathic healing. Ram had treated her menstrual cramps before she had left for Canada; Krishna had lessened the frequency of his daughter's epileptic seizures; together they had eased the suffering from Mira's grandmother's arthritic wrists. They were *healers*, even more powerful than doctors, but she wanted to tell them that nothing was wrong with her baby. No, she did not quite know this baby yet, and had no control over what had developed inside her, how the cells had divided, over what shaped the convolutions of his delicate brain, and this was her worst worry — that she might raise a baby like her brother, a changeling whose true identity might always be the most painful kind of enigma.

RETURNING AFTER HER bath, she found Gautham in the God room. Mira carefully stepped into the doorway and folded her legs to join her nephew cross-legged on the floor. They chanted mantras together in Sanskrit. The boy sipped droplets of water from a small brass spoon. Gautham asked for the *karpura*, camphor, and Mira broke a crumbling piece from a large block, placing it on a gold-plated dish with a handle and using a long match to light it on fire. Mira lifted her fingers to his nose and inhaled the sharp remnant smell of the camphor. Her mother kept containers of it in her basement prayer room at home, lighting it each evening as she and Ravi said their prayers. Gautham moved the plate in circles in the air, speaking in a monotone chant under his breath, and Mira could tell that the boy didn't even need to think about his actions, perfectly internalized.

Mira picked up Gautham's wilted paper copy of the mantra, which the boy kept in front of him even though he didn't need it, and read the words she hadn't ever seen in print, "*Om Bhur Buvaha Suvaha ...*" The left side of the page had the translation: *Om — The original sound, from which all sound originates; Bhur — The physical world; Bhuvah — The mental world; Suvah — The spiritual world. Om Thath Savithur Varenyam, Bhargo Devasya Dheemahi, Dhiyo Yonaha Prachodayath ... You, Lord, the Sun, the Creator, the Sustainer, you are power, love, illumination, and divine grace of universal intelligence. We pray for the divine light to illumine our minds.*

Mira chanted the words as though it were the first time, and thought that she might teach her own baby this someday, the words of the *Gayathri Mantra*, the rhythmic pace of a prayer chant, how to rest on the consonants and aspirate the *B*s.

Gautham used a rag to wipe dark spilled dots of lamp oil from the Lord's altar. Mira opened the dish of camphor again and broke off another piece.

"Take this," she said, placing it in Gautham's bony hand. "Keep it there on the windowsill. And check on it, maybe once a day. An experiment." He nodded solemnly and did as Mira had instructed.

"SHALL WE GO to town?" Ram asked one day as they stood for breakfast. "You must be wanting to shop." Mira agreed and Ram drove her to the Kasargod city centre in his white Maruti car. Mira had initially planned to buy H a pair of Bata shoes — "Bata, the world at your feet," he would quote, while proclaiming them the softest and most durable of the footwear market — and she had made a note of his shoe size before leaving home. But when they arrived in the city, she couldn't help but be drawn to Malabar Gold, the tallest building in Kasargod. Her father had once bought her mother a set of diamonds here. She decided she would purchase for H a piece of jewellery, something modest (lest he make one of his Liberace jokes), perhaps a wedding ring, since they had never bothered with bands, or a watch (he had wanted a Rolex, not realizing how much they cost until he looked it up online and said he would buy a counterfeit in India instead). Mira and Ram entered the store, feeling a cool air conditioned breeze. Deeply tanned employees moved over the burgundy carpets, carrying black trays with lemonade in paper cups, which they offered to Mira but she declined because the water hadn't been boiled. The employees wore crisp, white uniforms, a colour of white that barely existed in the India her parents had known, where teeth turned yellow-red from chewing betel nut, writing paper had a bluish newsprint tint. Mira sat on a plush red stool and pointed at items in locked glass cases. Men with oiled, parted hair brought her purple velvet boxes, and she shook her head at dozens of selections, pausing to weigh them in her hands, holding one up against another, impressing the men with her perfect English but letting Ram bargain in Havyaka as they quoted prices, to avoid being charged extra. She chose a watch with a sleek mesh strap, not too bulky, and — though she knew gold shouldn't be an impulse buy — she impulsively purchased a thin bangle for the baby's pudgy wrist. It was worth making the comparison: when you purchased a gift for a grown person or slightly older child, you considered the recipient's personality and preferences, whereas with a baby you considered only your own adult opinion, and functionality, how it would fit and for how long.

AFTER DINNER ON the night before H's arrival, Krishna and Ram approached Mira.

"There's nothing wrong with the baby," Mira said, trying not to sound defensive. She held the baby in her arms for the first time in days. The aunties and girls had grown fond of carrying him around with them or letting him play in the kitchen as they cooked and gossiped. Her great aunt liked to keep the baby with her while she slept. "We just had a checkup before we came here, his eyes and ears, everything; he's fine."

She could tell the men didn't catch all of her words, but Ram, the one with the better English, said quietly, "It is not his eyes. It is his mind."

It is his mind — she thought how terrible it is that there exist phrases, unremarkable and unbeautiful, that upon hearing you immediately memorize.

"What do you think is wrong with him?" she asked.

"It is not for-sure. He might be just-fine." He compounded his words and Mira would have found this endearing in another conversation. "But is there not something amiss in his reaction?" Ram said. He tried to get the baby's attention. He motioned for Mira to try, and Mira noticed for the first time that the baby wouldn't meet her eyes. Did babies know to look you in the eye?

"He quiets when I talk to him," Mira said. Ram just nodded.

Mira felt tears come to her eyes, though she knew this was an error, that her uncles were merely making guesses based on what they knew of her brother. It wasn't hereditary, what Ravi had. It was possible that her baby just didn't like her well enough to pay much attention to her.

"*Koogadda*." Krishna spoke for the first time, *don't cry*, touching Mira's arm.

"After *Namkaran* ceremony, we can perform a ritual," said Ram. "We will try to heal him."

H'S FLIGHT WAS to arrive after dark. Ram went alone to pick him up as Mira worked on preparations for the naming ceremony. Mira bent her legs under her on the marble porch ledge, washing mango leaves clean with water from a copper urn. She heard a sound, "Cooo … Cooo," in the distance, more human than bird-like.

"Could it be peacocks?" she asked Gautham, who sat with her on the other side of the ledge.

Gautham laughed. "It must be Ram Maawa and Harsha Maawa," he replied (this was what he called her husband), suddenly standing and hollering for the rest of the relatives. "During dark, the Jeep drivers refuse to come down the valley. It is too dangerous. So the person at the top of hill, they call, 'Cooo,' like birds."

Krishna brought a flashlight and began the trek up the hill. After twenty minutes had passed, Mira saw Krishna and Ram return, the beam of the flashlight shakily illuminating the path. H walked next to them.

Mira stood and watched her husband. He stepped forward into the fluorescent light from the house, his face spotlit, dark-eyebrowed and rectangular. He had worn a Nehru-collared shirt (embracing his culture), wrinkled from travel, with a pair of long khaki shorts, and brown sneakers with no socks. His hair was damp from sweat and his arm angled out behind him to pull a small wheeled suitcase, rolling foreignly across the red dust. Mira waited as the family embraced him.

Seeing his sweat made her feel the humidity renewed, and she reached her hands up over her shoulders and braided her hair, swiftly wrapping pieces into their neat pattern, securing the end with an elastic from her wrist. She never braided her hair at home, instead wearing it loose and straightened — H told her later that he had lost his breath as he watched his Canadian wife transform so seamlessly into a simple Kerala girl, into the person she might have been — and then he heard her call out, "H!" in the voice she might have had, had she grown up in this village, a voice developed by singing prayer songs over a tinny harmonium, by a childhood spent calling cows and chasing cousins and cooing down a steep, darkened path. The backdrop of mango trees and relatives turned her back into a child. Their parents, by career decisions, had taken them away from this.

Mira looked at H and told herself that despite the skepticism she held, she would protect him from whatever might be wrong with their baby. And after he had hugged her and she asked about his flight and released him to eat the many-course meal the aunties had prepared, she went to speak with Ram. She found her uncle washing his feet at the tap at the side of the house. Ram rubbed his feet against the stone ground, aged aquamarine from the copper tap's oxidation.

Mira said to him, "We're not going to tell him."

Ram looked up, using the towel on his shoulder to wipe his feet and slip them into his sandals. "Tell what?"

"We'll do the ritual, the healing for the baby. I don't want to tell H — Harshvardhan."

Ram paused and then nodded.

After dinner, Mira brought H over to her suitcase and pulled out the velvet case with the watch she had bought. "You know how I feel about men's jewellery," he said, and then opened it. "Oh, thank God," he said, and put it on immediately. "It goes with everything," he said.

HE WORE THE watch as the family gathered in the marble foyer, spreading and sitting in all corners, against all the walls, checking first for geckos. On some nights, they arranged themselves in the foyer and somebody would begin to sing. Mira's great aunt brought out three pomegranates and began to open them, spilling the pockets of seeds, and the family passed them around to each other, crimson fingers to crimson fingers. A girl began a pure-pitched Bollywood melody, and then an aunty belted a clear, solid prayer song. Smaller children grabbed tiny brass finger cymbals from the prayer room, and an uncle found a mrindangam to beat out the rhythms. Their voices carried easily into the mango grove, to the ears of the garden monkeys, gently disturbing the slumbering peacocks. A fat frog bounced heartily up the front steps and into the hall with them. A nearby uncle unceremoniously lifted the frog with both hands and dumped it back on its outside way. Mira recalled how, before their wedding, she and H had looked at brochures for possible honeymoons, advertising "exotic locales." This was one, technically, except that it had been her mother's norm. If her brother had lived here, he might have gone with the other men to work in the rice fields, and come home exhausted each night to sing along in his atonal voice, never marrying, staying here in perpetuity, unless — possible in this alternate world — he had been healed, he had become a normal boy.

The aunties admired H's new watch and praised Mira on her modest choice. Gautham, bored by the music and the talk of watches, stood and took Mira's arm, pleading with her to come with him. He led Mira to the room where he had left the piece of camphor untouched for days on the windowsill.

"Mira Athige, it is gone! So many days I watched it grow smaller and smaller. And today, it was no more!"

"Sublimation!" Mira said, almost as excited as the boy. "It went directly from the solid state to the gaseous state." His nephew looked confused, and Mira took a moment to explain it to him, punctuating her phrases with Havyaka words.

"It vanished," Gautham said, still not quite understanding, but Mira nodded. She put her finger to the windowsill and wiped away the dash of white residue that remained.

NORMALLY, THEY HELD Namkaran on the twelfth day after birth, but they had bent the rules so Mira's baby's ceremony could take place in India. The great aunt dressed the baby in new clothes, wrapping the raw silk around his warm round shape. She lined his eyes with black kajal and dotted a beauty mark on his cheek. The family had prepared the front yard for the ceremony, spreading thick straw mats over the flat ground. They had created a temporary roof for the area with a wide piece of fabric printed with swirls of purple, using twine to tie the corners to pillars and trees. The fabric undulated, ballooning in the breeze, creating shade over their bare heads.

A Hindu priest led the prayers, sitting shirtless at the front of the crowd that included the family and nearby neighbours. He cleared his throat frequently and adjusted the dhoti around him, his stomach piling over his waist. They offered petals of jasmine and hibiscus and chrysanthemum. The baby cuddled in H's lap, occasionally wiggling his arms and feet or gaping his mouth at the relatives. Following the priest's instruction, H took a small, clean betel leaf and curled it into a semicircle, holding one end to his mouth and one end to the baby's ear. He whispered the name, "Abhinay Gurunath Narayan," letting the leaf carry the sound to his son, who chortled and turned his ear to his shoulder. The crowd laughed. Mira dipped her right ring finger in a dish of honey and touched it lightly to baby

Abhi's lip. He flattened his lips together to taste the honey, and the crowd clapped. Then the aunties and uncles rose from their seats to present him with gifts, trinkets, and pieces of baby jewellery wrapped in silver paper.

THAT EVENING, WHEN H joined the other men to watch cricket on the television, Ram took Mira and baby Abhi to an upstairs room. He shooed away the gaggle of children and moved an old wooden chair to the centre of the room. Mira settled into the chair, holding Ravi, and closed her eyes. She heard Ram begin reciting words, his voice coming from different directions as he circled the chair, softly clicking his tongue. It was an experiment, she thought, just an experiment. Except that she didn't understand the exact starting conditions; she only knew the simple, desired outcome. Mira tried to clear her mind, concentrating on textures, on her bare feet sticking lightly to the red-painted floor. She sensed the crawling of skinny yellow geckos on the wall behind her, making their way up the furniture and then darting away from each other. The voices of chatting, laughing, singing women wafted from downstairs, the rhythms of rapidly spoken Havyaka floating through the shuttered, glassless windows, pattering against her ears. Air from the windows brushed against the sweat on her arms and cooled her. The baby didn't move, but Mira felt his breathing, a little congested, as the small body contracted and expanded sleepily against her chest. Mira's breathing slowed to match the baby's, and as she inhaled she could smell Abhi's light scent, like talcum and cooked almonds and fresh milk.

She thought maybe, too, she could smell camphor, a scent she would always cling to because it reminded her of hope and faith and belief, and of breathing eucalyptus deeply through a cold, and of her brother praying with his back rounded in her mother's basement prayer room, and of the first time she had learned about sublimation in chemistry class, and of how beautiful she thought it was that a solid could disappear into air.

Acknowlegements

I OWE GRATITUDE to Marc Coté and the rest of the brilliant people at Cormorant Books, without whom this book would still be a file on my computer. Thank you to The Writers' Trust of Canada for their early support. Thanks, too, to everyone at the Johns Hopkins Writing Seminars, in particular to Jean McGarry, Alice McDermott, and my workshop classmates for their incisive comments and wholehearted encouragement.